WHY YOU SHOULD NEVER KISS YOUR ROOMMATE

WHY YOU SHOULD NEVER...

ERIN NICHOLAS

Why You Should Never Kiss Your Roommate

Copyright 2023 by Erin Nicholas

Text previously published as Up By Five

Copyright 2014 by Erin Nicholas

All Rights Reserved.

No part of this book, with the exception of brief quotations for book reviews or critical articles, may be reproduced or transmitted in any form or by any means, electronic or mechanical, including photocopying, recording, or by any information storage and retrieval system without express written permission from the author.

This is a work of fiction. Names, characters, places, and incidents are the product of the author's imagination or are used fictitiously, and any resemblance to actual persons, living or dead, business establishments, events, or locales is entirely coincidental.

ISBN: 978-1-952280-80-1

Editors: Lindsey Faber

Cover artist: Najla Qamber, Qamber Designs

Cover Photo: Wander Aguiar

THE SERIES

Why You Should Never...

Kiss Your Boss (Ben & Jessica)
Kiss Your Blind Date (Sam & Dani)
Kiss A Grump (Mac & Sara)
Kiss Your Fake Boyfriend (Dooley & Morgan)
Kiss Your Ex-Husband (Kevin & Eve)
Kiss Your Brother's Best Friend (Ryan & Amanda)
Kiss Your Ex (Shane & Isabelle)
Kiss Your Enemy (Nate & Emma)
Kiss Your Best Friend (Cody & Olivia)
Kiss Your Roommate (Conner & Gabby)

ABOUT THE BOOK...

Conner Dixon has sworn to never live with another woman after raising his four younger sisters. He's retiring—from worrying, fixing problems, and cleaning up messes. But when a fellow paramedic's apartment burns down and she needs a place to stay, he can't say no.

Gabby's penchant for poker and her ability to overhaul a transmission definitely make her different from his usual women —not to mention her total lack of interest in getting involved with him. With her sights set on medical school, his crazy mix of family and friends is the last thing she needs right now.

But within forty-eight hours of moving in, she's up to her eyeballs in a family crisis and he's in uncharted territory with a girl he wants to rescue…who doesn't need him at all.

CHAPTER
ONE

LIFE WAS WAY TOO much fun to want it to end at age thirty-one. But a death wish was one explanation for why Conner Dixon was walking the hallways of St. Anthony's Hospital with a giant pink stuffed bunny.

The other, and more accurate explanation, however, was that Sara Gordon had had a baby girl last night.

Sara Gordon. The perfect woman. The woman Conner would do anything for. Including risking his life by showing up bright and early when her husband, Mac, was sure to be there.

Of course, Conner had made a point of showing up when her husband, Mac, was sure to be there.

Conner paused outside the door, adjusted the bunny's ears and the bright-pink bow he'd made the saleswoman add before he left the store, and put on his biggest, most charming smile.

"Conner!" Sara greeted him warmly, as always.

"You've got to be fucking kidding me," Mac also greeted him as usual.

"Sara, you're amazing," Conner said. He stepped to the side of the bed and handed the bunny off to Mac.

Mac growled.

Conner grinned and kept his eyes firmly on Sara. Not that it was any hardship.

Conner knew football—he could throw a perfect spiral as the game clock was ticking down to nothing and his team was behind by seven. Conner knew how to save a life—he could intubate a trauma victim faster than any paramedic in the city. In a burning building. With gunfire overhead. And a tornado bearing down on the city.

But there was something Conner knew even better than football or being a paramedic.

And that was women.

"Eleven hours of labor? You're a champ, girl. You're gorgeous, as always, and thank *God* that little girl looks like you."

"Dixon," Mac said, his tone completely exasperated, "how did you know we were up here?"

Conner grinned at the second-best paramedic in the city. It seemed over the last few months, ever since Conner had helped rescue Sara from a fire at the youth center where she worked, that Mac had become less angry and more...irritated by Conner's flirting.

That still worked for Conner. Yes, flirting with Sara was fun. She was sweet and beautiful and smart and sassy. All very important qualities in Conner's opinion.

Sure, her being married—happily married to a *big* guy—put a bit of a damper on things. But Conner had never intended to get serious with her, married or not. Conner never intended to get serious with *anyone*.

But Sara was married to Mac Gordon.

It had been an honest mistake. At first.

Conner had been a new paramedic and a newbie at hanging out at Trudy's, the local tavern where most of the hospital personnel kicked back, and he'd made the mistake of hitting on her one night.

He would have dropped it then and there had he not realized that her husband, the man glowering at him over the top of Sara's gorgeous curly, blonde head, was none other than Mac Gordon, the veteran paramedic who had been riding Conner's rookie ass from day one.

Conner got it. Rookies needed to be broken in. He was fine with that. But he was also used to being the cock of the walk and it was clear that Mac thought that title belonged to him.

So Conner didn't see anything wrong with messing with Mac's head. A little.

Conner was a hell of a paramedic. He was driven, determined, smart and confident.

Mac Gordon wanted Conner on the team. He just didn't *want* to want Conner on the team.

Which was very amusing to Conner.

Paramedic shifts could be long and boring. In many ways, boring nights for an ambulance crew were a good thing. But it left lots of time for bullshitting and pranks.

Conner had fit right in.

He shrugged. "I know people," he told Mac.

"I know people too," Mac said. "And I specifically told them to *not* tell you when Sara went into labor."

Conner propped his hip against the railing of Sara's bed.

He wasn't serious about his attraction to Sara. He liked her. If she'd been single, he would have pursued her until he had her for a long, hot weekend. But they'd have broken up by now for sure.

He reached out and tucked a strand of hair behind her ear.

He heard Mac's knuckles crack.

The thing was, Sara really was the perfect woman on paper. But that was exactly where Conner liked to have perfect women. He didn't need them any closer. He might do something stupid like wanting to keep one around if given the option. And that would never work out.

But Sara was a fantastic cover. He could pretend to be totally infatuated with her while nothing could, or would, ever happen. However, in the course of having this "crush", he had a chance to show any other women in the vicinity how sweet and romantic he could be.

Like when he'd taken the long route, past five different nurses' stations, on his way to Sara's room with the pink bunny.

That couldn't hurt him.

"I guess you just don't know them as well as I do," Conner told Mac with a grin that he knew would make Mac nuts.

"He *better not* know them as well as you do," Sara said.

Mac rolled his eyes. "I'm guessing I *do* know them better than he does."

"Excuse me?" Sara asked, sitting up straighter in bed.

"Conner might 'know' whichever nurse called to tell him you were here, but I'll bet he doesn't know if she likes hamburgers or hot dogs best or if she has kids."

No way did Mac know which nurse had texted Conner about Caroline Gordon's arrival into the world.

"*You* know every nurse's hamburger or hot dog preference?" Conner asked.

"I've been grilling burgers and dogs for every Employee Appreciation Day and hospital picnic for the last seven years," Mac said. "And I pay attention."

Conner narrowed his eyes. There were two Employee Appreciation Days and one annual picnic per year. Still…that was a lot of nurses.

"Seriously? No way you know that."

Mac looked smug now. "Well, it's not like I have to know *every* one of them. I know which ones are on your list, Dixon."

"How?"

Mac lifted his left hand and shaped it into a fist. He raised the first finger. "They're under the age of thirty-five, so that knocks several off the list." He raised the next. "They're single—" Mac's eyes flickered to his wife. "You don't *typically* go for married women."

Conner coughed. So far he was right. But so what?

"So that knocks a lot off." Mac's third finger came up. "They have to be gorgeous. That narrows it down a bit." He added another finger. "They have to be girlie—" Again he looked at Sara.

She smiled. Sara Bradford Gordon was definitely girlie.

Conner couldn't help it. He liked girlie girls. Very likely for deep, psychologically troubling reasons he preferred to not delve into.

"And," Mac said, lifting his fifth finger and pausing for a moment, "they have to be blonde."

Conner straightened. Mac was right on. And that was creepy.

"How do you know that?" Conner asked.

"Like I said, I pay attention." Mac crossed his arms. "And that leaves a much smaller list to keep track of."

Sara frowned. "That doesn't make any sense. You've been paying attention to the hot dog and hamburger eating habits of this list of women you think *Conner* would go for?"

"Yes." Mac scowled.

"Why?" Sara asked.

"Because I'm hoping to get him really interested in one of them."

There was a beat of silence, then Conner hooted with laughter. That was awesome.

He leaned in and kissed Sara on the head. "I gotta go. You did good, Mrs. Gordon. Congratulations on your sweet baby girl."

"Conner?"

He straightened and swung toward the female voice with a smile.

A smile that died immediately.

It was Katie. Ah, dammit.

"What are you doing here?" Katie asked, shoving a bouquet of flowers at Mac without even looking at the other man. Her gaze was glued on Conner.

"I'm visiting my friends who just had a baby," Conner said, moving a couple of steps away from Sara's bed. In case Katie decided to throw something. Which was likely.

Katie's eyes narrowed. "You know Sara?"

"Known her for years," Conner confirmed, inching toward the door.

What he hadn't known, of course, was that Katie knew Sara.

He looked over Katie's shoulder to Mac. Mac looked…entertained.

Of course he did. Mac could tell that Katie was a one-night stand gone bad.

Most men would be able to tell that.

"I'm just on my way out."

"You didn't tell me you knew Conner," Katie said, turning her attention to Sara.

Sara glanced at him, then back to her friend. "I didn't know that it mattered."

"*He's* the guy. The one I told you about."

Sara's eyebrows went up and she looked at Conner again. "Really?"

Something in the way she said it made Conner stop. What had Katie said? From the look of interest on Sara's face and the faint pink blush on her cheeks, it had been good.

Conner straightened. Well, maybe this wasn't going to be all bad.

He and Katie had had a hell of a night.

The next morning was another story.

"He's the one who…" Sara trailed off suggestively.

"Yes," Katie confirmed.

"And then…?" Sara asked.

Katie nodded.

Sara looked at him again. "Wow."

Okay, this was *definitely* going well. He glanced at Mac. Mac was now frowning.

Awesome.

"But then he…" Katie said, also trailing off purposefully.

Sara frowned. "Yeah."

Like some crazy teeter-totter, Conner's smile faded as Mac's grew.

"And then he never called," Katie concluded, the strange, largely wordless female conversation ending.

Conner knew all about strange, partially wordless—or entirely wordless—female conversations. His four younger sisters did that shit all the time. Very often about him.

"Yeah," Sara said again, turning her frown on Conner.

Hey. There had been pancakes thrown the next morning. Not by him. Never by him. He loved pancakes. And it had been a bitch to get that syrup cleaned up.

But the pancakes had been good. That had been sign number two that he needed to get Katie the hell out of his house. The adage about winning a man's heart through his stomach did, indeed, apply to him.

Sign number one, however, had been that she'd cried. And he didn't spend time with women who cried. Or yelled. Or had other less-than-happy emotions.

Well, okay, his sisters, but he freaking *hated* those emotions from them too.

Katie had been talking about how much sweeter Conner was than her last dickhead boyfriend, which had led to a rant about her last dickhead boyfriend, which had led to tears. Conner worked hard to always be better than the other men women dated. But that was hardly tear worthy. He'd given Katie four orgasms. Nobody should cry after four orgasms.

Which he might have mentioned to her. Just prior to the pancake-throwing episode.

And *now* would be a good time for him to go.

"Okay, well, congrats again," he said, making a beeline for the door.

"Conner." Katie's voice stopped him.

He sighed and turned. Sometimes women just needed to get

things out in the open. If she could rant and rave at him about his alleged assholeish behavior, maybe she'd feel better and this could be over.

"Ka—"

She didn't connect with his jaw, nose or eye directly. But she caught him hard on the browbone with her fist. And the big-assed ring she was wearing.

Yeah, not an open-palm slap. A gripped-fist punch.

Fuck.

His head snapped back and he immediately felt the skin split open.

"Katie!" Sara gasped.

Mac chuckled.

Conner lifted a hand to where he was now bleeding. Awesome. He sighed at Katie. "Feel better?"

"Better. But not good."

"You need to learn to throw a punch before you hurt yourself."

Katie's eyes narrowed and she stepped closer.

Mac piped up. "I'll teach her."

"Don't ever call me again," Katie said to Conner.

He hadn't called in the first place. "I promise."

"Congratulations, Sara," she said over her shoulder. "I'll come back later."

"Bye," Sara called.

Mac thrust a wad of paper towels at Conner. "Don't bleed on my wife's hospital room floor."

"Dammit, that hurt," Conner muttered pressing the towels to his forehead.

Mac chuckled. "I'll bet."

Conner crossed to the mirror above the sink on the other side of the room.

"You okay?" Sara asked.

He gave her a wink. "Will you kiss it better if I say no?"

"Come here. I'll give you something for it." Mac's tone held a mix of frustration, humor and warning.

Mac used that tone a lot when Conner was around.

Conner dabbed at the cut. "Nah, I think I'm good."

"You're gonna need butterflies at least," Mac said. "Want me to do them?"

Did he want Mac applying the adhesive strips he would need to keep the wound closed? Did he want Mac that close to him period? Uh, no.

"I'm good. Think I can handle it."

Mac shrugged. "Fine. If it helps, you can tell everyone I hit you."

Conner grabbed a new paper towel and turned. "Why would I tell them you hit me?"

"Isn't that less offensive than having a woman hit you?"

"I think it says a lot if a woman feels that strongly about me."

"Wait, the dreamy Conner Dixon who is desperately seeking the one woman who can heal his slightly broken heart since the woman he pines for is married to another might actually *piss someone off*?" Mac asked sarcastically.

"Don't forget the part about no other woman being quite able to measure up to the one I'm hung up on." He glanced at Sara, who rewarded him with one of her blushing smiles.

He knew she was flattered. He knew she found the whole thing a little funny. He suspected that she liked seeing her husband's possessive side—which was why the flirting-with-Sara thing really only happened when Mac was around. But Conner also knew that Sara knew he didn't mean anything other than the part where he thought she was great.

Not that he'd ever admit it to anyone, but if Sara did, by some huge miracle, want to have an affair—or more—with him, Conner would say no.

One, he wouldn't break up a marriage.

Two, he wasn't really the man Sara thought he was.

And three, Sara Bradford Gordon was the type of woman to

immerse herself fully in someone's life, wrap herself around every finger and tangle her issues up with his in a heartbeat.

He knew how this went. He'd been a fill-in father for his four sisters since he was seventeen. Now they were all happily connected to other men. Good men. Friends of Conner's, in fact. At the time it was happening he'd had more than a few reservations—to put it mildly. But now…he was *free*.

He didn't want to share a living space with, not to mention worry about, argue with or take care of another woman. Ever.

"Why would *you* hit me?" Conner asked, wanting to get the story straight if he decided to go with it.

Mac cocked an eyebrow. "Really? How many nurses saw you with that damned rabbit?"

"Hey, careful, that 'damned rabbit' is going to be sitting in your daughter's nursery," Sara protested.

Mac shook his head. "No, it's not."

"Of course it is," Sara said. "It goes perfectly with our baby-animal theme."

Mac rolled his eyes.

Conner smiled. He'd found out about the theme from Sam, Sara's brother. Inadvertently, of course. Kind of.

"Anyway," Mac went on, "as many women as possible saw the rabbit and deduced why you had it. It's not such a stretch to think you said or did something to make me want to hit you, is it?"

No, actually it wasn't.

Conner nodded. "Okay. You hit me. Because Sara was so happy to see me she threw her arms around me and kissed me."

Mac scowled. "No."

"Come on, it would have to be something big."

"No."

"How about the baby looks *a lot* like me?" Conner asked. He fought a smile and took a step toward the door as Mac drew up even taller.

"How about I really hit you and then we don't have to match our stories up at all?"

Conner didn't think Mac would actually hit him…but if he did, it would freaking *hurt*.

"Gee, look at the time," Conner said, heading for the door. He had a shift to get downstairs for anyway.

"Sorry you couldn't stay longer," Mac said dryly.

"Bye, Conner," Sara said sweetly.

He pulled the door open then blew her a kiss. "See ya, gorgeous."

The door bumped shut before he could hear Mac's response.

Gabrielle Evans came up short as she stepped into the break room. Conner Dixon was bending over the little sink in the corner, applying butterfly sutures to his eyebrow line.

The paramedic in her made a quick note of the cut, blood and sutures, but the woman in her simply could not ignore the bending-over thing for the first thirty seconds.

The guy really did very nice things to a pair of pants.

Then she got back to the blood thing. "You've got to be kidding me."

"Why do people keep saying that to me today?" Conner asked.

"You're *bleeding*? And treating yourself?"

"Yes." He muttered an expletive as the box of sutures fell off the edge of the tiny countertop and scattered.

"Here." She crossed to him and knocked his hand out of the way when he reached for the strips. She gathered them up and slipped them into the box, then looked up at him. "Let me."

He started to protest and she paused, a strip in hand, eyebrows up. "Really?"

"I've got it," he muttered.

"Don't be dumb."

He dropped his hand from his head. "Fine."

She opened a strip and stepped close to apply it. She reached for his forehead, then noticed the two strips he'd already stuck in place. They were terrible.

She sighed and gripped the end of one, pulling it off quickly.

"Hey! Ow!"

"*I've* got this," she told him. "Those were sloppy."

She tossed the used ones away, then leaned in to apply a new one. She pinched the edges of the cut together while laying the adhesive strip over it.

And ignored that Conner smelled really good. Or tried to anyway.

"Dammit."

"What?" Conner asked.

She realized she'd said it out loud. She met his eyes—and it hit her that she'd never been this close to him before. Well, maybe in the field working on a victim or something, but never somewhere she'd *noticed* how he smelled.

"Um…"

"Gabby?"

He frowned, which pulled his cut skin away from her fingers.

"Dammit…what?" he asked.

"Oh. Um…" she thought fast, "…glue."

The *last* thing she needed was to make some stupid you're-so-cute-Conner blunder. All the women at St. Anthony's fawned over him—well, except for her and Sierra Katz, the two female paramedics on his crew.

She liked Conner. He was a good guy deep down, an ace paramedic and pretty damned funny a lot of the time—sometimes intentionally, sometimes not. And of course she found him attractive. He was one of those guys any woman would have to admit was attractive. Because even if slender but solid, football-playing blonds with big green eyes and an easy smile weren't your type, he saved lives for a living and oozed charm like he exhaled carbon dioxide.

But she didn't giggle when he smiled at her and she didn't forget what she was going to say when he spoke to her and she didn't trip over her own feet when he came into a room.

At least, not usually.

She'd seen all of that happen with other women. And she'd seen the effect it had on Conner.

He was cocky all the time. He became downright insufferable when a woman acted stupid over him.

But he really did smell good.

"It needs glue?" he asked. "Damn."

It maybe didn't technically need glue, but it wouldn't hurt him and it would save her pride.

She was not the type of girl to stumble over a guy. And even if she were, the guy would *not* be Conner.

She'd grown up with three men like Conner. Her brothers were also handsome, charming and too smart for their own good. But having seen them at their worst as well as their best certainly took some shine off—of them and off of all men. It was very hard to impress Gabrielle Evans.

She knew a lot of things. She knew poker—she could hold her own at a high stakes table in Vegas and walk out with more than a little pocket change. She knew how to save a life—she could start a line in a trauma victim faster than any paramedic in the city. In a burning building. With gunfire overhead. And a tornado bearing down on the city.

But there was something Gabby knew even better than poker or being a paramedic.

And that was men.

"What did that to you?" she asked, forcing herself to turn away and dig the glue out of the box of supplies Conner had open on the table.

He hesitated just before he said, "Mac."

Glue in hand, she came to stand in front of him again. "Mac? Gordon?"

"Yep."

Gabby avoided Conner's eyes and concentrated on the gash that bisected his eyebrow and slanted off toward his temple. She applied the glue, then again pinched the edges together and held.

"So the woman who hit you must have been wearing a ring."

She felt Conner's surprise, but she kept her eyes firmly on her task.

"You don't think Mac would hit me?"

"I think if Mac wanted to hit you, he'd have done it a long time ago. Like when you kissed his wife."

She saw Conner's mouth curl in her peripheral vision.

Conner had this stupid crush thing going with Sara Gordon. Gabby knew it wasn't real, but he sure hung on to it. Like when he'd helped pull Sara out of the burning youth center, then planted a big old serious kiss on her.

Mac hadn't hit him then.

"No way he'd hit you for a stuffed pink bunny."

Gabby could feel Conner's gaze. "How'd you know about the bunny?"

She gave his cut another hard pinch, decided the glue was going to hold and let go of him.

"Because your nefarious plan worked. All of the nurses were talking about it. I heard about it when I went to get coffee."

Conner was full-out grinning now. "Mac will get to hear that talk for days."

Gabby sighed. Yep, he was just like her brothers—bigger was always better. Bigger rivalries, bigger contests, bigger arguments, bigger dares.

She propped a hand on her hip. "So who really hit you?"

He shrugged. "Doesn't matter."

"A woman, though. An ex-lover, I'm guessing."

He cocked his recently bandaged eyebrow. "Why's that?"

"Because you have three types of women in your life—future lovers, past lovers and sisters. Your sisters and your future lovers wouldn't hit you, so…"

Of course, one of his sisters—the youngest and sweetest, Olivia—*had* hit him once. And Gabby had been in the front row for that one. He'd totally deserved it. Still, his sisters generally thought Conner walked on water. The only females *more* enamored with him were the ones that wanted to date him.

"Fine, it was a woman. And a misunderstanding. And a big, gaudy ring."

Gabby snorted. "I believe the woman and the ring part."

He shook his head. "Seriously. A misunderstanding. About… what I wanted."

"Uh-huh. Like putting 'forever' at the end of all your sentences? Like when you said—" Gabby dropped her voice an octave, "—'baby, I gotta be with you', she heard, 'baby, I gotta be with you forever'?"

Conner pushed up from where he'd been leaning against the sink. "First of all, that is a terrible impression of me. Second, I never call women 'baby' and third, it was more like when I said, 'suck my cock', she heard, 'suck my cock forever'."

Gabby didn't even blink. If Conner wanted to shock her or shut her up with foul language or blatantly graphic or sexual talk, he was going to have to do a lot better than that.

She had three brothers, a dad, several uncles and a bunch of male cousins. All of the uncles and cousins lived nearby and were a regular part of her life. Her dad and one uncle were mechanics who owned a shop together. Another uncle owned a bar. Another farmed and another was a veterinarian. Growing up, she'd thought it was normal to put "fucking" in front of most nouns. Fucking engines, fucking cows, fucking weather, fucking politicians—it didn't matter.

Her brothers and cousins were no different and often forgot she wasn't one of the guys. They didn't just swear. They talked about women and sex and body parts at the kitchen table like it was a locker room.

One of her brothers, Reed, was a public defender, Grant was

a cop and Josh wanted to be a firefighter. Gentlemanly language was—well, she didn't even know what that was.

Women sucking on cocks though...that one she knew a little bit about.

"I understand why you wouldn't be inclined to put a definite time frame on a blow job," Gabby told him, repacking the first aid kit he'd pilfered the sutures from. "But maybe you need to be more specific with these women. Like, 'suck my cock until I come so hard I can't stand up'."

She snapped the lid shut, then turned to find Conner staring at her, his mouth hanging open.

"What?"

"You just said..." He trailed off, clearly unable to repeat it.

That was funny.

She grinned. "You didn't think I know what happens when cocks get sucked?"

He was looking at her like she'd broken out in green hives.

The break room door swung open. "You took a giant pink bunny up to Sara Gordon?"

Conner's face was still comically baffled as Sierra entered.

"He did," Gabby confirmed, turning away from him before she started laughing.

Conner went for the more obvious girlie girls. Gabby was sure most of them knew what they were doing in the bedroom, but Conner liked the ones that got all made up even to go to Trudy's, who wore high heels even when shooting pool—though most of them sucked, from what she'd seen—and the ones that drank pretty fruity drinks.

Maybe those girls didn't talk like truckers.

But most of them couldn't overhaul a transmission, didn't know the difference between a straight and a royal flush and had never won a hot-dog-eating contest either.

So there.

"You just strutted in there with that stupid rabbit, didn't you?" Sierra asked, grinning at Conner.

"I sure did. And Sara was thrilled to see me."

He sounded like he'd recovered.

"What happened to your face?" Sierra asked, coming closer

"A woman, a big, gaudy ring and a misunderstanding," Gabby recited. "Is that right?" she asked Conner.

"Well, the misunderstanding came before the ring, but yeah." He went to the freezer and grabbed an ice pack for his head.

"Let me guess, the misunderstanding had to do with how long you wanted her to stay the next day and when you'd be calling her again," Sierra said.

"The confusion was somewhere between never and forever," Gabby added.

They both grinned at Conner.

He didn't say anything as he rested the ice against his brow.

"You know what you need, don't you?" Gabby asked him.

"Two less talkative crewmates?" he asked.

Sierra laughed.

"You need to date a woman who knows you're full of shit," Gabby told him.

He moved the ice pack so he could look at her with both eyes. "What?"

She nodded. "Seriously. The problem with getting rid of these women after you're...done with them..." Even she flinched at her wording. But it wasn't her fault it was accurate.

Conner had raised that eyebrow again, but he didn't interrupt.

"...is that they believe all your charming, romantic bullshit," Gabby went on.

"Well, yeah. I sell it to them hard," he said.

"I know. And you're good. They fall for it. But then it's tough for them to stop believing it the very next day."

Conner sighed, as if the world really was unfair. "Hey, I'd love to date someone for a few weeks, even a few months. But I'm not doing forever. And I know women, I've even read

Cosmo." He glanced at Sierra. "It's like having the opponent's playbook."

Sierra snorted.

Conner went on. "By date five or six, they're assuming it's getting serious and they want more and more. If I'm not interested in long term, then it's really the fair thing to break things off sooner versus later, right?"

Gabby shrugged. He had a point. She read *Cosmo* too. "That's what I mean. You need to date someone who knows that all your romantic seductive stuff is just to get into a girl's pants. Someone who knows that what you really want is hot, sweaty sex and then to watch the game on TV with pizza."

Conner tossed the ice pack back in the freezer. "Well, G, if you run across a girl like that, you let me know. I'm all about that. But be sure she knows about the cock-sucking thing, okay?"

Gabby heard the door open again.

"You took a giant pink bunny up to Sara Gordon?"

Ryan Kaye, the fourth member of their crew, showed up just then. He squinted at Conner.

"What the hell happened to your head?"

CHAPTER
TWO

CONNER PULLED up to the fire scene in his own pickup. He and the crew were supposed to be off today, but the call had come for all crews to report. That was always a bad sign.

He'd been only five miles from the scene in the opposite direction, so he'd told Ryan he'd meet them there.

Ryan pulled their rig in only a minute later.

"Damn," Ryan said, climbing out and facing the apartment building that was ablaze.

Conner agreed. It was a newer building, not far from the hospital. It was also big. Which meant lots of potential victims. "No wonder they called us."

"Bradford's crew is on tonight," Ryan said.

Conner nodded. He'd already made note of the fact that the first rig on the scene was Sam Bradford's. Sam worked with Mac Gordon and his other two best friends, Dooley Miller and Kevin Campbell. Not that he'd ever admit it to Mac, but Conner was always glad to see them at a scene.

Conner had seen them in action. He'd done a lot of filling in for them before he'd been hired full time and given his own crew. They were damned good. They worked like they could read each other's minds and they definitely had each other's backs. It reminded Conner of how he felt working with Ryan, Gabby and Sierra. And how he felt when he pulled up and saw his buddies Cody Madsen, the Chief at Fire Station Three, and Shane Kelley, one of the best cops in the city on the scenes. Things always seemed to go better when they were all present.

"I'll go find Bradford," Ryan said.

There were no apparent victims. That could be good or bad—no one needed assistance, they'd all already been treated…or they were still inside or beyond help.

"Dixon!" someone shouted.

Conner pivoted and saw Cody striding toward him.

"We have victims coming out now," Cody said, his face grim. "There're a lot of people still inside."

Apartment fires at night were the worst—a lot of people in bed, disoriented when they awoke to the alarms, many trying to grab possessions before they evacuated.

"We'll take care of them," Conner assured him. "Just get those flames put out."

"You got it." But Cody didn't smile.

"Chief! We need you!" one of Cody's men yelled.

Cody and Conner exchanged a look that said *good luck, I'm glad you're here* and *take care of yourself* all at once.

Conner watched his friend jog off. He meant the "take care of yourself" more now than he ever had. He'd always wanted Cody to be safe, of course, but Cody was with Conner's sister Olivia now, and, damn, he made her happy. If he got hurt, Conner would kick his ass.

"Need a paramedic!" someone hollered.

And Conner was on.

He grabbed his bag from the back of the rig and headed for the area where firefighters were directing or carrying victims for treatment.

He glanced around as he knelt beside the middle-aged woman the firefighter had lowered to the ground.

Ryan was helping Sam Bradford with someone, Sierra was talking to two little kids, and he assumed Gabby was around somewhere. She was always the first out of the rig and into the fray.

Conner turned his attention to his patient. And then to the next one. And the next one. And the next. They kept coming. For over an hour.

Finally having applied his last dressing to another minor burn, Conner got to his feet and stretched.

There had been a lot of those minor burns requiring only first aid and reassurance. Thank God. He'd only intubated three patients to help them breathe and there had only been two third-degree burns that he'd seen.

It was possible that the other paramedics had treated the more severely injured patients, but he hoped it meant the fire damage was more to the building than to the people who lived there.

He looked up at the smoking skeleton of the building. There wasn't much left. The fire had burned quickly and it looked like the top half of the building was a total loss.

Conner shook his head and looked around for his crew. He'd helped Ryan with one of the intubations and he'd seen Sierra helping an older man into Bradford's ambulance at one point. He hadn't caught sight of Gabby yet, though.

He located Ryan, then Sierra. But still no Gabby. He turned a full three-sixty, searching the area. What the hell?

She had to be here. She wouldn't not show up.

"Kaye!" he shouted at Ryan.

"Yeah?"

"Was G in the rig with you?"

"Nope. Figured she'd meet us here too."

Conner was pretty sure she lived near here, so that would make sense. But then where was she?

"Anyone see Evans?" He approached Sam Bradford's crew and the third ambulance crew that had been called in.

"Uh, no. Sorry," Kevin Campbell answered.

"Me either," Sam said. He frowned. "She didn't go into the building, did she?"

They weren't supposed to, obviously, but Conner couldn't say for sure she hadn't. He had, on a couple of occasions, gone in for a victim when he was the only one or there wasn't time. It was stupid and risky, and he'd gotten his ass reamed and written up on disciplinary action both times. But if he had to do it again, he would.

And he could totally see Gabby doing the same thing.

"Hey, Dixon!"

He ignored the shout from Mac Gordon. Mac loved to give Conner a hard time when they were working. Or any other time. Conner deserved it, he knew, but he really wasn't in the mood. He needed to figure out where the hell Gabby was.

"Ryan, you need to call—"

"Dixon!" Mac bellowed again.

"Not now, Mac!"

"Yes, *now.*"

He turned to flip Mac off but his hand dropped back to his side when he caught sight of the woman Mac had been working on.

"Gabby?"

She pulled the oxygen mask to one side. "Hey." She gave him a sheepish smile.

"What the hell are you doing?" Conner strode toward her. Frustration warred with concern.

"Recovering from smoke inhalation and getting checked for burns," Mac said.

"There aren't any," Gabby said.

"I should make you prove it. There are some places on you I didn't check," Mac said with a wink.

She kicked him. "You wish," she said with a grin before putting her mask back in place.

Conner blinked. He'd never seen Gabby even remotely flirt with someone.

"What the hell…" Conner repeated. "You were already here?" She'd gotten there ahead of them? "You went in?" Dammit, he'd known she'd do something like that.

The idea of her charging into that fire made his entire body go cold. Jesus, she had no fear—and it scared the hell out of him.

"She was already in," Mac said.

His smile said he was making fun of Conner, but Conner didn't get it.

"You don't just go in. You know that. You wait for us…"

"She lives here, Einstein," Mac said. "She didn't report for duty because it's *her* apartment building on fire."

Conner stared at him. Then he stared at Gabby.

Gabby was watching him right back.

Mac spoke again. "She got almost twenty people out before the firefighters got ahold of her."

That didn't surprise Conner a bit.

"When they wouldn't let her go back in, she started treating people out of our rig. We didn't notice at first because she wasn't in uniform," Mac added.

That also didn't surprise Conner. Gabby was, hands down, the most dedicated paramedic on the team. That included Mac's crew. She wasn't the biggest or strongest, so there were things she needed the guys to do, things she needed help with at times, but she pushed herself and everyone else. There was no letting up, no resting when Gabby was around.

Conner admired the hell out of her.

"You gonna be okay?" he finally asked.

She nodded.

He nodded back. If Gabby said she was okay, she was. She

was smart. If she wasn't okay, if she needed something, she'd tell them. She was brave, but she asked for help, which helped Conner, and the rest of the crew, trust her.

Right now, though, he was having a hard time not hugging her.

She looked very different from the Gabby he was used to. Her hair hung free, for one thing. It was no wonder no one on Mac's crew had recognized her at first. Gabby always, *always*, wore her hair up at work. Ponytail or bun. Always.

Now it was free, spilling down her back and over her shoulders. It was long, way longer than he would have guessed—had he ever spent more than two seconds thinking about it—and it was a deep-mahogany color, the lights inside the ambulance catching red highlights throughout.

Her face also looked different. She never wore makeup, at least not the kind of makeup he was used to seeing, but tonight her cheeks were pale, her eyes were wide and her expression… vulnerable. That was absolutely not something he'd seen on Gabby before. She was typically taking charge, commanding, focused. But she was also typically on the other side of the scene, the side that took people to the hospital and then went home to their own homes.

This was her home. The charred, smoking, black mess behind them.

Fuck.

He definitely wanted to hug her. He had a soft spot for the damsel in distress, there was no denying it. It had always been that way and had only gotten stronger raising his four younger sisters. There wasn't a damned thing he could do about it. A woman in need would always flare up his protective instincts.

But he fought it. Hard. All the time. He'd tried the knight thing and it had blown up in his face—and heart—big-time. He was now allergic to women who needed anything more from him than romance and hot sex.

Or so he told himself.

Truthfully, he was like an addict—always drawn to it and having to fight not to get involved and try to fix everything.

Plus, he couldn't hug her. This was *Gabby*. There was something about her that held him back from the good-hearted teasing and flirting he did with Sierra, from the winks and smiles he gave the other women on staff at the hospital, from the hug he would have given any of them if they'd just watched their home burn down.

Gabby gave off this I've-got-it, I'm-good vibe.

But right now he couldn't look away from her mouth.

There was something seriously wrong with him, he was sure. The poor woman had had possibly one of the worst nights of her life and yet he was staring at her mouth and thinking about the cock-sucking comment from the day before. He'd said it to shock her, he'd admit that. To see how she'd react. But he had no way expected her to respond with something even more graphic.

He couldn't stop thinking about the suck-my-cock-until-I-come-so-hard-I-can't-stand-up thing. And he couldn't stop wondering just how much Gabby knew about cocks and all the related activities.

He'd never thought of her sexually before. Which was weird. She was a woman.

But she definitely gave no signs that she thought of him as anything more than a coworker and friend. He liked women who were interested. Who were very obviously interested. He'd had plenty of experience with reading female signals wrong—and the consequences of that. He liked the safe route now. The route where the women gave him big goo-goo eyes and flirted outrageously and whispered naughty things in his ear.

The route where he knew what they wanted and that he could deliver.

Which meant he should be very worried about the fact that the pull to hug Gabby was so strong.

Gabby wasn't the typical damsel in distress at all. She saved people. She made them feel better. She made them safe. People needed *her.* And she wasn't the oh-Conner-you're-so-amazing type.

She was neither of the types that typically drew him.

But he still wanted to wrap her up and take care of her.

He took a deep breath. "Let's get Sierra over here." Before he did something stupid. Like hugging her anyway and getting decked.

Punching some guy in the face…now *that* he could see Gabby doing. On her knees giving a blow job, not so much.

Though he'd spent the last thirty-some-odd hours thinking of exactly that.

"Katz!" he shouted to Sierra, his eyes on Gabby.

She pulled the oxygen mask off and stood from the back end of the ambulance. The plain-white cotton blanket they'd wrapped around her slipped off and she turned to toss it into the rig.

Conner froze.

She had, obviously, been in bed when the smoke alarms went off and she'd done the smart thing and had *not* taken time to change clothes or grab personal possessions.

The thin pink tank top with the spaghetti straps clung to her, curving over two small but firm breasts and hugging her flat stomach. The short-shorts were gray and also thin and ended only two inches below the curve of her tight ass. Her legs were long and smooth and Conner suddenly couldn't swallow.

Holy shit.

She might not need or want him, but his body suddenly thought it needed and wanted *her.*

He'd only ever seen her in uniform, or in jeans and T-shirts at Trudy's. And they weren't the fitted T-shirts with sequined logos calling attention to her breasts like a lot of women wore. They were plain old T-shirts.

"Oh my God, Gabby, there you are!" Sierra enfolded Gabby in her arms, hugging her tight. "Are you okay?"

"You knew this was her apartment building?" Conner

asked, stepping forward with a frown. Of course Sierra would have known that. He knew the girls were friends outside of work.

"Yes, of course."

"Why didn't you say anything?" Conner demanded.

Sierra scowled at him. "Because I went to intubate a three-year-old when we got here and I've been busy since."

"You should have said something."

Sierra kept her arm around Gabby's waist, but she turned to face him. "To you? Why? I told Cody."

Conner felt his frown deepen. Cody had known? And he hadn't said anything to Conner?

"And then I saw her working on a couple of vics, so I knew she was okay," Sierra said.

"She needed treatment," Conner said, his voice accusatory though he wasn't sure why.

Sierra shrugged. "Gabby's smart. If she was working, I assumed she was okay to be working."

"I was okay to be working," Gabby broke in. "Those people needed help more than I did."

"Mac had you on O2," Conner pointed out.

"Precautionary," Gabby said. "After everyone else was treated. I'm fine. My sats are good."

So the oxygen levels in her blood were good. That didn't mean she was fine. But even as the thought passed through his head, Conner realized how dumb it was. That was exactly what it meant.

"Fine." Sierra was here now. He could leave her alone. "So, um, Gabby…if you need anything, all you have to do is ask, okay?" he said. "I'm sorry about…all of this."

She gave him a small sad smile. "Thanks. I'm glad no one was hurt. And like they say, it's just stuff. But it was *my* stuff. So, yeah, this pretty much sucks."

He nodded. He could imagine. "Well, I'm serious—anything you need."

Her smile brightened and he felt stupidly pleased that he'd cheered her up somehow.

"Thanks, Conner."

"Okay."

He stood looking at her. Her hair was really long. And it looked thick. It was really shiny too and had a slight wave to it. She looked good with her hair down.

Sierra cleared her throat and Conner glanced at her. She gave him a what-are-you-doing look.

Right. What was he doing? Nothing. Leaving. He was done here.

But he didn't feel like he was done.

He had no idea what else he thought he might need to do, but he didn't feel done.

"You okay, Conner?" Sierra asked.

He nodded. "Yeah. I'm…glad you're safe, G."

"Thanks."

Her smile, even bigger than before, called his attention to her mouth again.

That along with the skimpy sleepwear and the surprising curves and the tousled hair…

One thing was clear—Gabrielle Evans was *not* just one of the guys.

She was a woman. And she did need something.

So, Conner did the typical Conner thing. "Okay, let's go." He stepped forward, grabbed the blanket and wrapped it around Gabby's shoulders again.

"Let's go?"

She looked up at him with her big brown eyes—he'd never noticed what color her eyes were before—and he caught his toe on the grass.

"Where are we going?" she asked.

"To my apartment."

Gabby stumbled this time. "What?"

"I have a guest room. You need a place to stay tonight."

"But, I—" She glanced at Sierra.

Sierra shrugged. "I have a couch. You know it's all yours if you need it."

"Yeah, Conner I'll just—"

"Stay with me," he said firmly, taking her elbow and starting for his truck.

"But Sierra—" Gabby glanced over her shoulder at her friend.

"Has a couch. I have a full guest room with a guest bath."

"But—"

He sighed. This was his instinct—to take care of the women around him—and this was the right thing to do. Gabby needed a place to stay, and he had a place for her.

Plus, she was a safe woman to take care of. She didn't *really* need him. She needed four walls and a roof. He could meet that need. But she didn't need comforting, she didn't need a hug, she didn't need him to make her feel better.

"This isn't a negotiation," he told her, putting her in the truck on the passenger side.

"I don't have any clothes," she said weakly as he started to slam the door.

Conner paused. Right. No clothes. He knew she meant that was a problem, but it took him a bit longer to come to that conclusion.

"We can swing by Carl-Mart," he said of the little-bit-of-everything store that had spun their name from the national chain of stores it rhymed with.

He started to close the door but she said, "Um."

"What's wrong?"

"I can't go into Carl-Mart like this."

He'd been doing a really great job of keeping his eyes off of her long, bare legs, but with her comment, his gaze dropped.

Yeah. Long. Bare. Legs.

"I'll run in." The door shut before she could say anything more.

"Conner, this is really nice, but I'm okay at Sierra's."

That was probably what she should have said. Or something like it. But Gabby found herself amused and, okay, comforted by his insistence on taking her to his place. She settled back into the seat in Conner's truck, tugged the blanket tighter around her and let him drive her to Carl-Mart.

Waking to the sounds of fire alarms going off in her home had been the scariest thing she'd ever been through. Trying to orient herself in the dark, graphic scenes from fires she'd worked as a paramedic flashing through her mind, desperately evacuating her neighbors, caring for injuries on people she knew—her heart had been in her throat. Then she'd looked over and seen the rig—*her* rig. Her crew. And she'd breathed. For the first time since being jolted awake by her screaming smoke detector.

Seeing Sierra and Ryan on the scene had calmed her and allowed her to take a deep breath and truly assess what was going on around her.

Then she'd seen Conner.

He was their leader. There was no question that they worked as a team. A fantastic team. They were all bright and skilled and totally committed. But there was something about Conner that was…bigger than all of that. The way he carried himself, how sure he was with everything he did, the command in his voice, his quick decisions. Working with him had always been a pleasure. When Conner was there, everyone was going to work their asses off, everything that could possibly be done was going to be done and everyone was going to be accounted for, from the oldest to the youngest victim, crew and staff, even pets. It was true he was a little crazy about it all—he'd once gone into a building after a goldfish. Still, it did give everyone around him an incredible sense of security.

When she'd seen him there, her on the victim side of things, she'd felt a sense of…*I'm okay*. She couldn't explain it better than that. Conner was there and she mattered to him and that made her feel better.

And now that she realized he hadn't even known she was there, that she'd been a victim of the fire, she knew he was over-compensating.

He hadn't rescued her, he hadn't treated her, he hadn't fussed about Mac treating her—nothing. He hadn't even known she was *there*.

So now he had to take her home and ensure she had everything she needed.

That was who Conner Dixon was. A person only needed to know him for about a day to know that, and she'd known him for two years.

Conner pulled into a parking space in front of Carl-Mart and turned to her. "What do you need?"

She thought quickly. "Probably a T-shirt, sweatpants and a toothbrush?"

He looked at her as if waiting for more. "That's it?"

She shrugged. "I'll shop tomorrow."

"Wow."

"What?"

He shook his head. "It's just that I don't know any woman who wouldn't ask for shampoo and soap and body spray."

She blushed. She was trying to get through the night. "I guess I assumed you had shampoo and soap that I could borrow."

His gaze ran over her hair and she felt her scalp tingle.

"I do. Yeah, of course."

"And toothpaste?"

"Definitely. In fact, I have some extra toothbrushes."

For his overnight guests, Gabby filled in mentally. "Then I just need stuff to wear to shop tomorrow, I guess."

"None of the women I know would wear sweatpants to shop."

She felt her face get hot again. Dammit. She was practical. Was that so bad?

"Just get me something to cover me up until I can shop for more stuff," she said. "I'm not picky."

"Okay." He started to get out, then stopped. "Oh, do you, um…"

She waited.

He turned back. "Do you need…underwear or anything?"

She almost laughed at that. Womanizer Conner Dixon was hesitant to say the word *underwear* to her? But she couldn't laugh. Because it simply further illustrated that Conner hadn't thought about her as a woman and didn't feel flirtatious toward her at all.

"No, it's fine," she said, trying not to let her irritation seep into her tone. *She* was the one who had downplayed her femininity around Conner for the past two years.

"No?" he asked. "What will you wear?"

"I'll go without."

Strangely, the air in the truck seemed to heat slightly. Conner's gaze dropped to her breasts. They were hidden behind the blanket and certainly weren't much to speak of in the first place—nothing like he was used to—but she still felt her nipples harden with the *idea* that he was looking.

"I, um…" He cleared his throat, then opened the door and got out. He paused before shutting it though. "Anything else?"

Gabby took a deep breath and willed her nipples to stop tingling and her ego to stop stinging from the clear contrast she was to the women Conner was used to spending time with.

This was Conner. He was taking care of her. She didn't do well with people coddling her, but she recognized that it was important to him to feel like he was doing something to make things better for her.

"I'm starving," she told him. It wasn't *entirely* untrue. "Could you grab some crackers or something?"

He looked like she'd just told him he had superpowers.

"Yes, of course."

Conner was back in the truck in fifteen minutes. He tossed her the Carl-Mart sack. "Put those on, okay?"

"Um." She dug into the bag and pulled out a huge hot-pink T-shirt and an even bigger pair of turquoise sweatpants. He'd also added a travel-sized bottle of shampoo, a bar of soap in summer-floral scent, a box of crackers and a candy bar.

And not a plain old chocolate bar, but a dark-chocolate truffle candy bar.

Damn, the guy was good.

Except…"These are huge."

He glanced over at the T-shirt she was holding up. "You think?"

She laughed, realized he was serious, and frowned. "Hey, what size do you think I wear?"

His gaze ran over her, then he shifted on his seat and started the truck. "I haven't given it a lot of thought before," he muttered.

She knew that. Of course she knew that. But it stung a little.

It was *good*, she insisted. Her efforts to stay off his girl radar had worked. But he thought she wore an XL T-shirt and sweats? Seriously?

"Just put them on, okay?" he asked, pulling out onto the street.

"I will as soon as I shower," she told him, stuffing the clothes back into the sack.

"Now would be better." He pulled up at a stoplight.

"What I'm wearing smells like smoke, my hair smells like smoke, I've got soot and dirt on me. I'm just going to ruin the new stuff."

"Gabby," Conner said, his voice tight.

"Yeah?"

"Put the damned things on. Please."

She looked at him. It was clear he was clenching his jaw. "What's with you?"

"I just need you to be more covered."

"I'm wearing a blanket."

"But I've seen what's under the blanket." He pulled away from the light.

"But—" Then his words sank in. He was thinking about what was under the blanket? And it was making him want her *more* covered. She felt herself grin. "What's under the blanket is what's going to be under the huge sweatpants, you know."

"Yeah, but those huge sweatpants are ugly. It will help." He dropped his voice to a mutter. "Like the uniform has for the past two years apparently."

She glanced over. "You know I heard that, right?"

He shook his head. "Sorry. I promise to be good."

"What's that mean?"

"It means I haven't really noticed that…" He trailed off, looking a bit sheepish. "I haven't appreciated…" He sighed. "You don't have to worry about me hitting on you, Gabby. You can stay with me and we're friends like always and that's it. I don't want you to be uncomfortable around me now that I've realized…"

She didn't wonder at why he'd trailed off—he'd noticed she was a girl.

Fuck.

This was exactly what she'd been avoiding all this time.

"Are you kidding? My apartment just burned down, I look like hell and the thought of hitting on me has occurred to you *now*?"

He grimaced. "I know. I sound like a complete asshole who's led around by his dick."

"Well…yeah, a little."

"In my defense, the thoughts started with your cock-sucking comment the other day."

Thank God he was driving. If he'd been looking at her he would have noticed that she had a hard time swallowing.

She should have never said that. She'd said it to get a rise out of him, but she hadn't thought through just how affected *she* would be by the exchange. Especially when he brought it up again. But she wasn't used to carefully choosing her words around men. The men she hung out with were relatives or had known her since she was a kid. There was no chemistry there.

With Conner...that was definitely not the case.

She'd felt the spark the first time she'd met him. And she'd promptly done everything she could to squelch it. Or at least keep it from fanning into something more.

"I was wearing my uniform the other day when I said the cock-sucking thing."

He took a deep breath. "It would be great if you could not say the word *cock*."

She raised an eyebrow. "That's all it takes? You really are a slave to your libido."

"No, it's usually harder than that."

There was a beat of silence, then he groaned as she laughed.

"I didn't mean *that*."

She snickered. "What did you mean?"

"I meant, that it's usually *more difficult* for a woman to get me wound up than just saying one word."

"So, what's going on here?"

"I'm going to chalk this up to the damsel-in-distress thing." He was staring resolutely at the road in front of them.

"The damsel-in-distress thing?" she repeated. Then her eyes widened. "Are you referring to *me* as the damsel?"

He lifted a shoulder. "Yeah. A woman I know and care about is in trouble and I get all protective."

There was a crazy warm feeling that filled her stomach at that. She frowned. *That* was a bad idea.

"Protective and turned on aren't the same thing," she pointed out. "And I wasn't in distress the other day when I said—"

"We both know what you said," he broke in. He gave a disgusted sigh. "If it's not that, then it's simply that I finally realized you have boobs. And *that* does kind of make me an asshole."

She couldn't help her grin. "You're an asshole because you just now realized I have boobs—"

"It would also be great if you didn't say *boobs*."

Her grin grew. "Or you're an asshole because you're all worked up simply because I have…those."

He shifted on his seat again. "Yes."

She laughed at that. "In all fairness, I've been hiding…them…from you. So it's not totally your fault that you didn't notice."

He glanced over. "What do you mean?"

Did she want to get into this? It seemed like they were putting it all out there and maybe that was a good idea. They were going to be living together and she did *not* need Conner to hit on her now. She did *not* need any further complications in her life. She was trying to simplify. Nothing about being involved with Conner Dixon would be simple.

"I've been downplaying the whole girl thing. I dress down, avoid makeup, wear my hair up."

His gaze went to her hair. "I do like your hair down."

"Exactly. I've kept you from noticing that."

"Why?"

"Because I didn't want you hitting on me."

"And all it takes to *keep* me from hitting on a woman is her hair up and no lipstick?"

She smirked at him. "Apparently."

He narrowed his eyes at her, then looked back to the road. "And you were so turned *off* by me that the idea of me flirting was disgusting."

Gabby wondered if any female, anywhere, would find Conner disgusting. "No," she said honestly. "I knew if you flirted, I'd flirt back and it would be distracting. We work in situations that require our full concentration and dedication. And I definitely didn't want to deal with working with you after we broke up."

He looked over again, his eyebrows up. He looked mildly

amused. "How do you know it would have gone beyond flirting?"

"It would have." She couldn't say exactly how she knew, but she did. She'd been around men all her life. All of her brothers and cousins had friends. She'd been flirted with plenty. And it was very rare to feel a spark like she felt with Conner.

His smile grew. "Then how do you know it would have gone beyond just a one-night thing?"

She gave *him* a look. "You would have never been able to keep it to one night."

He chuckled. "You might be right about that. I like you. I don't always really like the women I take home."

She didn't say anything, but she did roll her eyes.

"I know how that sounds," he said, even with her lack of response. "What I mean is, I don't really know them. I know you. We probably would have dated for a while. If you were my type."

"I thought we just established that I do have boobs."

"*Touché*," he said with a tip of his head. "But I'm not into tall brunettes. I like curvy blondes."

Uh-huh. It did seem that way.

Gabby didn't analyze her actions. She simply let the blanket fall away from her shoulders as she reached for the Carl-Mart bag.

Conner glanced over and she felt the truck swerve slightly. "What are you doing?"

"I realized you were right," she said, pulling the candy bar from the bag.

"Right?"

"I'm not your type. So there's no reason to worry about being modest."

"Put the sweatpants on."

She looked at him as she bit into the chocolate. "No. I'm warm now."

He hit the button to turn the AC on.

CHAPTER
THREE

GABBY GRINNED around her gourmet candy bar.

"Gabby." Conner's voice sounded tight and a little frustrated.

"Conner."

"I was wrong. You're my type. I definitely realize you have boobs. And I'm going to flirt like crazy. You should cover up since you don't want to get involved."

"Well, see, here's the thing. I've only got two months left to worry about being uncomfortable with you at work. I figure it'll take you at least that long to convince me you're worth the trouble and then we won't have anything to worry about," she quipped.

Then realized her slip.

"Two months left? What do you mean?"

Gabby grimaced. She hadn't told Ryan—or Conner—about giving the hospital her sixty-day notice.

She was starting medical school in August and would be leaving the crew except for rare on-call instances if they needed her. It was only April, but she needed a couple of months to get her life transitioned from working full time to full-time student status.

For one, she needed to move. Even before the fire, she wouldn't have been able to keep her apartment without her full-time salary anyway and she was really trying to avoid moving in with her parents. And she needed books and to complete everything that was required for orientation and, most of all, to make sure her family was ready for the big life change. Yes, it was *her* life change, but in the Evans family, the ripple effect was phenomenal.

She was always around, always available to her family. And she loved it. Brothers and cousins dropped by to watch a game or play poker. Her mom would get in the mood to bake and call everyone over for dessert. Uncle Andy, who owned the bar, would put together game-day or holiday promotions where everyone in the family helped out. If things got busy and backed up at the shop, Gabby and her brothers would spend a Saturday helping their dad and uncles do oil changes and tire rotations.

For Gabby, if you were in someone's life, you were *in* someone's life, whatever they needed—and whether they wanted you to be or not.

So her decision to back off and have more space and time outside of the family was going to be hard on all of them.

"I...um..." she took a deep breath, "...I start med school in August."

Conner was clearly surprised. He seemed to think about it for a moment. "Here in Omaha?"

"Yes, at the medical center." A part of the University of Nebraska, it was one of two medical schools in the city.

"But you're leaving the crew."

She pressed her lips together and nodded. She loved being a paramedic and she loved their crew. Conner would understand that it would take something big to make her want to leave them.

"Well, congrats." He didn't sound particularly enthusiastic.

"Thanks." She was the least enthusiastic she'd been when telling anyone about her medical school acceptance.

He cleared his throat and shifted on the seat. She took another bite of chocolate.

Finally he said, "It would *not* take me two months to convince you to sleep with me."

She laughed, almost spitting chocolate onto his dashboard. She covered her mouth with her hand and looked at him. He gave her a cocky grin.

He was right. It would take him about two seconds if he really tried. Which was the point of all her Conner-flirtation-avoidance maneuvers in the past.

"You're not *my* type," she told him.

"Romantic and good in bed is every woman's type."

Gabby knew that was exactly why he concentrated on those things. She understood that he was used to being *the* man. Raising four sisters and helping his mom after his dad's death had put him in the position of hero at an early age. A position he loved. He loved having women think he was the best thing since someone invented the concept of double chocolate. So he carefully focused on things that would make women put him on the Conner-is-so-amazing pedestal.

"I like long-term relationships," she told him. "And you're allergic to them."

Conner gave a funny grunt in response.

She rolled her eyes. But she knew this was who Conner was. And she knew who she was.

Committed relationships were something Gabby believed in. It sounded cheesy, but she had a big, boisterous, loving family that was built on a series of long-term, committed relationships —from her grandparents to her aunts and uncles to her own parents. It was a foundation, a solid place to come from—and to come home to.

They pulled up in front of his apartment complex and Gabby gathered up what was left of her chocolate bar and her no-way-am-I-wearing-these clothes in the Carl-Mart sack and got out of the truck, wrapping the blanket around her shoulders again.

He led the way to the steps, then gestured for her to precede him.

She was halfway up when she thought of something. "Hey, Conner, I know that you have this thing about keeping things light and easy with women and I know that two months is a lot longer than you typically spend with anyone. But I want to promise you that I won't *need* you. I won't be difficult. I won't need to cry on your shoulder. None of that. Roommates only, okay?"

He didn't say anything.

She turned back.

He was checking out her ass.

She grinned. "I guess blonde or brunette doesn't matter from behind, huh?"

He lifted his gaze to her face, but he took his time about it.

Gabby felt warm everywhere by the time he looked her in the eye.

"You could have green hair with big purple polka dots all over and *this* view would still be phenomenal," he said sincerely.

She felt her smile die.

Holy crap. She could not let on how much he'd just turned her on with that one sentence.

"It's only two months. And I'll get some baggy pants. Or wear my uniform all the time."

She bit her lip. Because she was babbling. And she would *not* turn into one of those babbling, I-have-no-pride-when-you-smile-at-me girls that fed Conner's ego.

"What's only two months?" he asked.

"Me staying here."

"You need to stay *here* for two months?" he repeated. Then he almost immediately seemed to regret it. "Sorry. It doesn't matter. Sure, two months is fine."

"My lease was ending there in two months and I have a

deposit down on a new place, but it won't be available until June fifteenth."

She had to stop. She did not babble. What the hell?

"June fifteenth. Fine."

It sounded more like he'd said, *Root canal. Fine.*

He passed her, ascending the rest of the stairs ahead of her, and unlocked the third door on the left. Then he grabbed the duffle bag sitting right outside the door.

Gabby grinned as she recognized it as one of Sierra's. That woman was a really good friend.

Gabby followed him into the apartment.

He tossed the duffle bag on the couch and kicked his shoes off as she looked around.

His apartment was surprisingly cozy. Her brothers each had apartments and they varied in layout and décor as much as her brothers themselves differed. But they were guys. They all had the basics. Entertainment centers, a couch, a recliner, a table with anywhere from one to four chairs for meals. But they didn't have things hanging on the walls, they didn't have plants, they didn't have throw rugs.

Conner Dixon had throw rugs.

His living area consisted of a matching sofa, love seat and oversized chair with an ottoman and a beautiful coffee table. A coffee table that was not covered with magazines, remote controls or empty glasses.

Conner's held a stack of four books, a set of coasters—Gabby wasn't sure her brothers even knew what a coaster was—and one remote control. *One.* Unbelievable.

The living room was separated from the kitchen by a long, marble-topped bar with three tall stools. The bar held a bowl of fruit. *Fruit.*

The kitchen was huge, with a center island—that was not covered with junk mail. Even Gabby's center kitchen island was covered with junk mail. There were a few dishes propped in the sink and there was a bag of chips and a twelve-pack of bottled water on the counter, but otherwise it was clean.

And there was a throw rug covering the faux-wood floor in front of the sink.

"Did your sisters decorate for you?" she asked, facing him again.

He frowned. "No, why?"

"Your place is really nice."

Even the lighting in the living area was bright but warm, provided by nice lamps that sat on matching end tables.

Gabby suddenly felt her eyes well with tears. She sniffed. Crap.

"You okay?" Conner stepped close, his hand closing around her elbow.

She nodded. Then shook her head.

"Here." He pushed her into the chair. He disappeared into the kitchen and returned with a cold bottle of water that he held out.

She took two big drinks before she gave him a small smile.

"Sorry. I just got a little choked up."

"Your apartment?"

She nodded. "All of my stuff was hand-me-downs, not worth a quarter at a rummage. None of it matched. But it all had a story. The kitchen table and chairs had been my grandmother's. My couch was the first thing my uncle bought after he graduated from law school. My bed was the one my mom slept in growing up. My coffee table was from my other uncle's frat house. It had the best stuff scratched in the surface."

She looked up at Conner, feeling stupid. He was sitting on his coffee table, facing her, their knees almost touching.

"I am really sorry that happened to you, G," he said quietly. "And I'm sorry that I hesitated for even one second when you said you needed to stay here. Of course you can. However long or short you need."

And then there were the sweet Conner moments. They spent

most of their time together at work, of course, but she'd seen him calm an older woman after she'd fallen and broken her arm, she'd seen him with kids at the scene of a car accident, she'd seen him go into a condemned building after a litter of kittens.

"Thanks, Conner."

He nodded. "I like it better when you smile."

She smiled. "Doesn't everyone always like it better when other people smile?"

"Probably. Except IT guys. I think the ones at the hospital like to see people cry. All that 'have you tried restarting the computer?' bullshit and using big terms just to make us feel stupid."

She grinned.

"And personal trainers. If you smile around them, they make you do double reps."

She chuckled.

"But dammit, Gabby, I really like it when *you* smile. When you smile it means things are okay. I always look for your smile at scenes. Once I see it I can breathe deep again."

Her smile died and she felt her eyes widen. "What?"

He nodded. "I didn't realize it until just now. But there's always this churning in my gut when we're at a scene. Adrenaline, all of that. And it doesn't stop until I see you smile."

She swallowed hard. "I don't always smile at a scene." There were too many times that the smile didn't come for several hours, sometimes a day or two, after a scene. They all knew that there would be bad scenes and that things wouldn't always go their way. But none of them took that particularly well.

He nodded. "I know. But I don't think that churning stops until you do."

"That's..." She didn't really know what that was.

"Because I trust you. And because you're smart and dedicated and you have a lot of heart. If you're smiling, things really will be okay."

Gabby had no idea what to say to all of that. It was deep. And sweet. And way too emotional for her and Conner.

"You better be careful, Dixon," she said softly. "It almost sounds like you did notice a girl even without makeup and a push-up bra."

"That's the damnedest thing. I did. But I didn't. How's that possible?"

She rolled her eyes. "You mean how was there a bra—push-up or otherwise—nearby and you didn't notice there were boobs?"

His eyes narrowed. "Something like that."

She wet her lips.

His gaze followed her tongue.

The entire upper half of her body tingled.

Damn.

She was *not* going to be that girl. She was not going to fall at Conner's feet.

He was not perfect, he was not a God, he had no magical powers.

Probably.

She cleared her throat. "That's easy. You like the girls who gaze up at you adoringly and I'm not the type."

"You don't gaze?"

"Not adoringly."

"At me?"

"At anyone."

"Ever?"

"Nope."

"Why is that?"

She shrugged. "Maybe I like being gazed *at*."

His eyes did that thing again where they dropped to her lips, then roamed over her hair and ended on her mouth again.

And her body did the same *oh yeah* thing that she didn't really understand.

She was responding to something from him that she couldn't even really define.

"Being gazed at is good," he finally said.

"Yeah."

"I'm not really good at that."

She gave him a small smile. "Yeah."

He looked surprised. "Yeah?"

She laughed. "Yeah."

"I'm generally known as quite the romantic."

She nodded. "You are."

"And sweet. Sexy."

"Yep and yep."

His eyes narrowed again. "You don't agree?"

"I think you're *very* romantic and sweet and sexy…with the girls who pursue you first, the ones who come on to you."

He opened his mouth. Then shut it.

She laughed again. "We've spent thirty-six hours a week, every week, for two years together, Conner. You didn't think I'd notice a few things?"

He leaned in. "What do you think you've noticed, G?"

"That you like the obvious girls, the ones who are all about you, the ones who will do anything for you. You flirt, but you never ask them out before they've thrown themselves at you. You love being doted on. You love the view from that big old pedestal they put you on."

Something flickered in his eyes, but he gave her a slow grin. It didn't make her tummy flip like it should have. Because it was practiced. She could tell he was faking it.

"So you know my secret."

"That you're full of shit?"

He raised an eyebrow. "What?"

She nodded. "You're full of shit. You only like the sure things, but none of them know that. You make them feel like they're special and beautiful and wonderful, and they never realize that they did all the pursuing."

"What makes you think that I don't really think that they're special and beautiful and wonderful?"

"You do," she said, knowing that Conner really was a good

guy who appreciated women. He treated them all well. "But not before they think *you're* special and beautiful and wonderful."

"Yeah, well, I'm not really the romantic type deep down. It's an act."

She snorted. "Bullshit."

"Seriously."

"No. You want to be romantic, but something holds you back from doing it first, from making that first move. So you let all your sweetness and romance out on Sara Gordon."

Gabby could tell she'd shocked him. Again.

"You don't think I'm really head over heels for Sara?"

Gabby laughed. "Sara is safe. You flirted with her, but you didn't really turn it on until she showed you her wedding ring. You kept with it because you can romance her, get all that stuff out of your system on a woman who can never really do anything about it."

She tipped her head, realizing for the first time that she'd *really* psychoanalyzed Conner.

"Why is that anyway, Dixon? You don't want to go all crazy for a girl who's unattached?"

He sat back. "I have no idea what you're talking about."

Ah, she'd gotten too close. Good to know.

"Yeah, probably not," she said with a shrug. "But just so you know…you're safe with me. You can be yourself. I'm not the girl to be pursuing a guy on a good day and certainly not right now."

She'd grown up around men. Tough guys. "Real" men. They worked with their hands, they drank beer, they told raunchy jokes, they preferred denim over all other fabrics. But as loud and passionate as they were about their sports, poker and cars, they were more so about their women. The men she knew—her father included—were romantic and protective while being all about women's lib. They respected women and they picked women who would be their *partners*. Not one of them got away with thinking women—theirs or any others—were the weaker sex. She supposed that's why Conner was able to make her tummy flip at times. She liked a protective guy, a guy who would insist she sleep in his guest room when she was homeless, but who would also get out of the way when she needed to stitch someone up and would admire her ability to deal with a drunk who'd put his car in the fountain in the park.

"Not right now?"

She pushed up from the chair, the blanket slipping off one shoulder.

Conner's eyes immediately went to the bare skin.

Definitely not right now. Or ever.

She was nervous about medical school. It would be demanding, and she wanted it bad. She needed to reduce the chaos as much as possible and then control what was left as best she could. With her family there would always be some craziness going on.

Getting involved with Conner Dixon would be like adding an earthquake to the hurricane that was the Evans family.

She didn't need any more shaking up than she already had.

"Medical school is all I care about right now," she told him, pulling the blanket back up to her neck. "I don't have the time or energy for anything else."

Conner rose, standing way too close, something she couldn't quite define in his eyes.

"My sisters have always sucked any extra time and energy," he said. "I haven't had anything left for a woman. And women are a lot of work."

Gabby smiled and stepped back. "What you need is to live with a woman who's *not* a lot of work. For about two months. Then you'll see we're not all so bad."

Conner shook his head. "Women aren't bad. Women are awesome. That's the problem."

Hmm. Not exactly the word she'd been expecting. "Con—"

"And now *you're* a problem."

"Wh—"

He reached up, his thumb going to the corner of her mouth. He drug it across half of her bottom lip and her body exploded with what felt like a thousand Fourth of July sparklers. He held his thumb up. There was a smudge of chocolate.

His eyes were on hers though. "I can't believe that for two years I thought of you as just Gabby. You were one of the crew. Someone I could trust and depend on. Someone I respected and valued. And now, within a few hours of realizing you had boobs, you've become trouble. Typical." He wiped his thumb on his jeans and headed for the kitchen.

She frowned and followed. "I'm not going to be any trouble."

"You already are."

"How?"

He grabbed a beer from the fridge, popped it open and drank. "Until about an hour ago," he went on after swallowing, "I was finally, fully girl-free. Olivia and Cody got together a month ago. *One month* I've been *not* the primary guy in someone's life and now here you are, moving in with me, wearing your hair down, with your boobs and your mouth…" He trailed off and took a huge swig of beer.

And now it was her turn to stare at him, amazed.

She took the beer can from him and took a long, cold drink.

She set the can on the counter and propped a hand on her hip. "What about my hair and my boobs and my mouth?"

"They're all *here*, with me, in my apartment. This is my girl-free zone!"

"Girl-free zone?"

"Not even my sisters are allowed here. I moved here a year ago and that was the rule we put down. This is the one place in my entire life I can go without girls!"

"You don't bring girls here?" She *knew* that wasn't true.

"Sex girls," he said. "Not *real* girls."

She just looked at him. This was Conner. Nothing had changed. But it felt very different standing here now with him and it wasn't all about her attire—or lack of attire.

"You're scared of me."

"Excuse me?"

She nodded as the realization sank in. "You're scared of me. Because there's no definition for me."

Conner grabbed the can and drank again. "What are you talking about?"

"I'm a girl, but I know you pretty well, and you like me and trust me. I'm a friend, but you want to see me naked. I'm a crewmate, but you want to sleep with me."

He scowled at her. "What makes you think I don't want to sleep with Sierra?"

"Because she's not the type to fall all over you."

"Neither are you. Or so you say."

Gabby nodded. "But you're still attracted to me. Which is what makes you nervous."

"I'm not scared of you, Gabby."

She didn't believe him. "Okay. That's good. Because having sex with a friend, someone who knows you and who you really care about outside of the bedroom, is a very different experience than a hookup or a relationship that starts with sex."

"You sound like you know what you're talking about."

"I've only had fairly long-term relationships and they were with guys I was friends with first."

"How many?"

"Three."

"How long is long term?"

"The shortest was ten months. The longest was two years."

Conner stared at her. "You were with the same guy for two years?"

She nodded.

"What happened?"

She shrugged. "Life." She'd been sad at the time that she and Greg broke up, but she hadn't been heartbroken or unable to move on. Which was her sign that the breakup had been a good idea. "We changed. Grew apart."

He watched her for several long seconds. Then he said, "I'm not scared of you."

Uh-huh. This was new for him. She knew that. "I would offer to move out and stay with Sierra, but I think this will be good for you."

"Good for me?"

"To live with a woman who doesn't fit into any of your categories. Someone you like, who you're not related to, who isn't in it just for you and who you're attracted to."

Conner frowned. "With a woman who isn't in it just for me?"

"Oh, come on." She laughed. "I work at St. A's, Conner. I've heard the girl talk. They're all so impressed with your reputation as a lover that they all want so bad to be good for you. To be memorable. To rock your world. They'll do anything for you, right?"

He stepped closer to her. "They all have a fantastic time doing it too."

She couldn't help it. Her breath hitched a little at the low, almost dangerous tone in his voice. Still, she had to roll her eyes. Such a guy reaction. "I'm not saying they're complaining."

"Then what are you saying?"

She huffed out a breath. "That there's maybe a little more 'suck my cock' than there is 'suck my clit' going on."

Gabby knew instantly that she'd just poked a little too hard.

Conner's eyes darkened, he moved in close and his voice dropped low. "I can't fucking believe that Gabby Evans has now said the word *cock* and the word *clit* to me within forty-eight hours."

Suddenly she couldn't swallow. "Um…"

"Yeah, um," he said, leaning closer yet. "Now all you have to say is um?"

"Um…"

Fuck. She *could not be that girl*. But she couldn't come up with any other words.

He gave her a slow, sexy smile that made her hormones start

doing the cha-cha. Because *that one* was real.

"Would you say 'suck my clit', Gabby? Because, if so, then hell yeah, I'm attracted."

She wet her lips and his gaze burned hotter. Would she say "suck my clit" if she were naked with Conner? Would the sun rise in the east?

It was all hypothetical anyway. That was the *type* of girl she was, the type he should spend some time with rather than with his adoring fans. It didn't mean she was going to actually have a chance to say that.

"It's not the same if you tell me, or ask me, to say it," she told him. Did she sound breathless? Dammit. "I'm talking about you being with a girl who can be just as demanding of you in bed. Who's as concerned about getting what *she* wants as she is about giving you what you want."

"A girl like you?"

His voice was husky and she swore she could feel him touching every nerve, sending zings of pleasure through her whole body.

Damn, the guy was good.

"I would definitely make you give me what I want," she said. Because it was true. And because she wanted to prove it right that very second.

He lifted a hand and she held her breath as he traced his thumb over her bottom lip, like he had with the chocolate. "Intriguing." Then he dropped his hand and stepped back. "It's really too bad you're not my type after all."

He finished off the beer, tossed the can into the recycling bin next to the sink—the guy had a *recycling bin*—and headed down the hallway toward the back of the apartment.

"Guest room is the second door on the right. Towels are in the hall closet."

Gabby was still staring after him, her body humming, everything in her warm and wet and willing, when he called, "Night," and shut his bedroom door behind him.

Conner awoke the next morning hard and horny.

He rolled to his back and stared at the ceiling, replaying the dream—that had replayed seemingly twenty times throughout the night—again.

Gabby. And the skimpy tank and shorts from the fire scene. And her long, dark hair flowing down her back. In the dream, she was still talking about him liking girls who were all about *him*…as she went down on her knees and unzipped him. She kept talking about how he kept women at arm's length and how she could show him that he deserved more, as she took his cock in hand and mouth. And proceeded to give him the best blow job he'd ever had—dream or otherwise.

He certainly hadn't pushed *her* away. Not during *any* of the dreamworld blow jobs. In fact, he'd sunk his hands deep in her heavy, long hair and pulled her as close as he could get her.

Fuck.

Conner dug the heels of his hands into his eyes.

Intriguing? Hell yes she was intriguing.

He wondered if she'd noticed how he'd run from her last night. Scared of her? Damn right he was. For all the reasons she'd said. She wasn't his type—meaning she hadn't come on to him. In fact, she'd been pretty clear about not wanting to get involved with anyone with med school coming up.

Still, he wanted her.

And the idea of her leaving the crew made his stomach hurt.

Fuck.

She was messing with his head. And she was living here. Perfect.

He rolled and looked at the clock. The crew didn't work today or tomorrow. But who knew what time Gabby got up in the morning? Paramedics and ER staff were used to crazy sched-ules, sleeping when they could, doing everything when they could. There was no routine, really.

He listened closely, trying to determine if the shower was running or if there was any noise coming from the kitchen. Nothing.

But he could swear he smelled cinnamon.

She was baking for him. Oh hell no.

Cinnamon rolls were one of his favorites.

And the last thing he needed was *another* reason to be surprised—and turned on—by Gabrielle Evans.

Conner got out of bed, pulled on sweats and T-shirt and headed for the kitchen.

Which was empty. Of hot brunettes and anything resembling cinnamon rolls.

He turned a three-sixty. He smelled cinnamon. What the hell?

He noticed the coffeepot was on. That was probably it—some girlie-flavored coffee. But he poured a cup anyway—it was coffee, after all, and he was going to need as much help as he could get today. But when he tasted it, it tasted like plain coffee. Good plain coffee, but still.

Cup in hand, he searched the kitchen. The oven, the microwave, the fridge.

Nothing.

"Morning."

He jumped, sloshing coffee onto his bare foot. "Dammit!" He swung to face her, fully expecting her to be standing there holding a plate of…something.

But if she was, he never would have noticed it. All he noticed was that she was wearing a tiny, silky camisole and a pair of tiny, silky panties that left *a lot* of bare skin. Very nice, smooth, tan bare skin.

She crossed to the coffeepot, her bare feet with bright-pink toenails padding softly on the wooden floor. Bright-pink toenails. If anyone had asked him if Gabby got pedicures, he would have lost that bet.

He couldn't tear his eyes away from her. She reached for a coffee cup, the camisole riding higher on her back, exposing more silky skin and firm muscle. She filled the cup and Conner let his eyes wander down over her ass, the long length of thigh, the curve of her calf, to the back of her foot. He wanted to suck on that spot where her calf muscle met her heel. What the fuck was that?

She turned, sipping the coffee. She hadn't added sugar, cream, milk, nothing. She leaned back against the counter and just looked at him.

Conner forced his gaze to stay on her face. But it was damned difficult. Even if he hadn't dreamed about her on her knees, pretty mouth around his cock all night, he would have still been painfully hard right now. But he *had* dreamed of her. Over and over.

He was about to lose…something. His cool, his mind, his temper, his…battle to not touch her.

"What the hell are you wearing?" he demanded, blatantly taking in the view.

It was a relief and torture at the same time.

She wasn't wearing a bra. The pale, cream-colored silk clung to her, the lacy V neckline plunging between her breasts. Her nipples pressed against the soft material and he could imagine perfectly how one would feel against his tongue.

There was about an inch of skin visible between the hem of the cami and the top of her panties. They were also cream colored and silky. And there wasn't much to them.

He studied her, realizing that she waxed or shaved very thoroughly, and suddenly wanted to know how far she went like he wanted his next breath.

Holy damn. This was Gabrielle Evans. One of the best paramedics he knew, one of the nicest and most practical people he knew, one of the people he most wanted at his side when in the field and one of the people he most looked forward to seeing in the break room at the start of a shift.

He frowned. He hadn't ever specifically realized that until now. If someone had asked, he would have said, yes, he enjoyed working with Gabby. More, he appreciated her. Her cool calm, her quick decisions, her skill. Her smile. Fuck, there was the thing about her smile again. He'd only realized last night how it calmed him after a trauma. And then he'd said it out loud.

Not good.

But, thinking about it now, it didn't feel like a new insight, more like something he'd taken for granted.

"I'm wearing some of the only clothes I own at the moment," she said.

He took his time moving his gaze back up her body. "Sierra didn't pack you any jeans?"

She sipped her coffee and nodded. "She did. But I don't sleep in jeans and I just got up."

"I don't sleep in sweatpants, but I pulled them on before coming out here," he said, grumpily.

"What do you sleep in?" she asked, her eyes tracking down over his body just as thoroughly and slowly as his had studied hers.

"Nothing," he said.

"Nice."

The way she said it and the way her eyes felt on him was nice, that was for sure.

He frowned. "And you sleep in that?"

She shook her head. "No."

"What do—" He stopped before playing right into her hands. Barely.

She smiled and sipped again. "It's a good thing I'm not your type, don't you think?"

Christ.

His body—and his imagination—clearly didn't give a damn that she was a brunette. Or that her breasts were small and perky instead of voluptuous like he typically went for. Or that she was at least three inches taller than most of the women he was attracted to.

Or that she hadn't baked for him this morning.

Women who spent the night always cooked for him in the morning.

"You're not," he said, with an apologetic shrug.

"I know. You told me." She put one hand back on the counter behind her.

The motion pressed her breast forward against the barely there covering.

Conner didn't groan. But his attempt to keep from groaning came out as a strange grunt that he then had to cover with a cough.

"And it's a good thing," she reiterated, "because if I was, we'd never get anything else done during these two months I'm living here."

"Anything *else*?"

"Besides sex, I mean."

Stupid. Stupid, stupid, stupid. *Anything else?* Really? He'd asked that? He'd known exactly what she'd been talking about.

"We'd be going at it on every surface in this place. We'd never make it to work. We'd lose our jobs. It is a *very* good thing that I'm not your type."

She rinsed her cup in the sink before setting it in the top rack of the dishwasher.

Conner imagined taking her over and over again on every surface in the place.

"Did you make something with cinnamon this morning?" he asked as she started to leave the kitchen.

Maybe she'd put on body lotion that smelled like cinnamon.

She stopped. "No, why?"

"You didn't bake?"

Her eyebrows went up. "No."

"Did you light a cinnamon candle?" He could *swear* he smelled cinnamon.

"No."

"Do *you* smell cinnamon?"

"Right now?" she asked, then shook her head. "No." She frowned. "Do you?"

"Yes. It fucking smells like cinnamon rolls in this kitchen."

She tipped her head to one side. "Are you having a stroke?" she asked, looking mildly concerned.

"I don't believe so," he said dryly.

"But you smell cinnamon."

"Yes."

"That's not actually here?"

He sighed. "Apparently."

"Did you hit your head last night? Do you suffer from migraines?"

"No and no." He was evidently just crazy.

She shook her head, and damned if she didn't look like she felt sorry for him.

"Let me guess," she said. "Girls always cook for you the morning after. So you automatically woke up thinking 'there's a girl in my house' and expecting cinnamon rolls."

Conner stared at her. Holy hell. If that was true he was… fucked. And more than slightly pathetic.

"No. It smells like cinnamon in here," he insisted. Because the other alternative was that he was crazy. And maybe a bit of an asshole.

She smiled. "I actually make amazing cinnamon rolls," she said. "But," she added with a shrug, "they're probably not the *type* you like."

Then she sashayed her sweet little ass out of the kitchen.

And Conner finally let out the groan that he'd been holding back since she'd walked in.

💋

Living with Conner for two months was going to be fun. The bed in his guest room was amazing, his apartment was clean and comfortable. And it did her female ego good to know that she could affect him.

She didn't want to do anything about it, but it was nice to know that a guy like Conner—who had lots of women giving him attention—could find her…what was the word he'd used?… oh yes, *intriguing*.

She grinned. Intrigued was probably not something he routinely felt about women who ended up in his apartment.

She liked shaking things up for him a little. Conner Dixon had always been very clearly comfortable in his life, with everyone doing what he told them to do and staying in the roles he'd assigned them. So it had been fun to be in the front row to see his sisters and friends rattle him when they started pairing up and falling in love.

Being the cause of some rattling was turning out to be even better.

Considering her apartment had burned down and all her worldly possessions had been destroyed, Gabby felt pretty good walking through the mall replacing her wardrobe. She did really hate that she'd lost the hand-me-down furniture. That was dumb. There wasn't anything she could have done to prevent it and there was nothing she could do about it now. But she was sad to have lost the things her family had given her. She hadn't actually thought she would always live with furniture donated from family members, but every time she'd walked into her apartment, she'd smiled and felt at home. From the bookcase in the corner to the desk by the window in her bedroom, her furniture had a story.

But with a family as big as hers, there was plenty more furniture sitting around in attics and basements. And maybe it was time for her to get some furniture of her own and make some stories to pass down to the next generation.

Gabby found herself smiling. She had new shoes, new pants, new tops and new underwear and was heading for her car, when she felt her feet slowing as she passed the makeup counter.

She didn't do makeup much. And on the rare occasion that she did, the stuff she got at Carl-Mart was just fine.

It was the photo in their advertising that had caught her eye. A woman, her hair up and makeup perfect, her head tipped to the side, with a man—a very hot man—standing behind her, kissing her neck.

It was a sexy photo.

And it made Gabby want to buy makeup.

Which made it an effective photo as well.

"Can I help you?" the girl behind the counter asked.

Gabby looked at the girl, then back at the photo.

She'd never made herself up for a man. But she was tempted to for Conner.

Which was incredibly stupid. She liked that Conner was attracted, but she didn't want to get *involved* with him. Did she? And besides…he hadn't seemed to mind her lack of makeup last night. She'd been in a fire and working an emergency scene, but thinking about the look in his eyes and the feel of his thumb on her bottom lip the night before could still make her tingle.

Yeah, he'd wanted her. Even without makeup.

He also respected and liked her.

That mattered. Whether he wanted to admit it or not.

And he'd liked her—and her smile, she couldn't forget *that*—before he'd noticed her boobs.

That also mattered. A lot.

So Gabby might just have to kiss him. Conner Dixon had probably never kissed a girl that he sincerely liked, who truly knew him. And who didn't have lipstick on when he did it.

He'd never been flirtatious or sweet or romantic with her.

He deserved to be kissed by someone who liked him anyway.

"What do you say?" the girl behind the counter asked.

"Actually, I think I'm good," Gabby said. "I think I'm really good."

CHAPTER
FOUR

AN HOUR LATER—AND four hours after leaving the apartment—Gabby climbed the stairs to Conner's third-floor apartment.

Before she'd walked half the distance from the staircase, she heard them.

Men. A lot of them.

And she knew she was related to most—if not all—of them.

Son of a bitch.

Her brothers had found her already.

She let herself in with the key Conner had left by the door for her. The noise level was high enough that no one heard the door open or her dropping the shopping bags to the floor.

Indeed, six big men filled the apartment. Two were her brothers, one was a cousin and two were uncles. And one was Conner.

Oh God.

They'd brought food—of course they'd brought food. Her uncle Steve was here and his wife, Lori, always made sandwiches for poker night. Uncle Jeff was also there and Melissa, his longtime girlfriend, was a fantastic cook and always sent dessert along. Her brother Grant and her cousin Lance were in charge of the beer—and they didn't bring crappy, cheap beer. Her younger brother, Josh, was worthless in the kitchen—one of the main reasons he showed up for poker night, even though he preferred to play "real" poker at the casinos and private clubs—so he'd brought the usual umpteen bags of chips. Which went perfectly with the dips that Gabby always made. Except that her apartment had *burned down*. Not that any of them were, obviously, going to let that keep them from letting her kick their ass at poker.

They were also all talking at once. Which was typical and something she'd grown used to.

But she wasn't so sure about Conner.

He was sitting on one of his barstools, a beer open in front him—thankfully—and a sandwich in hand. His attention was bouncing between her brother Josh and her cousin. They were arguing—shocker—at a speed and volume that made it impossible to interject. Even if you wanted to.

Her uncles and other brother were taking over Conner's couch and love seat, with his flat screen on—another shocker—ESPN.

She knew Conner was in to sports. He was the quarterback for the Hawks—the winningest team in amateur football league—and he and Ryan routinely talked everything from baseball to hockey. Gabby had participated in several spirited conversations about NCAA rules and regulations, contract negotiations in the NBA, and spring training for the MLB.

But she didn't know that he was in to having strange men invade his house and make themselves at home. Even if they did bring food and beer.

She slammed the door, instantly quieting the room—the reason the women in the Evans family all slammed cupboards, drawers and doors on a daily basis.

"I assume you're all here with gifts and condolences over my ordeal last night," Gabby said sweetly when everyone's eyes were on her.

"Finally. Where the hell have you been?" Lance groused as he stretched off the barstool he'd occupied.

"How did you find me here?" she asked rather than answering. Lance didn't really care where she'd been, only that she was here now.

Lance frowned. "Grandma."

"Mom," Josh said.

"Lance," Steve said.

Gabby rolled her eyes. She'd called her mom that morning before leaving the apartment—she'd also had to replace her phone today. Her mom had been concerned, but had accepted Gabby's assurance that she was fine and asked if she needed anything. Since she'd just spent the night in a queen-size bed more comfortable than her own and had a shower with a dual-pulsating showerhead and a cup of some of the best coffee she'd had in a long time, she'd said no.

"Where's the care package from Mom?" she asked her brother Grant.

He pointed down the hall. "Conner put it on your bed."

Gabby grinned. She'd known there would be a package and she already knew what would be in it. Cookies—Marilyn Evans's cookies were a staple hope-you-feel-better item. There would also be shampoo—she'd used the travel bottle that Conner had picked up that morning but hadn't gotten any of her own, knowing what her mom would send. It would be strawberry scented. Exactly what Gabby had used all through high school. She thought it was sweet her mom always sent that whenever she thought her daughter needed a pick-me-up and she was amazed that it worked every time. There would be wet wipes (Marilyn believed no one could ever have too many wet wipes) and socks (fuzzy ones in bright colors), a book or two (always romances) and a pillow. Always a pillow. Marilyn had sent her a pillow at summer camp, one to college, one to her first apartment, somehow knowing that Gabby was incredibly home-sick, and one after she'd had her tonsils out at age twenty-three. That surgery had really kicked her ass.

There was something about the pillows, though, that always made Gabby feel better. Her mom made the pillowcases and they always smelled like her childhood home. Falling asleep was a piece of cake on those pillows. She had four of those pillows on her bed.

Gabby stopped and actually felt her eyes sting for a moment. She'd *had* four of those pillows on her bed.

Damn.

The final thing in the box would be a note. Something sweet and mom-like, with a cartoon cat or a flower or a goofy smiley face at the bottom.

"I didn't make any food," Gabby said, hand on her hip, glaring at her relatives. Surely the lack of Gabby dip would get them the hell out of here.

"Conner ran to the store," Josh said, moving to the table by the window that she now noticed was set up for poker.

Her eyes found Conner across the room. She'd been purpose-fully not looking at him, unsure how to adequately apologize for all of this.

"He did?"

"We told him you were always in charge of dip and he said 'not today' and went to the store."

With Josh out of the way, she could see the containers on the bar top—salsa, French onion and spicy cheese.

She smiled.

She'd be hearing from her family for days about how they'd had to eat *store-bought* dip during poker. But she didn't care. That was nice and they were big, spoiled babies.

"Thanks," she said to Conner. "And I'm sorry."

He just lifted an eyebrow.

"So, we playing or what?" Steve asked, pulling out a chair at the table as if the "yes" had already been given.

Gabby sighed. "No, we're not playing. For God's sake. You don't even know Conner, yet you show up here on his doorstep and take over his apartment? Seriously? You guys need to get out now."

"We do too know Conner," Josh said. "He's one of the paramedics on your crew. He fell through the floor in that big apartment building downtown about a month ago."

"Two months," Grant said. "He's the one that's always driving Mac Gordon nuts."

"He threw that forty-two-yard pass in the division championship this year," Steve added. "The Hawks have been number one for three years because of him."

"And he's got those four hot sisters," Lance added with a grin.

Gabby was staring at her relatives, her mouth hanging open. Yeah, so her brothers and Lance hung out at Trudy's once in a while and many of her uncles and cousins followed the Hawks, but seriously?

She glanced at Conner. He was grinning with a full-of-himself grin that made her roll her eyes. Okay, so it wasn't just women who put Conner Dixon up on a pedestal.

"How did you know about me falling through the floor?" Conner asked, pulling out one of the chairs and taking a seat at the table.

Josh pointed at Gabby. "Gabs tells us all about you."

Oh no he didn't.

Gabby froze, staring at her brother. What the hell had he said that for? As if Conner's head wasn't big enough?

She was going to kill Josh.

"Is that right?" Conner looked up at her with a big smile.

"All the time," Steve, her father's youngest brother, agreed.

Well, crap.

There was no way she was getting rid of them. It was poker night. And she was shacking up with some guy they didn't really know.

Yeah, they were staying.

"I do not talk about him all the time. Not any more than I talk about Ryan and Sierra." She bravely met Conner's eyes. "I tell them about our calls and stuff."

Grant nodded. "She loves to tell gory, bloody stories during dinner."

She did, actually.

"That's why she became a paramedic in the first place," Lance said.

"To tell gory stories?" Conner asked.

She narrowed her eyes. He seemed interested.

"Our Aunt Linda asked her what she wanted to be after she graduated," Lance said.

Gabby chewed on her bottom lip. She wasn't sure how she felt about her family spilling her secrets—even if they weren't embarrassing secrets.

"Gabs said she wanted to go into medicine," Lance went on. "So Linda said, 'Oh, you mean like a nurse or something'. Gabby got this look her face and said, 'I want to be an ER doctor'."

Gabby felt Conner's eyes on her but she refused to meet his gaze.

"Linda laughed and said, 'Oh, you should do something nicer. Be a baby doctor or something'." Lance looked at Conner. "You have to know Linda. Everything is supposed to be 'nice' or 'sweet', especially for Gabby, since she's the only girl."

"The only girl?" Conner interrupted. "In her family?"

"In the *whole* family," Lance said. "There are sixteen of us grandkids on this side. Gabs is the only girl."

Again, she felt Conner's gaze on her, but she slugged Lance in the arm. "That's not the only reason I did the paramedic thing."

"She's been saving up to go to med school," Grant said. "And getting experience."

In her peripheral vision she saw Conner nod. "She's definitely getting a lot of that. She'll be great in the ER."

Her gaze flickered to him at that unexpected compliment.

He raised his eyebrows. "What? It's surely not a surprise that I think you're great at what you do."

For some stupid reason, her body flushed with heat at that and all she could think for a moment was *I'll show you just how great I am at what I do.*

And *that* couldn't happen with her family here. She was thinking dirty thoughts about Conner with her uncles right here?

But yeah. She sure was.

"Thanks," she finally managed. "That's nice to hear."

"If you want to go into emergency medicine, you'll be awesome," he said. "You planning to come back to St. A's?"

She would *love* to do her residency and then work at St. Anthony's. She smiled. "From what I hear, their paramedics make the doctors' work a lot easier around there."

Conner grinned. "Damned right."

And there was that feeling of camaraderie she loved so much.

"Yeah, yeah, Gabby's awesome, Conner's great. Can we play poker now?" Lance asked, picking up a deck of cards and shuffling.

She looked at Conner. Only if it was okay with him.

He gave her a little smile. "Love poker."

"We should warn you," Jeff said. "Gabby's great at poker too."

"Yeah?" Conner didn't look concerned. "She's full of surprises."

"And you haven't even had her dip yet," Lance added.

Gabby told the men that she needed twenty minutes before she'd be ready to play. They'd groaned and griped, but no one had outright argued.

Conner couldn't help it—he found this whole scenario fascinating. She clearly held some authority over the men in her family, even the ones older than she was.

He'd been thinking about her all day. Her and her tiny-assed sleepwear. When he'd heard the pounding on his front door an hour and a half ago, he'd hoped it was his buddies. He needed a diversion, badly.

Well, it had been a diversion, that was for sure. The five men had come in like they were old friends. They introduced themselves, explained that it was their weekly game night and told him he was welcome to join in.

Nice of them, considering it was his apartment.

But Conner hadn't minded. The talkative, loud, jovial group seemed like the perfect thing to keep his mind off of the fact he was living with a woman who had blindsided him.

Gabrielle Evans was a surprise from her long, dark hair to her bright-pink toes.

He'd been working next to her for two years without a clue that he did, in fact, like small, perky breasts.

Which was very much for the best. If he'd felt this pull, this— okay, *heat*—before this, they would have never been able to work together. And he could face anything in the field if he knew Ryan, Gabby and Sierra were with him. Not just Ryan, not just one of the girls, but them as a team.

And now Gabby was going to be leaving them.

But hell, it was medical school. That was nothing to blow off. And he was completely serious when he said she'd be perfect in the ER.

Still, he'd—*they'd*—miss her.

But as far as distracting him from Gabby…Gabby's family sucked.

They talked about her constantly. About the dips she made, about how she'd chewed her Uncle Dave's ass the other day for not taking her grandmother to the doctor, about how she'd planned a baby shower for her cousin Grant's wife and then let her aunt Tami take credit, about her apartment fire, about where exactly in *this* apartment she was sleeping.

They were clearly a fun-loving bunch, but Conner had no delusions about why they'd shown up to play poker at a stranger's house, without an invitation, the day after Gabby had moved in. They were checking him out.

He would have done the same thing with any of his sisters.

So, he'd let them in. He had nothing to hide. He wasn't sleeping with or seducing their sister/niece/cousin. In fact, he was fighting the urge every second so far. He was her *friend* and was letting her sleep in his *guest room*. Temporarily.

Once the guys accepted that, they'd been a lot of fun. Even though Gabby came up constantly. Conner had been a little suspicious at first. Now that they'd established he was a nice guy with good intentions, were they trying to push Gabby and him together?

But it had only taken about a half hour to realize that they talked about her because they liked talking about her. They liked her. And she was clearly a part of *everything* their family did.

It had been fifteen minutes since she'd left the room and Conner found himself glancing toward the hallway for the third time. The bags she'd dropped by the front door when she'd first come in and then gathered up to take to her room indicated that she'd spent the day shopping. No doubt replacing all the stuff she'd lost in the fire.

He wondered if there was more stuff in there like she'd had on this morning. Then he wondered if he hoped so or if he hoped *not*.

Finally, he shoved back from the table. "Gonna hit the bathroom," he said.

As if they'd just been waiting for someone to stand up first, they all scraped their chairs back and headed for the kitchen and more food and drink.

"Tell Gabby to move her ass," Grant, her oldest brother, called to Conner.

"You got it." Perfect. An excuse to find her.

He was *not* going to think about how he'd wanted an excuse to find her.

The bathroom door in the hallway was wide open, as was her bedroom door, but as he approached, *his* bedroom door swung open and Gabby stepped out.

Along with her came a cloud of something that smelled delicious—and girlie.

She came up short when she saw him.

She'd pulled her hair back and changed clothes. Instead of the fitted jeans from before, she now wore loose-fitting yoga pants and a green T-shirt that in no way hugged her breasts as nicely as the camisole from that morning or the tank top from last night.

Which was too bad. He was quickly becoming comfortable with his newfound attraction to small breasts.

"Conner," she said, as if relieved to see him. "Oh my God." She looked over his shoulder, then grabbed his wrist and pulled him into his bedroom and then into the master bathroom.

Wait. Conner blinked. His bathroom was *not* decorated in pink and black.

He glanced around. But, yes, this was his bathroom. In spite of the fact that every towel rack, the shower-curtain rod, even the hooks behind the door had pink, white and black silk and lace hanging from them.

Tiny pieces of silk and lace.

Conner swallowed hard. "You went shopping today."

Gabby stopped talking about…whatever she'd been talking about. He honestly had no idea what she'd been saying. His bathroom looked like Sexpot Barbie's closet had exploded.

Gabby followed his gaze to the pink thong that was draped over the toothbrush holder.

"Yeah. Obviously I needed to replace a few things and I had to wash them out tonight so they could hang to dry by tomorrow and I couldn't really hang these out all over the bathroom those guys are going to need to use when the beer catches up with them."

Conner managed to focus on her face. Her hair was pulled up now and he wondered what kind of idiot he was to not have noticed how beautiful she was, even without her thick, long hair falling free.

"Did you buy all this stuff because you knew it would drive me nuts?"

He'd never given Gabby's underwear a single thought before she'd paraded through his kitchen that morning, but now he really thought she seemed more the basic cotton type.

Gabby looked around again. "Sorry. I'll move this stuff as soon as they leave."

Loud laughter from the kitchen drifted in to them and she rolled her eyes.

She was damned cute.

How the hell had he not noticed that?

Because you don't want cute and you don't want someone you like. You want hot and gone-in-the-morning.

"I'm not...upset that you hung this stuff up in here, G," Conner said, shoving his hands into his front pockets. He needed to *not* reach out and see if the lace on the white panties hanging closest to him was as soft as it looked.

"You're not?" she asked, watching his eyes. "Then why do you look like I hung dead-animal carcasses up in here?"

He snorted. "I didn't realize that I look disgusted when I'm turned on."

She opened her mouth, then frowned. "You're turned on?"

"Uh, yeah."

She seemed a little puzzled, but also amused. "Good to know I can get to you with a nine-ninety-nine five-pack from Carl-Mart rather than needing to spend fifteen bucks for one at Tease."

"These are not Carl-Mart panties," Conner said.

She snagged one off the towel rack. "They are."

He took it from her. It was pale pink and silky, with lace around the top. "These are…"

"Cheap underwear."

"They're hot pink and black see-through with…*lace*."

She laughed and looked around. "And purple and light blue and peach." She grabbed another pair. "And there's no lace on this one."

Conner looked again. Now he saw the purple and other colors. What the hell?

His eyes landed again on the hot pink and black that had first caught his eye though. "*Those* are not from Carl-Mart."

"They are," she assured him. "They're sexy, I'll give you that. I couldn't resist. But they were only five bucks each."

Conner lifted his hand to rub his forehead, realized he still held the light-pink panties and handed them back to her.

"I'm seeing things and smelling things."

"What?"

"Cinnamon this morning, hot-pink crotchless panties now."

"Crotchless?" Her voice sounded a little choked.

He shrugged. "That's what I see."

"Seriously?" She looked concerned. "Have you been having headaches or any other symptoms?"

A raging hard-on for about twenty-four hours, actually. But he wasn't going to mention that.

He looked around his bathroom with a sigh. So she wasn't *trying* to drive him crazy with her panties. And yet he was going crazy anyway.

Living with a female…he *knew* it was a bad idea.

There was a loud crash from the front of the apartment, followed by several expletives, then more laughter.

Gabby's eyes slid closed. "I'm so sorry about *them*."

He wasn't bothered by the guys. They were loud, but they were harmless. Funny. They even had the potential to be interesting. "You have a big family."

"Uh, yeah."

"You dick!" someone in the living room shouted.

There was more loud laughter.

"I'm *really* sorry."

Conner chuckled. "It's not a big deal. They're just worried about you." His gaze wandered to the dark-purple bra hanging over the shower rod.

"No, Grandma told them to come."

He looked at her. "Your grandma sent them over?"

Gabby nodded. "I mean, I'm sure Lance, Steve and Jeff won a game of pool or something to get to be part of the posse that came over to check you out, but it was Grandma's idea."

Conner felt his mouth twitch. "Josh and Grant didn't have to fight to be included?"

She shrugged. "Brothers are automatic."

Right. "I can see why your grandmother might be concerned about you living with some strange guy."

"Nah. She knows who you are and that you're a good guy," Gabby said, waving her hand.

Something made Conner reach for her and grab her wrist. She stopped talking, her eyes wide.

"How does your grandmother know that I'm a good guy?" He tugged slightly, bringing her closer.

And was gratified to see her gaze flicker to his mouth before returning to his eyes.

"I've talked about you."

Her brother had said that earlier and it had given Conner a stupid warm feeling in his chest. Hearing her say it, however, made him warm a little farther south.

But it was still stupid.

"What do you tell her?"

Gabby licked her lips and cleared her throat. "Um, you know. Just stuff."

"Stuff?" He felt her pulse hammering in her wrist and smiled. "Like how brave and strong I am?"

She rolled her eyes. "I might have mentioned *one* time when you were really *stupid* and went climbing into a car hanging on the edge of a big ditch to pull a kid out before the car was stable."

"Stupid. Uh-huh." He stroked his thumb over the soft skin of her inner wrist. "And I bet you tell her how great I am at calming people down in traumatic situations."

The way her breathing had sped up didn't exactly illustrate his calming techniques. Then again, he didn't necessarily want her calm right now.

What do you want her feeling, Ace?

He ignored that question and concentrated on Gabby and her big brown eyes.

Brown didn't seem quite right though. They weren't chocolate brown. They weren't the color of coffee. More like the color of scotch. Or whiskey. Something intoxicating.

Conner shook his head. Christ. Where had *that* come from? That was a bit poetic for him. There were three eye colors—brown, green and blue. And he really liked *blue*.

"I might have mentioned *one* time when you hit on a woman who was pinned inside an SUV after she'd rear-ended a semi."

Conner grinned. He hadn't been hitting on the woman—not really. But the flirting had worked to calm her down and take her mind off the tools they were using to pry her loose.

He ran his hand from Gabby's wrist to her shoulder and down again. She shivered and the warmth he was feeling spread. "I bet you tell Grandma how hot I look in my uniform though."

Gabby shook her head, but she was smiling. "I did mention the time when you and Ryan got stuck in the sauna when we were working on that heart attack victim at the gym."

Oh fuck, that had been *hot*. Not in any good way at all.

He chuckled. "So your grandmother thinks I'm a stupid, inconsiderate jerk. No wonder she sent the guys over here."

Half of Gabby's mouth curved and she sighed. "Grandma thinks you're great."

"Because *you* think I'm great?"

Something in her eyes softened. "Of course I do."

It wasn't exactly heat that spread through him this time but it was *something*. Something unexpected. Gabby thought he was great. That was…something.

Women often thought he was great. Lots of them. Most of his life. But Gabby had made a point yesterday that had stuck with him—most of them had no idea how full of shit he was.

He had been faking the confident, I-know-what-I'm-doing, I'm-always-right thing since age seventeen. It was second nature now. The fact that Gabby had seen through it was scary. And kind of cool. Because she thought he was great anyway.

He pulled her in closer.

She came, her toes nearly on top of his, her breathing even quicker now, her pupils dilated. "Conner."

It wasn't really a question. Or an answer. It was just his name.

And the heat was right back and spreading quickly.

"You don't think I walk on water," he said.

She shook her head slightly. "I think you'd do your damnedest to walk on water if you thought someone needed you to. But," she said softly, her eyes on his mouth, "you don't need to be able to walk on water, Conner."

Later, he planned to blame this all on the pink and black lace surrounding them, but at the moment he knew that the urge to kiss her was far more complicated than that.

It was no less strong, however.

He leaned in and brushed his lips against hers.

She sighed and he tipped his head to deepen the contact.

Just as someone shouted, "Holy shit, Gabs! Get your ass out here!"

She pulled back and Conner settled back on his heels.

She was staring up at him, clearly surprised by the kiss. She pressed her lips together and Conner felt a surge of satisfaction hit him in the gut. He'd seen that stunned, *wow* look from women before, but it had never been from something that had barely happened. And it had never been from Gabrielle Evans.

Impressing Gabby seemed liked something that would be hard to do.

That he had accomplished it with a simple kiss made him feel like puffing out his chest and crowing.

And he couldn't help but anticipate the look on her face if he really turned it on.

"I am *really* sorry about my family" was the first thing she said.

Conner couldn't help his grin. "I'm okay."

"I didn't give them the address," she assured him. "Grandma probably found it on her website."

Conner suddenly had the urge to meet Gabby's grandma. And *that* had definitely never happened before. "Your grandma has a website?"

Gabby took a deep breath and stepped back. "It's one of those websites that gives home addresses and phone numbers and for additional money you can get background checks and criminal records. Yeah, she pays the additional money. She loves it."

Conner laughed. "Is she nosy or worried?"

Gabby puffed out a breath. "A little of both. She has sixteen grandkids."

"So your grandma knows about my speeding ticket?" He didn't have anything to hide. At least, nothing that would show up on that website.

"And any overdue library books."

He smiled. "That's kind of...cool."

"Oh my God," Gabby said, her eyes widening. "You're thinking that you should have signed up for one of those sites when your sisters were young, aren't you?"

"I'm thinking I should sign up now and run Ryan, Shane, Nate and Cody through it."

She grinned back. "There's caring and then there's crazy, you know."

There was a crash from the other room as if one of the barstools had been knocked over.

Gabby sighed. "And mine are crazy."

"They love you." Conner was trying really hard not to grab her and pull her back up against him. "They're just making sure you're okay. It's not a big deal." Her brothers, uncles and cousins were right down the hall. He could *not* pull her up against him again.

And that's all that's stopping you now?

Fuck.

"Well, they could have all cared a little more last week when I needed my oil changed," Gabby said. She reached up and pulled the holder from her ponytail, then drew her fingers through her hair and refastened it.

Conner felt like he couldn't breathe.

He'd seen women—his own sisters, in fact—do that exact thing thousands of times. But he had *never* before had the nearly overwhelming urge to grab the ponytail and use it to hold her head where he wanted it while he kissed the hell out of her.

He did now.

He coughed. What were they talking about? Oil changes. Right. "The place down by the park on twenty-fourth has ten-dollar oil changes Wednesday mornings."

"Oh, I can't pay someone else for an oil change."

"Why not?"

"My dad and one of my uncles own a shop."

He tipped his head. "Do *you* know how to do an oil change?" That seemed like something she'd be able to do, for some reason.

"Well, yeah," she said as if it were obvious. "And faster than any of those yahoos out there. But I was busy last week."

He shook his head.

"What?"

"I'm just thinking that there's a lot about you I don't know." And he was intrigued. In spite of himself. Living with a female was trouble. Having her underwear scattered all over his bathroom was trouble. But being intrigued by her? The biggest trouble of all.

And he could honestly not remember the last time he'd been intrigued by a woman. Probably Ashley. And that had been years ago. And had ended in big trouble.

"Are you surprised because you thought there was a lot less to me or because you thought you did know me?" she asked.

He thought about that. "I don't know," he said honestly. He'd simply never thought about Gabby much beyond her skills in the field and that she was easy to get along with in the break room.

She didn't seem bothered by his answer. She searched his eyes. Then said, "Well, we can go out and tell everyone there's nothing to worry about. They can go back and tell Grandma that I paraded around here in my underwear this morning and you did nothing about it."

The memory of that morning slammed into him. It hadn't been far from his consciousness all damned day, but having her mention it brought it all back in vivid Technicolor. "Is that something you would typically tell your brothers, uncles and cousin? And grandmother?"

She grinned. "No. Because then they'd think something was up."

"What do you mean?"

"They'd think that I was trying to get something going with you."

Why wasn't he grabbing her ponytail and kissing the hell out of her again?

"Are you?" he asked. "Trying to get something going with me?"

She hesitated for a moment. Then she stepped in close again and pinned him with a serious look. "You're a great guy, Conner, but I'm going to medical school in a couple of months."

"We could have a lot of fun in two months."

Had he actually just said that? Maybe the stroke thing wasn't so far-fetched. The last woman he'd dated even close to that long was Denise McDonald. Or was it McDaniel? No, McDermott. Something like that. Two years ago. And it had been not quite three weeks.

But the idea of hanging out—and kissing—Gabby for two months didn't seem long at all.

"We could," Gabby agreed.

Which was one hell of a good idea from where he was standing.

Other than the detail about Gabby knowing he was full of it and being willing to call him on it, of course.

His guy friends knew that Conner was a go-to guy. They saw him in action at emergency scenes and on the football field. Those were two places he *did* fucking know what he was doing.

It was the female-relationship thing where he faltered. Exactly as Gabby had said. Sisters, friends, women, his mother… he was pretty much faking it all. He truly cared, of course, but as far as always saying and doing the right thing, he had it covered on the surface only. Basic advice, being there to change tires, throwing birthday parties—those things he could, and did, do. If things got more complicated or went deeper, though, he covered with humor, charm…and presents.

For instance, he'd really thought that keeping his sisters from dating his friends was the right thing to do. But now it had happened to all four of them. All. Fucking. Four. It was still enough to make him wonder just what he'd done in a previous life to deserve all of that. But damn if his sisters weren't happy. And loved. Protected. Safe.

Not to mention how happy and settled and *normal* his friends were now.

It had clearly been wrong to think he should keep them apart.

And it was one more example of Conner not knowing what he was doing.

But there were women—lots of them—who thought he was great, who would go on and on about how great he was and who wouldn't hesitate to show him how great they thought he was. And who would leave in the morning. He *did* know what he was doing in those situations.

Flattery, flirting, fucking. Those things he had down pat.

Why, then, would he choose to have a relationship—however short—with a woman who apparently saw past at least some of his BS? One who was *not* leaving in the morning? At least not for a couple of months?

Still, he said, "I remember you mentioning something about me needing a woman who's as concerned about getting what *she* wants as she is about giving me what I want."

"Most of the women you end up taking home have spent a lot more energy getting your attention than you ever give to them," Gabby said with a nod. "It might be good for you to be with a woman who makes you spend some time on her."

"Are you saying you want my undivided attention on you, Gabby? 'Cause I think I can do something about that." For two months. Or for a couple of years.

He should also get an MRI scheduled.

She raised an eyebrow. "See, it's really hard to say no to that. As you know."

It was stupid, but the idea that she cared about him…and that he could make her breath hitch…wasn't *de*flating his ego. Or anything else. He shifted, aware of the near-constant pressure behind his zipper when she was around.

He lifted his hand to her ponytail and drug his fingers down the length of it. The silkiness and scent made him wonder what it would feel like spread out all over him.

Her breathing was definitely shallower again.

"No way would she be having sex when we're in the same house!" someone yelled from the front.

"I'm telling Grandma!" someone else yelled.

Gabby covered her eyes with her hands. "Oh my God," she muttered.

Conner laughed and stepped back. He was actually grateful those guys were here. Gabby was drawing him in, making him think about some things that should make him very nervous.

"We'd better get out there," she said with a sigh. "Lord knows what they might be doing to your place."

They left the bathroom and as Gabby pulled the bedroom door open, the scent of popcorn hit him.

"Hey, uh, G?"

She stopped and turned back. "Yeah?"

"Do you smell popcorn?"

She gave him a puzzled frown. "Well, yeah."

He sighed with relief. "Okay, good."

"Why?"

Because he was losing his mind. "I keep smelling some of my favorite smells when you're around. Wanted to be sure it wasn't like the cinnamon rolls this morning."

She laughed softly. "Nope, this is real."

Real.

Yep, it sure seemed real.

And *that* should have made him back off faster than anything.

CHAPTER
FIVE

THE GAME WAS GOING WELL. For Gabby. As usual.

She scooped the pile of chips from the center of the table and grinned at the guys. "I love this game."

Lance sighed. "I wish you were cheating."

"That would make you feel better?" she asked, separating the different-colored chips into stacks.

"Well, yeah. Then the reason you always kick my ass wouldn't be that I suck."

The truth was, none of the guys sucked. They just weren't as good as she was. She could bluff better than anyone in her family. Which came in handy when they wanted to know how things were in her love life, how she'd done on the chemistry midterm, who'd dented her car's fender and who'd jimmied the lock on the back door so they could sneak in after curfew.

"And yet, you keep playing with me," she said. "Even barging into someone's apartment without an invitation so I can kick your ass and take your money. Seems less than intelligent."

Lance grinned, unfazed. "I do it for your self-confidence,

Gabs. What would you do without us all acting like idiots so you can feel superior?"

She flipped him off. The men in her family weren't idiots. They were simply…easily distracted.

"Thank goodness you made some dip," Josh said.

All the guys agreed and reached for more chips.

"No offense," Josh said to Conner.

"None taken. Her dip is way better than mine."

Gabby hid her smile as she shuffled. She'd found a can of chili in Conner's cupboard and added it to the cheese dip he'd bought and warmed it up. Big deal. But in her experience, if it was hot and served in a nice bowl, men thought it tasted better.

Conner had nice bowls. Who'd have thought?

She glanced at him across the table, then flushed when she realized he was watching her. She gave him a smile. He returned it. And her tummy fluttered.

What the hell was *that*?

Conner was cute. He was funny and intelligent. He was heroic. She'd seem him save lives, for God's sake, and while she'd been impressed, her tummy had never *fluttered*.

Geez.

She concentrated on the cards in her hands. The last thing she needed with her family sitting around was to send the cards flying in all directions while she tried to shuffle. They'd definitely know something was up then.

And something *was* up…kind of. Not really. She wanted to help Conner break out of his one-night-stand rut. That was all.

But after a few minutes in the bathroom with him and one tiny, not-even-quite-a kiss, she could see why women went along with it—everything and anything Conner wanted from them. Their common sense simply stopped working.

A tiny brush of his lips and she'd been tempted to take her clothes off—or more, to take *his* clothes off. If he ever touched her with any kind of sexual intention, she'd be lost.

Dammit.

She didn't want to be one of those girls, one of the girls Conner was so used to. She wanted to be different, to show him he wanted different, a woman who wouldn't fall for his sweet-talking BS and would make him be *real* to win her over.

"Fuck, they're shuffled already." Lance reached over and grabbed the deck of cards from Gabby. "What's wrong with you tonight?"

She looked around and realized she'd been daydreaming while shuffling.

She never did that. Poker was serious.

"Do you have a fever or something?" Josh asked.

She frowned at her brother. "Would you all go home if I was sick?"

No way. This was Josh. He hadn't passed up a game of poker since he was sixteen. Ever since he'd learned that he could win candy bars, video games and, in one very memorable instance, a motorcycle. The motorcycle hadn't run and their mother had put her foot down against it—hard and fast—before he could fix it up, but Josh had been thrilled.

And hooked. From there on out, he took every opportunity to play and the pots had grown and grown.

The problem was, he was good. He won more than he lost. And it fed his compulsion.

"Hell no. That might be our only chance of winning some of our money back," Jeff said, picking up his cards.

Gabby sighed. The rest of the men in her family weren't much better. Their love for chips and dip kept them playing and their competitive natures made them take it seriously.

"If she was sick, you'd all get the hell out. Right after you made sure she was okay, right?"

They all looked at Conner. He was frowning. At her brother Josh.

Oh boy. They'd riled the protective big brother. Conner was mostly easygoing and funny but he didn't joke well about his sisters and their well-being.

Josh gave him a look that said Conner's question was strange. "Gabby's always okay."

"And bitchy when she's sick," Grant added.

Conner swung his frown to her oldest brother. "You still make sure she's okay, though."

Grant was unconcerned by the hard edge in Conner's voice. "She doesn't like fussing."

"Maybe because none of you fuss," Conner said. "My sisters can all be bitchy too, but that doesn't keep me from taking care of them."

"Hey, we told you, Gabby's tough. She doesn't ask for help because she doesn't *need* help," Grant said, his smile fading slightly.

She glanced around the table. "You've been talking about me?"

"Yeah. Conner here thought someone should check on you in the kitchen when you were cussing so loud," Lance said.

"We told him that the *last* time someone should go after you is when you're cussing. Especially in a room that has knives," Grant told her.

She rolled her eyes.

"You found the Band-Aids on your own," Conner asked, his gaze dropping to her thumb. She'd sliced it on the sharp edge of the chili can after she'd opened it.

It clearly bothered Conner that she'd been hurt. And that she'd attended to it on her own. She smiled. That was nice. Ridiculous, but nice. She was a paramedic and it was a Band-Aid. "I have some of my own."

"I'm telling you, she can take care of herself," Josh said, reaching for more dip. "If you get in her space, she'll threaten parts of your body that most men are fond of keeping attached."

Gabby puffed out an irritated breath. Her family made her sound like a ball-buster. And, she supposed, she could be. Sometimes they needed it. She didn't like them trying to help because they often made things messier and more complicated than if they just stayed out of it. She didn't like them hovering and fussing either—or she didn't think she would like it…it's not like any of them had ever done it—because they sucked at it. And she could put a damned bandage on her own damned finger. But she wasn't a bitch all the time. She liked to laugh and have fun. She and her brothers had a great time together. They were some of her best friends.

When they weren't turning on her.

She glared at them, then glanced at Conner. Who was still watching her, but with something new in his eyes. Concern? That was…weird. Then again, if he wanted to kiss her finger to make it better, she wouldn't stop him. And if he wanted to keep going with the kissing, she wouldn't stop that either.

Oh boy.

She looked down at her cards. She was being sucked in. She was going to have to be careful here. She was beginning to think she should feel sorry for all the women Conner flirted with. He was potent stuff.

"I'll look at the cut later," Conner said, picking up his cards.

She looked up, surprised. It was clearly not a request. "What?"

"Your cut. I'll look at it later and make sure it's okay."

"It's okay," she told him.

"I'll make sure."

"Con—"

"Ooh boy, you're brave," Lance said. "When she had mono and I tried to keep her company, she threw a bowl of soup at me."

Conner looked at her, clearly amused.

She rolled her eyes. "You came in, plopped down on my couch and started changing the channel," she told Lance. "And wouldn't stop after I told you to."

"You could have caused burns that would have haunted me all my life," Lance said.

The soup had been cold by the time she'd thrown it. And the bowl had been plastic. And had missed him by several feet.

Conner shook his head. "You must not know anything about women."

Gabby snorted. "That's an understatement."

"Gabby's not really a *woman*," Lance said, rearranging the cards in his hand.

Gabby met Conner's gaze and immediately felt warmer from the way he was looking at her. She definitely felt like a woman when Conner was around. She felt like freaking *basking* in being a woman when he looked at her like that.

She had to shake that off. She was on the verge of babbling and batting her eyes again.

"And *you* know a lot about women?" Steve asked Conner.

"Raised four of 'em," he said with a shrug.

Gabby laughed. "And that makes you an expert?"

"Well, his sisters are definitely *women*," Josh said.

Conner raised an eyebrow and managed to look very intimidating with only that.

Josh shrugged. "It's true."

Gabby waited to see if Conner would argue. It was true. His four sisters were beautiful, smart, fun, successful and had men wrapped around their little fingers. Even the ones they weren't married to. But wow, those girls had landed some awesome guys who were so obviously crazy about them that it made everyone in their presence yearn for a little of it.

Conner needed some of that.

"I'm not saying it's easy to understand women," Conner said. "It takes work. But if you care, you can figure them out."

Grant leaned forward, out of his casual, card-playing posture. "We care about Gabby. We try to stay out of her way because that's what she wants."

"You sure about that?" Conner asked evenly, *not* leaning out of his casual posture.

"I'm sure," Grant said firmly. "I've known her kind of a long time, Dixon. You don't need to give me advice on my sister."

"No advice," Conner said, tapping his cards against the table. "Hell, guys who aren't related to her should be thrilled that you guys are what she's used to. Makes us look a lot better."

Grant glared at him. "What's that supposed to mean?"

"It means if *this* is what she's used to, it wouldn't take much for a guy to impress her."

Gabby frowned. "Hey." But then she felt like smiling. Conner was sticking up for her? Wow. But she kept her frown. Conner was sticking up for her to her family. They were going to be around long after he'd moved on.

Conner glanced at her. "Women, even the independent, feisty ones, like to be paid attention to. With the right kind of attention."

"What kind of attention are you talking about, Dixon?" Grant asked, clearly suspicious.

Gabby kicked Grant under the table.

But Josh was frowning at Conner too. "I sure as hell hope the attention you're giving your sisters is different than the attention you're giving Gabby."

Gabby huffed out a breath. Idiots, all of them.

"Very different types of attention," Conner said easily.

Her gaze snapped to his.

"Oh really?" Grant asked.

"Okay." Gabby clapped her hands together. She had to stop this testosterone war. This was stupid. "Let's see who knows me...and women in general, better."

She headed to the bathroom she was using and grabbed some items. She knew her brothers and cousin would crash and burn on this contest, but it was better than them all yelling at each other and someone saying something unfortunate. Like that he'd kissed her in the master bath just a little while ago.

Returning to the living room, she found six men drinking beer and acting annoyed. She swept all the chips away from the middle of the table and set three hair accessories in the center—a hair straightener, a ponytail holder and a can of mousse that helped create soft curls when she was in the mood.

"What does each of these mean?"

"I'm sorry?" Grant asked.

"The hair stuff. You've seen all of it, right? So what's the difference? What do they mean?"

The guys stared at the items she'd put down like they were rare relics from an ancient civilization.

"You use that for ponytails," Lance said pointing to the elastic band.

"Yes," she said. "But what does it *mean*?"

They all looked at one another. Finally Grant focused on Conner. "Well?"

"You're going for practical or running late," he said. "Women pull their hair back when it will be in the way or when they don't have time to do more with it."

Gabby was a little impressed. "Very good. The ponytail holder means I'm focused on work and don't want to mess with my hair. Or, if I'm not at work, I'm having a lazy or sloppy day. I might not feel good, or maybe I just want to relax and kick back. It means I'm comfortable with you and am okay with you seeing me without my hair done."

"That's a lot from one little ponytail," Lance said.

She shrugged. "What can I say, it's how it is. Can you figure the other stuff out?"

No one, including Conner, said anything.

"No idea?" she asked Conner.

He gave up with a shake of his head. But he was smiling.

She picked up the mousse. "I use this to make my hair curl. It's soft and sexy that way. Wearing it like that means I'm feeling feminine and want you to notice me that way."

"I would *never* notice you that way," Josh said.

She frowned at him. "I know. And I never wear my hair curly around you, do I?"

He seemed to be thinking about that.

She shook her head and picked up the straightener. "I wear ponytails or buns at work to keep my hair out of the way. But for everyday when I'm not at work or if I'm going out after work, I use this to straighten it. It's easier to do than make it curl. When I wear it down and straight, it means I'm good, confident, things are routine and normal. If you're around," she said, directing the comment to Conner, "it means I'm not trying to impress you, but I'm trying to look nice."

Grant simply sighed.

She grinned and picked up three bottles of nail polish. "Red, purple or black means I'm feeling daring, sexy, like going out and having fun," she said holding up a bottle of purple.

"You said *sexy* again," Lance pointed out.

"And I never wear any of these colors around you guys."

"So, how are we supposed to know that's what those colors mean?" Josh asked.

"You couldn't make an educated guess?"

He rolled his eyes.

Conner took the light-pink polish from her. "Okay, I'm guessing this means you're feeling soft and romantic. You would wear that on a date."

She smiled. He was right about men paying attention to women. It did feel nice.

"And this?" she asked, holding up clear polish.

"Everyday. Nothing flashy, just basic."

This came from Grant. Gabby looked at her brother with surprise. "Nice."

He gave Conner a smug grin.

"Okay, this should be easy," she said. She started to hold up a pair of cotton panties, then realized she was about to show them to her brothers. Her different types of underwear all meant different occasions and moods too, but she hadn't thought that fully through before bringing them out here. "Uh, never mind." She tucked it behind her back.

Conner leaned to look. "Everyday, practical, simple."

She looked down at him and couldn't help her smile. "Right." She dropped the underwear and then stood on them so no one else would see her panties.

Conner leaned again. "Relaxing at home, end of the day, feeling comfortable and maybe a little playful?"

"I'm not holding anything," she said.

"I know." He gave her a wink.

She felt her eyes widen. "Commando is playful?"

"Depends on who you're expecting to come over later, I guess."

Grant cleared his throat.

Josh flat out said, "Knock it off."

Conner shrugged. "I win that one too."

"You only knew a few of those other things," Lance pointed out.

"Okay, how about this?" Conner asked. "If she's eating cereal for dinner it means she's had a long day at work and didn't want to cook, but she's trying to eat something a little better than delivery pizza. If she makes asparagus, salmon and rice—things are going well, she's feeling good about herself and is eating healthy. Protein bars—feeling fat. Chocolate cookies—dough or baked—something isn't going well, a breakup, something at work, fight with a friend…something. Leftover Chinese food— been really busy, some work project or something, trying to juggle a new boyfriend and work…needed something fast that she could eat while she worked. Leftover pasta—left over from a date where she didn't want to overeat but it was delicious and now that he's not there she can eat the rest."

There was a long silence after his recitation. Gabby knew she was staring at him.

"Wow," Josh finally said. He looked at Gabby. "How close is he?"

"It's scary really."

Conner grinned and took a drink of beer.

Gabby's uncles laughed and got up for refills of food.

Lance shook his head. "I'm gonna need a pen and some paper and for both of you to start over from the beginning."

It was two hours later before anyone left, but thankfully when they did, they all left at once.

Gabby was carrying an armful of beer bottles to the kitchen when Conner stopped her. "Let me look at your finger."

She rolled her eyes. "My finger is fine."

"Let me look, G."

She had been around enough stubborn men in her life to know that it was sometimes easier—and took less time—to give in, than to stand and argue about not giving in. Besides, the idea of Conner wanting to be sure she was okay made her feel kind of tingly.

Which was probably a very good reason to *not* let him look at it. Still, she found herself setting the bottles down and holding her finger out to him.

He unwrapped the bandage and studied the cut and her first aid. Which was, of course, perfect.

"You satisfied?" she asked, taking her finger back before she asked him to kiss it better.

"Pretty good" was all he'd give her. But he studied her face. "You don't like people fussing over you? Why is that?"

She tucked her cut finger into her front pocket. "I don't need it."

"Everyone needs it sometimes."

"So you don't like living with a girl. Why is that?" she asked him.

He grinned at her turning the tables, but answered, "Lots of reasons."

"Such as?"

"You want a list?"

"Yes. And a chance to prove to you that some of it may not be that bad."

He chuckled. "Fifteen years with five women, Gabby. I know what I'm talking about."

She moved in a little closer. "Yeah, but *I'm* not your sister."

He cleared his throat. "Yeah, I've noticed."

She grinned at that. "Let's see what you've got. What's the first thing you don't like?"

"The drama. Everything is always ten times better or worse than it *really* is."

She thought about that. He had a point. But not all women were like that. In fact, she knew that his sisters played it up sometimes just so he'd be able to do that you-exasperate-me-but-I-like-taking-care-of-you thing.

"So, let's pretend you had some excitement at work. You got shot at, you saved some guy's life and you're tired and sore and hungry. You walk in here and I'm all 'Oh my God, Conner! I'm so glad you're okay! Here, sit down. Here's some lasagna. And wow, you were so brave. I was so worried. I was pacing around here for hours'. Then I throw my arms around your neck and hug you tight and say, 'Can I give you a massage? Or rub your feet? Or here, lay with your head in my lap and we can watch whatever you want on TV…' That's not so bad, is it?"

He was nodding. "No. That's not so bad."

"Okay, what else?"

"Getting your feelings hurt easily."

"All right. So, I'm at work and someone says I look fat in my pants. I'm totally beside myself. I mean, okay, I've skipped a week or so on the treadmill, but come on. I can't be *fat*. So I go into the bedroom and I put on a tight pair of jeans and I come out and ask you to look at my ass. You do, being the good friend you are, and you assure me I look okay. But then I need to be *sure*, so I go in and put a skimpy dress on. And this one shows a ton of cleavage and leg. I twirl around and ask you to check me out. Which you do, because you're a great guy. But I'm still not sure. I put on my short-shorts and a tank top. Then I have to try on my bikini, to be *sure*. And through the whole thing, you are so sweet and reassuring, and in the end I feel better about myself and you've saved the day."

"Uh-huh. Okay, you might have something there."

She grinned. "What else you got?"

"How about all the *stuff*?"

"The stuff? Like the stuff all over the bathroom counter that's taking up all the space?"

"Yeah."

"Well, let's see. You don't mind when I lean in close when we're in the kitchen." She stepped close and leaned in to demonstrate. She felt Conner's breath against her neck and goose bumps danced down her arm. He breathed in deeply. "Or when I pass you in the hallway, and you get that little waft of my body spray?" She moved back and looked up at him. "That's okay, isn't it?"

He swallowed "Yeah, that's okay."

"And that's from that purple bottle."

"Well, there're tubes and jars and stuff."

"Yes. One is face moisturizer. It's what makes my skin soft and smooth. Like if you put your hand like this…" she lifted his hand to her cheek, "…you feel how nice that moisturizer is."

He drug his thumb across her cheekbone. "That is nice."

She slid his hand down her arm. "And the bottle of body lotion makes this skin soft and smell good. Nice, right?"

His fingers wrapped around her wrist and he lifted her arm, his eyes on hers. He took another deep breath. "Delicious."

She had to swallow hard now. "And there're the razor blades in the shower. But those make this…" she turned and propped her foot up on the table and ran her hand down her leg, "…soft and smooth too."

Conner moved in close, his chest against her upper back, and reached to touch the same leg with his hand. His palm ran up and down the length of her leg and Gabby blew out a slow, quiet breath.

"You've got a great point," he said.

He was so close that it felt like his deep voice rumbled through her whole body.

Gabby set her foot on the floor and turned to face him, absorbing the heat of his big body. "Maybe all the girl stuff isn't so bad."

"I'll admit I never looked at it all like that before," he said. "And then, of course, there's your dip."

She laughed. "You can be impressed by food too?"

"Absolutely."

"It's a bunch of premade stuff mixed together."

He nodded. "You owe me a can of chili."

"I'll make a note of it." She grinned. "Good to know that I can get you to do anything if I mix stuff up in a Crock-Pot."

"What kinds of things do you want to get me to do?" Conner asked moving in closer.

A dozen delicious fantasies danced through her mind. She moved in closer too. "My brothers will rearrange my furniture and my uncles will do dishes for my dip."

"Even though it's just premade stuff mixed together?" he asked with a small smile.

"I'm the best bluffer in my family," she said. "I've convinced them it's the best stuff they've ever had."

He paused, an eyebrow going up.

"What?" she finally asked.

"Just wondering what else you might fake with me."

She wet her bottom lip and Conner's eyes followed the motion with heat. She'd never fake an orgasm, anyway, but she was pretty sure that wasn't going to even be an option with him.

"In poker and cooking I'll keep you guessing," she said. "I like everything else very real."

He ran his thumb over her lips. "Damn right," he muttered.

She held her breath, waiting for him to do...something. She

could kiss him. He was right there, the desire in his eyes real. But he needed to make the move here.

For one thing, Conner didn't do that with women. They made the moves, offered themselves up. But she'd warned him that sex with someone he actually knew and liked would be different. He needed to make this decision. He needed to realize what he was doing here and do it intentionally.

For another, she often made the first move. It might be nice for the guy to take that initial risk for her.

Not that it was a huge risk for Conner. He'd have to be an idiot to miss that she wanted him.

"So…" she finally said, "…probably bedtime."

Damn, that was pretty obvious. *Chill, Gabby, let him do it.*

Conner dropped his hand and stepped back. "Yeah, okay."

Back. Not the direction she wanted him going. She took a deep breath. "The bed in the guest room is really comfortable."

He swallowed. "I'm glad."

"Have you ever slept in it?"

Let him do it! Do not throw yourself at him. Relax.

"Um, no."

Is your *bed comfortable? Do you want to try the guest room out? Or we could do it right here…*

She gave him a smile that hopefully didn't look as forced as it felt. "So…sleep well."

"You too."

He needs to make this move.

Or not.

She took another deep breath, then turned and headed for her bedroom.

He didn't stop her and she hated that she was disappointed by that.

Conner was sure that he'd been attracted to interesting women in the past.

Sure of it.

He couldn't think of one off the top of his head, but *surely* he'd been intrigued before.

Conner headed for his bathroom to get ready for bed. Alone. In spite of the fact that there was a gorgeous, intriguing woman just down the hall.

Who had cleaned up all the lace and silk in his bathroom.

He kicked the door shut and reached for his toothbrush. A flash of pink caught his eye and he turned to find a hot-pink thong still hanging from one of the hooks on the back of the door.

He stared at it, scrubbing his teeth.

He could see how she might have missed it. It was tiny.

He spit out the toothpaste and scrubbed again, harder.

Fine, she *was* scaring him. He wanted her. Despite every-thing. She was attracted to him, but she knew him and wouldn't be swayed by his usual flirtations. He didn't really know what to do with her.

But he still wanted to do…everything with her.

Dammit.

Women made the first move with him. He liked it that way. He didn't like guessing. Gabby had seemed on the verge of grab-bing him and kissing him. He'd been waiting for it. She'd even babbled about how comfortable the bed was in the guest room and asked if he'd ever slept in it.

Gabby was definitely the type to grab and kiss a guy she wanted.

But then she'd turned and walked away.

He should let it go. If she didn't want to grab him, then…it was okay.

But dammit, it didn't feel okay. Why hadn't she grabbed him? She'd been affected by the sweet kiss in the bathroom. He'd made the first move there. It should be her turn. He should wait her out.

But it only took him three seconds to swear, pull the thong off the door and stomp out of his room.

He was going to regret it, no doubt, but he was never going to survive living with Gabby and knowing what she wore under her clothes and that she could play poker, change the oil in her car and apparently make the best taco dip in the history of the world.

Hell, he was already fascinated with the feel of her hair.

Already.

That was the word—the truth—that bugged him the most.

She'd been here twenty-fourish hours and he was *already* a goner.

He lifted his hand to knock on her door, but she swung it open at the same time.

He held the thong up. "I think I'd look better in the black."

She grabbed it from him, seeming to smile in spite of herself. She pressed her lips together and shifted her weight to her other hip. "Okay, listen, I was thinking about you."

"I sure as hell hope so," he said sincerely, "because I can't stop thinking about you."

She studied his eyes and seemed to be pondering something. Finally, she took a deep breath. "Then there's something I need to do." She stepped forward and wrapped her arms around his neck, pressing the entire length of her body against the entire length of his.

When her mouth met his, Conner actually felt his knees wobble.

That had absolutely never happened before.

Gabby cupped the back of his head with her hand and opened her mouth under his. He groaned and traced his tongue along her full bottom lip, the lip that had been taunting him. Then he stroked in deep, tasting her fully, absorbing her moan, and took the kiss from hot to nuclear.

They kissed like they were starving for one another for several long moments before she tore her mouth from his.

He stood, staring into her eyes, panting.

Slowly she shook her head. "This is a really bad idea."

He felt his mouth drop open for a second. Then he shook *his* head. "*This*, Gabby girl, is the very definition of a good idea."

She let her head fall back against the door and closed her eyes. "No, this is dangerous. Bad and dangerous."

Not exactly adjectives he was used to attaching to sex.

Women. Everything with women was complicated.

"You kissed me, you know," he felt compelled to point out. And he'd loved it.

She nodded, pulling her tiny little top down as far as it would go. Which wasn't far. "Yeah. I had to know."

"Know?"

"If it would be amazing."

He sighed again and crossed his arms. "What's the problem?"

If this had been any other woman, he might have chalked this up to teasing and foreplay, but this was Gabby. She was the most straightforward woman he'd ever met.

"You like me more now than you did yesterday."

He waited for her to go on. She didn't.

"How is me liking you *more* dangerous and bad?"

"It's dangerous to like each other too much and have sex."

He leaned in, bracing a hand on either side of the doorjamb. "I'm not scared of you, G."

"You should be."

He laughed lightly. "What are you in to, girl? I can keep up. Or happily die trying."

There was a tiny twitch of a smile at the corner of her mouth. "It's not that. I'm going to medical school."

Yeah, she kept saying that.

He tipped his head, still grinning. "You afraid you won't want it to end after the two months?"

"No," she said firmly. "I'm going to be fine."

Yeah, an inflated ego was *not* going to be a problem.

Conner sighed. "Then what?"

"*You* might not want it to end. And that's not fair to you."

That made him lean back and drop his hands. "What?"

"You don't know how to have a real relationship with a woman you're not related to. You've never had sex with a woman who was a friend first. But with me you're going to get all of that if we do this. It's not fair to get you invested in this if I'm going to end it in two months."

Conner didn't really know what to say to that. From anyone else it would have sounded incredibly conceited for her to assume that this was going to be such a big deal, but somehow, with Gabby all he could think was…she was right.

"We'll circle two months from now with a big, fat, red magic marker on the calendar," he said, moving in close again. "We'll both end it."

"Okay. But it's really hard to walk away from the best sex you've ever had."

He blinked at her, then started to grin, then realized she was serious. And the craving for her only grew. "You think I'm going to be the best you've ever had?"

"I hope so," she said with a slight shrug. "But I'm really afraid I'm going to be the best *you've* ever had."

Again, if this were any other female on the planet, Conner would think she was being shamelessly flirtatious. But this was Gabby. If nothing else, she was genuine. Always.

He gave her a slow grin. There was nothing that had happened so far that made him think she was wrong. He was up for the best sex of his life. Bring it on. "Well, hell, G, how can I not want to find that out?"

"I'm not kidding," she said with a very not-kidding expression. "I knew we liked each other, but in the last two days I feel like it's changed. We like each other more. And that could be bad. Like I told you, sex with someone you really like, who's a friend first, is very different from sex with a hookup that you know is going to only be one night."

And just like that a stupid flash of jealousy went through him. "You've slept with a friend before?"

That put a soft smile on her face. "Yeah. I've had a couple of friendships turn into more."

Yep, definitely jealousy. "But they didn't work out."

"No. But I can tell you, the sex was *not* the problem. There's something awesome about being able to *really* let go with someone you trust, when you really want it to be good for them too."

He absolutely wanted her to *really* let go with him. "You've had sex with nonfriends too?"

She laughed. "Uh, yeah. A couple."

Evidently there was nothing that was going to cool his need for her. "You know a lot about men, right?"

She shrugged. "I think so."

"Then you know that saying stuff like that only makes me want to show you that this can be the best *you've* ever had too."

"Good point." She paused. "I'm not going anywhere for *two months*," she reminded him. "That's a lot more than just one morning-after."

"Not a deterrent at all, G." Two months was sixty days. And sixty nights. Nothing wrong with that. At all.

She stood, watching him, chewing her bottom lip.

He reached out, freeing her lip from between her teeth. "Sex with a friend is amazing, huh?"

She took a deep breath, but nodded.

"Show me."

She pulled in a quick breath, then without another word went up on tiptoe and kissed him again.

Well, hell, there was really only one thing to do in a situation like this. Conner put both hands on her ass and lifted her up, putting her against the door and pressing close.

Gabby wrapped her long, gorgeous legs around his waist,

and his cock lined up perfectly with where he needed to be. Now. More than anything he'd ever needed before.

Suddenly he didn't like the little scrap of silk covering her as much as he had. It was in his way.

He rocked against her, causing another delicious moan. She nipped at his bottom lip and Conner felt heat streak down his spine. He squeezed her ass and she squeezed him with her thighs.

She was secure against the door and her hold on him made him sure she wasn't going anywhere. He slid his hand from her ass, along the back of her thigh and back up, his fingers tracing over the hot, wet silk between her legs.

She pulled her mouth away to suck in a sharp breath.

He looked up into her eyes. "You okay?"

"No, but if you move your fingers about three centimeters left, I'll be really good."

He grinned. Damn. There was no way he was going to be able to leave her alone. Even if she moved out now.

She wiggled against him and Conner was the one to suck in a breath now.

He brushed his fingers over her again and loved watching her eyes almost cross. He had no idea how this had happened so fast. One minute she'd been Gabby, one of the best paramedics he knew, and the next he was going to die if he didn't get inside her and make her scream.

"No more talking and thinking," she said. "Let's just make this all nice and hot and dirty."

She was amazing. "You had me at hot and dirty. But I don't know about nice."

She laughed lightly. "You're right. Don't be nice. Be...very not nice."

"That I can totally do."

At least, he usually could. He wondered if he'd be able to be vulgar and dirty with Gabby. The woman saved lives for a living. At that very moment, even with her hot and wet against him, he could picture her crawling through the smashed back window of a pickup to free a three-month-old baby from the wreckage. The fucking truck could have gone up in flames at any minute, but there was no holding her back. And then there was the time he'd found her in the surgery waiting room, holding hands with an older gentleman as they waited for word on his wife. The crew had brought the woman in with a broken hip and bad concussion, and Gabby hadn't left until the woman was resting comfortably in her hospital room hours later.

Then she moved against him and moaned, "I need you, Conner. It's crazy, but I knew it would be like this."

Oh yeah—he was all in. She needed him. She was turned on, babbling, but that's all he needed to hear.

"You knew it would be like this?" How the hell had *he* missed it?

"That's why I never..." She wiggled again and he had to readjust his grip on her.

"Why you never what, G?" he asked huskily.

"Why I never let you see me as a girl."

With his hand against hot, wet pussy and breasts with rock-hard nipples pressing into his chest, that drew a soft chuckle from him. "Well, I'm definitely noticing that you're a girl now, G." He slipped his finger past the elastic leg of her panties.

Her smile died as she gasped, though all he'd done was stroke over soft skin. That was nothing compared to what he intended to do. Soon.

"I'm glad," she said, her head falling back against the door behind her.

"And can I say...you're very good at it."

Her head came up. "Good at being a girl?"

He nodded and ran his finger over her soft, very girlie skin again.

"You said you weren't going to be nice," she reminded him breathlessly.

"You want not nice?" he asked.

She moaned, her eyes slipping closed. "So much."

He slipped his finger through the wet folds, making her shudder. "Pull your top up."

Her eyes flew open. "What?"

"Your breasts have been driving me nuts since…" He trailed off. Being turned on at the scene of her apartment fire might be a little insensitive.

Her mouth curled. "Since…you realized I had breasts?"

"Something like that."

"You go for bigger breasts usually."

"I don't care about any breasts but yours right now. Pull it up."

She sighed. "It's like I can't think straight when you're around. I know I should make this harder for you, make you work for it, but I just want to strip down and rub myself all over you."

His cock throbbed at that. "Gabby," he said through gritted teeth.

"I'm starting to think the other girls don't actually *want* to be so needy around you, but they can't help it."

"Thank you." It sounded kind of like a compliment. "Now pull your top up and show me your nipples."

He felt her thighs squeeze him, but she still insisted on talking. "You know that whole thing about you being with a woman who is as demanding as you are with sex?"

Why was she still *talking*? "Yeah?"

"That's supposed to be me. I thought I was going to be showing you what it's like to have a woman taking as much as she's giving. But I'm up against the door, panting and moaning and ready to let you do whatever you want."

"*Good*. Now stop talking and take off your top."

She bit her bottom lip. And did not take her top off.

Conner sighed and moved his hand away from her sweet heat to hold her leg more securely. "G, what's going on?"

"My breasts are *really* not what you usually like."

His gaze dropped to the slight swells, the hard tips begging for his tongue. "First of all, they're *breasts*. I'm going to like them. Second of all…they're breasts."

She snorted softly.

He met her gaze as he lifted a hand, dragging his thumb over the stiff peak of her right breast. She sucked in a breath. "Does playing with your nipples make you wet?" he asked gruffly.

She nodded.

"Does sucking on them make you beg?"

She licked her bottom lip and nodded again.

"Then I'm going to *love* them."

She reached slowly for the bottom of her shirt, then pulled it up and over her head.

He had no idea where she threw the top. His eyes were riveted on the sweetest, most perfect breasts he'd ever seen. They were small, but they were firm, the long pink tips making his mouth nearly water. She had a bikini tan line. The lower two-thirds of her breasts was two shades paler than the tan that ran across the upper curves and into the valley between.

He ran his thumb over the tip again, now with no silk barrier. She gasped.

Then he lifted her, bringing one nipple to his mouth. He licked, feeling her fingers curl against his scalp. When he sucked, she cried out.

"Yep, love them," he said. He put his lips against her neck, kissing, then licking. "Gabby, you have exactly ten seconds to tell me to go away, or I'm not going to stop touching you until the sun comes up."

Her voice definitely breathless, she still smiled. "There you are being nice again. It's almost like you can't help it."

Oh, he'd show her nice. He leaned away from the door, bringing her with him. "Bed, now."

"I have a better idea."

He stopped. "Oh?"

"You have to promise something, though."

He raised both eyebrows. "At this point? Anything."

A sexy smile stretched her mouth. Her delicious I'm-going-to-have-those-lips-around-my-cock mouth.

"You have to promise not to let this make you fall in love with me."

He narrowed his eyes. Now she was teasing him. And she was cute as hell doing it. Cute and hot and…fun. He couldn't remember the last time sex had been fun.

No, that was stupid. Sex was always fun. But it wasn't…like this.

But the love thing was easy. If nothing else—and there was a lot of "else"—Gabby didn't need him. For anything. There was nothing he could give her that she didn't already have or couldn't get. "Okay."

"Promise?"

"I promise."

"Then I want to ride you on the poker table."

He stared at her. He was hot and hard and *needed* her. "Damn, girl. I'm glad you warned me not to, 'cause you're right…that might have done it."

She grinned. "Is that a yes to the poker table?"

He turned and strode toward his living room, still holding her. "You say I want to ride you and my answer will always be 'anywhere, anytime'."

"Duly noted."

He flipped on the light for the dining area as they passed, then deposited her on the green felt that still covered the table. Her breasts bounced slightly and he thought about pointing out that was hot, no matter what she thought, but she shimmied out of her panties then and, frankly, he lost all ability to speak.

She propped up on one elbow, one long leg dangling off the edge of the table. "You okay?"

He shook his head and pulled his shirt off. He wasn't okay. Not at all. He felt like he'd never seen a naked woman before. He couldn't decide where to touch first, what he most wanted to taste.

His gaze toured over her body. She was taller than most of the women he went for, with long, toned limbs. He'd already felt those legs around him and he was a big fan. Her skin was sun-kissed everywhere but for the mouthwatering, paler skin on her breasts and a gorgeous pale strip of skin between her legs. But even the lines across her hips were tiny and he knew she wore a very skimpy bikini. And she clearly waxed accordingly. There was the tiniest patch of trimmed dark hair on her mound and everything else was deliciously smooth, all a pretty peach or pink color.

"I think I owe you thanks for any career achievements I've had," he told her.

"Ooookay."

"If I'd known all of this was under your uniform, I'd never have gotten a damned thing done in the past two years."

She grinned. "You're welcome."

He stepped forward, between her knees, all seriousness then. "Gabby, you're gorgeous."

Her smile faded and her eyes widened slightly. He could only imagine what his face looked like. He was barely holding it together. This was crazy. He was far from sex starved, but he felt like it with her. He was experienced. He'd done it all, pretty much. But he felt like he was on the verge of making a first-time bumbling idiot out of himself.

He put a hand on each of her thighs, stroking up and down over the smooth, firm skin.

She licked her lips. "You okay, Dixon?"

The use of his last name pulled him back to reality a bit. This was Gabby. He could be himself.

"I'm thinking if you cowgirl me right now, I'm gonna last about three seconds."

CHAPTER
SIX

SHE GAVE A SOFT LAUGH. "I'd take that as a compliment."

"Yeah, well, we can't have you thinking I don't give as good as I get. So I'm going to do this first." He pulled her hips toward him as he went to his knees. He heard her soft gasp and it fired his blood further. As did the gorgeous, wet pinkness before him. "Besides, you did say there needed to be equal amounts of clit and cock sucking, right?"

Before she could answer, he leaned in and kissed her inner thigh, then licked the spot, moving closer to her center.

He heard a soft *thunk* and looked up to find that she'd slumped back on the table. "I love clit sucking."

"*That's* hot as hell."

She laughed softly. "I mean, I love having it done to me. I've never done it."

He grinned. "You have no idea what you're missing."

She lifted her head and smiled. "Do *you* know how great it feels to wrap your hand around a big, hard cock, then bring a man to his knees just by sliding it into your mouth?"

"Holy…" He trailed off, staring at her. "I'm on my knees now, babe, and I'm pretty sure I'm down for the count."

She looked far too smug as she laid her head back on the table. "Well, while you're down there, I could use an orgasm."

He couldn't help but laugh, even as lust flooded through him. Damn, the girl was something. He'd heard her tell some raunchy jokes but he'd had no idea she would be like this. She was uninhibited and so fucking hot he wasn't sure he was ever going to want to leave his apartment again. Some women hesitated at even having the lights on in the bedroom, not to mention being spread out on a poker/kitchen table with a light shining right above like a spotlight. Gabby not only reclined like she was in a lounge chair at the beach, but *she'd* suggested it.

He kissed her inner thigh again and was rewarded with a soft moan. And he kept going. Up her thigh to the line where her hip bent, then over her mound, before coming front and center. He kissed lightly at first, but at the strangled sound she made he flicked his tongue out and over her clit.

She didn't jerk or buck or even arch. She widened her legs with a simple, "*Yes.*"

Feeling pretty damned full of himself, Conner licked again, then suckled. He felt her fingers curl into his hair and her breathing was coming in short, shallow pants, but otherwise she was quiet and still.

He licked with a long, wide swipe over her clit, then down lower into the sweetness there. She whimpered slightly and her fingers gripped his hair a little harder, but she didn't move a muscle otherwise.

"Everything good up there?" he asked with a smile.

"Good, bordering on great," she said, her voice huskier than usual.

"Aw, well, I like great, but I was kind of hoping for amazing," he said, unable to keep from licking at her again.

He could tell her butt tightened, but there was no other movement.

"You want amazing?" she asked. "How about you give me a couple of those very capable fingers of yours and suck a little harder?"

And why the hell wouldn't he do exactly as he was told? Right after he started breathing again.

"Amazing is coming right up," he muttered, leaning in.

He sucked her into his mouth as he slid a finger into her heat. She felt so sweet. She sounded even sweeter.

"Please, Conner."

There was something about hearing this very capable woman, who didn't need anyone or anything, panting and moaning because of him. He had never wanted to make a woman come as hard as he wanted Gabrielle Evans to come.

He swirled his tongue around her clit, stroking his finger in and out, then added another finger. As he started to slide a second finger into her, he felt her muscles pulling him deep. He sucked harder and heard her gasping, then moaning.

He'd be quite happy to stay right here like this for...ever.

Not that it would take her forever to climax. Not if he had anything to say about it.

And he most definitely did.

He pressed his fingers deep, separating them slightly to stretch and glide firmly along her inner walls. She moaned and now her hips did lift away from the table.

He raised his head, looking from the sweet pinkness up her body. Her fingers gripped the edge of the table, and he could see her tummy quiver. Her breasts stood proud, her chest was flushed and her neck arched, giving away the delicious tension he was creating in her body.

What a view.

"So, so good at being a girl, G," he said huskily before flicking his tongue over her again and again. He moved his fingers in a steady rhythm and felt the beginning ripples of her orgasm.

He sucked harder and thrust faster, and within moments her muscles clenched his fingers and she cried out.

Knowing her clit would be hypersensitive, he lifted his head, but kept his fingers moving slowly, riding her climax out with her.

Once she was spent, her legs and arms flopped loosely onto the table, and Conner got to his feet with a cocky grin.

"So that was pretty great," he said, loosening the tie at the front of his sweatpants.

She lifted herself onto her elbows and gave him a slow smile. "Nice to know at least some of the rumors about you are true."

He paused in pushing his pants off his hips. "The rumors?" he asked.

"Hey, keep going," she said, motioning with her hand toward his pants.

"What rumors, Gabby?"

She looked up at him. "That you know what you're doing when a girl gets naked."

Was she really teasing him about his reputation? As if she didn't mind that he was good at this because he'd done a lot of it?

"You've heard rumors?"

She laughed. "Practice makes perfect, right?"

And then there was that damned stab of jealousy *he* felt, because, honestly, she was pretty damned good too. Women who were new to the sex thing, or shy about it, sure didn't climb up on poker tables and tell guys to add fingers and suction.

"How about you, hotshot?" he asked, shucking out of his pants. He hadn't bothered putting underwear on.

She checked him out unabashedly. He stepped closer to the table.

"Hang on there, slick," she said with a grin. "You got up close and personal with my goods—give me a minute to appreciate what you're bringing to the table." She laughed and patted the tabletop. "Get it?"

He couldn't help his smile. "You're hilarious."

Had he ever said *that* during sex before?

But he did pause so she could get a good look. And she didn't even blush as she took in the sight from head to toe—and back again.

"Very nice, Dixon."

"So how about you?" he repeated. "You perfected a few things?"

Gabby sat up. "I've had a compliment or two."

He fucking hated that. He gave her a cocky grin though. "I don't give compliments lightly."

"Oh, you'll be singing my praises."

"Don't hold your breath."

"Challenge accepted."

He also didn't remember the last time he'd had this much fun with a woman.

That was probably a bad thing. But Gabby slid off the table and stood, pressing her body against his as she slid around him and he couldn't remember why.

"Get on the table, Conner." She said those five words with a deeper note in her voice and heat in her eyes. She gave him a little push.

He obliged.

He sat, then leaned back, bracing his hands on the table behind him.

Gabby didn't hesitate taking him in hand. She wrapped her fingers around his throbbing shaft and stroked him from tip to base with exactly the right amount of pressure to make every neuron in his brain focus solely on his cock.

Fuck. It was already unbelievable.

She continued to stroke him, studying her hand on him as if it were the most fascinating thing she'd ever seen. "You're huge," she murmured. "I don't know if I can take all of you." Then she looked up at him through her lashes. "I hope you'll take it easy on me, Conner."

She was messing with him. He could tell by the mischief in her eyes and the tiny curl at one corner of her mouth.

"Knock it off."

She laughed. "Come on, that's what all guys want to hear."

She wasn't exactly *wrong*. "Only if you mean it." She still had her hand on him and was still moving, though, making it difficult to be irritated with her.

"Oh, you all want to hear it even if we don't mean it." She looked up again. "The guys in my family often forget I'm a girl too, Conner. They talk like it's a locker room even when I'm around."

"Hey, G?" Conner said, his lower body already tightening in spite of the banter.

"Yeah?"

"You got anything better you could be doing with that mouth of yours?"

He'd certainly talked during sex before, but never like this. It was a whole new experience and he was enjoying it. Which was probably a bad thing too, but he was still having a hard time remembering why.

"Get your compliments ready," Gabby said.

"You give good head?" he asked, intentionally putting challenge in his voice.

"So I've been told. I mean, I prefer to have you on your knees, but I don't mind spending some time down there too."

The hot surge of jealousy warred with the hot surge of lust in his gut. He put a hand on the back of her head. "Gabby?"

Suddenly she caught her breath. "Yeah?"

"Suck my cock until I come so hard I can't stand up."

He knew she recognized the words from the other day in the break room. *Her* words. Her suggestion for being more specific with the women he brought home.

Her lips parted and she took a deep breath. "You know, I would," she said, clearly trying to keep her tone light...and failing a little bit, "but then I'd have to wait for you to get it back up to get my cowgirl ride."

"And this is where you turn into that girl who is going to be demanding and who's going to be sure she gets what she wants from me?"

Yes, he did remember *all* the words Gabby had said about sex.

She gave him a slow, sensual smile. "That's right."

She pushed against his chest. He laid back. "Where are the condoms?"

"There are some in the silverware drawer or in the table by the couch."

She paused. "You keep condoms in your silverware drawer *and* by your couch?"

"They're wrapped. It's not like they're open and used, touching all the forks." Which was exactly what he'd said to Ryan when he'd found them.

She shook her head and started for the kitchen, gloriously naked—Conner propped up on one elbow to keep her in sight—and uninhibited about it.

"I don't care if they're touching the forks," she said with a shake of her head. "But why the kitchen *and* the living room? Don't you ever go into the bedroom?"

"I have some in the bedroom and bathroom too."

She looked up over the bar. "Seriously? You have them stashed all over the house?"

"You never know where you're going to be when you need one."

She came back toward him, condoms in hand. "Okay, you got me there."

And not a twinge of jealousy on *her* part? Really? If he'd said something like that to *any* other woman, they would have been bitter about it.

"Even though you're never more than ten feet away from a condom in this place, I brought a couple, okay?"

He grinned. "You don't think you'll be able to wait to get all the way to the kitchen the second time?" He loved that she obviously thought there would be a second time too.

"I'm hoping to be too tired to move that far."

She climbed up on the table with him, the sight enough to make his whole body throb again. She threw one long leg over him, straddling his thighs.

She ripped the condom open and slid it on with a practiced hand.

And a moment later, Conner forgot about being jealous or conflicted or that there was a reason some of this was a bad idea. As Gabby moved over him and eased herself down on the aching length of his cock, all he felt was that this was exactly where he'd wanted to be for a very, very long time without even knowing it.

She took him in slowly, adjusting to his length and girth as she went.

Conner made himself stay still when he wanted to grab her hips and thrust home in one stroke.

Instead, he watched the adorable little wrinkle between her eyebrows and the way she pulled her bottom lip between her teeth as she slid down his length, watching the point where they were joined the whole time.

His body screamed at him to take her, to stroke, to thrust, to *move*. But he only lifted one hand to her thigh, squeezing gently.

When he was as deep as he could go he focused on breathing.

When she lifted her hand to her breast and fingered her nipple, he closed his eyes and focused on breathing.

When she lifted her hips, gliding up his length, then lowered herself again slowly, he kept his eyes closed, gritted his teeth and focused on breathing.

But when she said "God, Conner" in the husky, hot way she did, he opened his eyes, put his hands on her hips and thrust.

"*Yes*," she hissed. Her eyes met his. "Show me what you've got, Dixon."

He grinned.

He thrust again, his fingers curling into her hips, holding her still to take him over and over.

Gabby sat up straighter, one hand still on her nipple, the other going to her clit.

His thrusts grew harder and faster, the table creaked and groaned, and Gabby stayed with him every step of the way. Conner felt his climax building quickly, the visual stimulation as good as the physical. Then she leaned back and swiveled her hips just right and he knew he was a goner.

"Come on, Gabby, keep up, babe," he said through gritted teeth.

She flashed him a smile. "I'm with you."

He felt her muscles begin to tighten and he gripped her harder, burying himself as deep as he could go.

The table rocked under them and he felt Gabby grip him hard. Her head fell back and she gave a heartfelt groan as she went over the edge, her pussy milking him.

Conner was right on her heels. His climax gathered, tightened, then erupted.

Just as the table leg under them cracked and buckled.

The table tilted and they slid to the floor in a jumble of limbs.

Gabby rolled away from him as his ass hit the hardwood floor.

"*Fuck.*" He sat stunned for a moment. Then he reached for her where she was lying on her back. "Gabby, you okay?"

She was shaking and he crawled to her side, only to discover that she was shaking with *laughter*.

He flopped onto his back beside her. "Fuck," he said again.

"Damn, Dixon, where'd you get that table? A garage sale?"

He turned his head to look at her. "What if I said yes?"

She laughed. "Well, I guess you've now done that one too many times."

He chuckled too. "Never done that before. Glad the felt was on there or I might have splinters in my ass from the slide."

She rolled to her side. "You've never done it on that table before?"

He shook his head.

"Why not? It's the perfect size and height."

She was…something. And she was right. "Guess I've never had anyone want to before."

"*You've* never wanted to?"

Was the sky blue? "A gentleman lets the lady make those decisions."

She laughed again. He loved her laugh.

"A gentleman lets the lady decide where he's going to fuck her brains out?"

Heat grabbed him and he reached for her. Fucking *her* brains out sounded like a hell of an idea. Again. "Don't want anyone to say I wasn't considerate," he said, pulling her close.

"I'll say very nice things on my comment card," she said, letting him pull her close. She put her hand against his cheek.

He grabbed her hand, nipping her fingertips, trying to distract her. The look of tenderness in her eyes—especially considering they'd just broken his table having sex—was too much.

"I had this picture of women batting their eyes and saying 'whatever you want, Conner'," Gabby said. "But that's not what happens, huh? You make sure they have what *they* want, right?"

"Why wouldn't I?" he asked lightly. "As much as I enjoyed breaking this table, if I get to see a naked woman, why would I care *where* I'm seeing her?"

Gabby grinned. "Okay, you got me there. I'm just surprised."

"That I'm a gentleman?"

"That even when you're being a man-whore, you're sweet."

Conner chuckled at that. "I don't know about sweet. It's pretty simple—happy women make me happy, and romance and great sex make women happy."

"Well, ain't that the truth," Gabby said, resting her head on his chest.

He ran his hand over her hair, most definitely feeling happy. Maybe even more than happy. He hadn't done much in the romance department with Gabby. They'd played poker and joked around with her family. That wasn't romantic.

Or was it? And why did he feel like maybe *he'd* been romanced?

He prided himself on providing whatever experience the woman he was with needed. Whether it was a night of candle-light and pampering, or a chance to let loose and try some new naughty things, Conner was the man. He didn't worry too much about what he wanted, one way or another. It was all good. He loved the flirting, the romance, the seduction and the sex—all the fun that happened at the beginning of a relationship.

So he kept his relationships at the beginning.

Once things moved beyond that to the place where things got emotional and complicated, where they were more involved in one another's life—where it was harder to make women happy —he was out.

He'd done emotional and complicated for fifteen years with four very strong-willed women. Four women he couldn't break up with—or get away from. He wasn't about to *choose* to have a relationship that involved emotional and complicated.

"So how do you get away with it?" Gabby asked, her hand on his stomach, her breath teasing his chest.

"Get away with what?" He really wanted to run his hand down her back to her butt. He really loved her butt.

"Well, you like making women happy. How do you get away with breaking it off with them and still keeping them happy?" She draped her leg over his and scooted even closer.

Conner fought to pay attention to the conversation. "I tell them the truth—I can't have a serious, lasting relationship with anyone because I have to worry about my sisters."

That had been the truth. For a long time.

Gabby laughed. "You can't use that excuse anymore, Dixon. Your sisters are all well taken care of by their guys."

"And I'm loving every minute of it," he said with feeling.

Gabby lifted her head to look him in the eye. "What? You're *loving* that your sisters are all engaged to your best friends?"

He nodded. "Completely."

"When did that happen? 'Cause that sure wasn't the case about a month ago."

A month ago he'd found out that his baby sister, Olivia, had fallen for the best of his best friends, Cody. That had not hit Conner particularly well at first. Olivia was—or at least had been—the most sweet and vulnerable of his sisters. And Cody had a history with women that made Conner adamant about keeping Olivia far away from him.

Not that it had mattered. True love was true love. And now, a month later, Conner could admit that he'd been wrong. Not out loud. Not to the guys. But to himself, when he was feeling especially self-aware and mature.

And maybe to Gabby.

"My sisters being in loving, committed relationships is the best thing to ever happen to me."

"Wow," Gabby commented, clearly surprised. "You really, really sure that you haven't had a stroke?"

He laughed and lifted her hand to his lips, needing to taste her again, even if it was just kissing her palm. "I'm really, really sure. In fact, I've never felt so clearheaded and rational in my life."

She sighed softly as he drew his tongue over the middle ridge in her palm to her wrist. "What brought about this huge change of heart?"

"Being free."

"Free?"

"I put in fifteen years with the girls." He'd dealt with a plethora of emotions, mistakes and problems. He'd worried and lectured and advised and disciplined and shown up at every hour of the day or night and picked up the pieces. "And now I'm retired."

He deserved a break. Any sane person would agree. He'd done okay. The girls had turned out great. Now he could relax.

Gabby curled her fingers against his jaw as he continued kissing up her arm to her elbow. "Retired, huh? No more worries? Just like that?"

The full truth of that had sunk in only over the past two weeks.

His sisters were grown and had wonderful men who loved them very much.

And they were now those wonderful men's problems.

Conner could, for once, simply enjoy his sisters.

He shrugged and licked the inside of Gabby's elbow. "It sank in when two weeks had gone by and none of the girls had called me for anything. I was sitting here one night and realized that I'd heard from them only about things like what time we were all getting together for dinner and that Emma's OB appointment had gone well. Stuff like that. And it occurred to me that I wasn't even worried. I knew the guys were there taking care of stuff."

Conner tugged slightly, bringing Gabby up to lay on top of him. He kissed his way up to her shoulder, loving the little shiver he felt go through her.

"So you're enjoying just being a big brother?" Gabby asked.

If she could still concentrate on their conversation, he wasn't doing a very good job. Conner moved his lips to her neck. He ran his hands down her back to rest on her butt, pressing her against him.

"I am," he told her. "I haven't done much of that."

She wiggled against him enticingly. But she kept talking. "You haven't enjoyed your sisters?"

He chuckled. "Uh, no. I was a normal teenage boy, a typical big brother—teasing them, arguing with them, finding them incredibly annoying, staying out of their way as much as possible."

No one wanted to be in the path of the whirlwind that the Dixon Divas created wherever they went, even when they were little. The noise and drama they'd produced had never been little.

"And then…" He trailed off. He simply didn't talk about his father's death much. Or at all.

"Your dad died," Gabby said quietly.

He cleared his throat and nodded. "Massive heart attack. It was really sudden."

Gabby lifted her head. "You jumped from typical big brother to not-so-typical father figure."

Conner could only nod again. He'd become the only male in the house when Amanda, the oldest, had been fourteen.

"And now that the girls are in love and with these amazing men, you can relax a little," she said.

"You got it."

He could attend parties, buy gifts, show up for surprise lunches. The girls were in a fun time of life. They were planning weddings and getting ready for babies and enjoying being madly in love.

Conner loved seeing them happy and he loved being just their brother. Not their father figure, not their disciplinarian, not their guardian or protector.

"Now Ryan gets to deal with Amanda's perfectionistic ways as she plans their wedding and Shane can deal with Isabelle's meltdowns about her fibromyalgia getting in the way of things and Nate can deal with *everything* that goes with Emma being pregnant and Cody can deal with Olivia remodeling their kitchen."

Gabby smiled. "You're free."

"I feel like I'm kicking back in a hammock on a sunny beach with a fricking piña colada in hand."

"But not just a vacation?"

He shook his head. "Full retirement."

"What if one of the guys bails?" Gabby asked.

"I'll hunt him down, kick his ass and haul him back here."

Gabby laughed. "Ironic, isn't it? You'd now kick their asses for *leaving* your sisters?"

It was. But he didn't care.

Making women happy over the long term was hard work.

It wasn't like he'd never worry or that he didn't care if one of the girls was upset, but he wasn't the *main* guy in charge of taking care of the problem and making them happy again anymore. And he knew too well that when one of the girls had a problem, the others got involved and made it their problem too.

Ryan, Shane, Nate and Cody deserved it all.

"Well, imagine that," Gabby said, pushing up so she straddled him.

His hardening cock pressed against her butt as she ran her hands along his upper arms to his shoulders then up the sides of his neck. She laced her fingers at the back of his head and pulled him forward.

He sat up with her in his lap.

"Imagine what?" he asked, running his hands up and down her back.

"I was wrong."

"About?"

"I thought maybe you were feeling a little left out now that all the girls are matched up with all your friends. You might be feeling like a…" she paused, looked up at the ceiling, then back him, "…ninth wheel," she said with a grin.

He shrugged. There had been a few of those moments, but overall he was feeling quite content. "I'm pretty comfortable hanging out with them all. As long as there's no kissing."

Gabby leaned in and put her mouth against his. "But kissing is so fun."

He gripped her butt and took her mouth.

Kissing was definitely fun.

The kiss got hot and intense, fast. Gabby ran her tongue along his lower lip, much the way he craved doing to other parts of her again.

"Where's the other condom?" he asked against her lips.

"Right here."

Without breaking contact with his mouth she reached between them and slid the condom on, then lifted herself and took him deep.

"Christ, Gabby," Conner groaned.

She started moving immediately. Conner leaned back, needing to see her. Her hands were flat on his chest and her hair was falling over her shoulders.

"Put your hands up," he said. "Hold your hair up."

Her eyes on his, Gabby gathered her hair up on top of her head.

She looked gorgeous.

Conner took a nipple between his thumb and finger, rolling, tugging, then squeezing.

She gave a soft hiss and her hips ground harder and faster.

He lifted the whole breast to take the tip into his mouth and her hands went to his head, pressing him close.

"Hands up, G," he ordered.

She complied and he sucked again.

"*Conner.*"

"I fucking love that," he told her, sucking harder.

She started moving faster, her thighs flexing, her hips lifting and falling rapidly.

"You feel so good," she said breathlessly. "I can't move fast enough. I'm so close—"

He pressed his hand against her lower back, making her arch farther. "Take me, Gabby. Whatever you need."

Her eyes snapped to his. "Whatever I need?" she asked.

"Anything."

"I want you on top," she said without pause. "I want you to take me hard, right here on the floor."

He was buried deep, her breast in hand, and still lust flooded through him.

Without another word he flipped her to her back. He braced

his hands on the floor beside her as her legs wrapped around his waist and he thrust hard.

"Yes, damn, yes, Conner," she panted.

He had the sudden urge to get really dirty with her. It was stupid. It was amazing he was even able to *think* at all, but he sensed that Gabby would like things really naughty.

He pushed himself up until he was kneeling between her spread thighs.

Her neck was arched and her eyes shut.

"Gabby," he said, holding still until she opened her eyes and met his gaze. "I want you to watch me fuck you."

He felt her inner muscles tighten at that and he gave her a cocky smile.

She licked her lips and slowly propped up on her elbows.

He put a hand on either thigh, spreading her even wider. The sight was almost his undoing. It was hot as hell to see her like this. Not just the position, not just the look on her face, but that this was Gabby. He'd seen her stare down a guy who was pointing a gun at another guy in a bar. He'd seen her work even after spraining her ankle so badly that she'd been on crutches for a week after. He'd seen her give CPR while shoulder deep in the river.

She was courageous, caring, talented and driven.

And she was letting him see, taste and feel her in the most intimate way possible.

It was humbling.

Which was the stupidest thing he'd ever thought of during sex.

He moved slowly, pulling out and pressing in, watching her watching where their bodies were joined.

Her lips were parted as she breathed, her chest flushed a pretty pink that matched her cheeks. He didn't think for a second that she was embarrassed. He knew she was incredibly turned on and loved that her body gave her away.

"You like it slow?" he asked, demonstrating. "You like feeling every inch of my cock sliding in and out?"

She nodded.

"Or do you want it fast?" He thrust hard, in and out several times, watching as her fingers tried to curl into the floor to anchor herself.

"All of it." She tightened her muscles around him. "Any of it. I'm going to come either way."

That's all he needed to hear. She wanted him in any way. He moved his thumb to her clit, pressing and circling.

"I love how I look moving in and out of you," he told her gruffly. "The way your wetness looks on my cock. Makes me want to taste you. Makes me want to make you taste me."

Her muscles clenched and she moaned.

"Conner," she said between gasps.

"Yeah, G. Anything."

"Later you can put your mouth wherever you want, but if you stop fucking me right now, I will kill you."

Torn between groaning and laughing, he slipped his hands under her ass, lifted her and thrust hard and fast until she'd climbed and tumbled over the edge.

He finished right behind her.

He stayed between her knees, catching his breath and letting his body cool, thinking that nothing had ever looked as good to him as the sight of Gabby, spent from sex, lying spread out on his floor.

Eventually he became aware of how hard the floor was beneath his knees, and he collapsed beside her, both of them on their backs.

"So I was also wrong about this," she said, still sounding a bit short of breath a few minutes later.

"What's this?"

"That you need a woman who can be demanding with you. You actually love that, don't you?"

He chuckled. "If you're asking if I like dirty talk, then hell yes."

She rolled her head to look at him. "But you like when a woman tells you what she wants."

"Of course."

She shook her head and went back to studying the ceiling. "You're like a chameleon. You're always whatever the woman you're with wants. You can be the charming playboy, the romantic gentleman, the dirty scoundrel."

His chest tightened at her words. She wasn't wrong. He was surprised, however, that she'd realized it.

She reached over and linked her fingers with his. Conner closed his fingers around hers, the contact making the tension in his body ease slightly.

"You want the women to tell you what they need sexually so you can be sure to be what they want." She almost sounded like she was talking to herself. "So much of your life has been about helping women—your sisters, your emergency victims, even the women you date." She looked at him again. "You've always been the best with our adult-female victims."

Yep, he knew that. He had a way with women. It was a fact.

"There's nothing wrong with being what women need and want."

She squeezed his hand. "No, there's not. Until it's keeping you from having what you need and want."

He should have known that even hot sex with Gabby would turn into some big discussion of feelings. She was female, after all.

"I have what I need and want."

"Yeah?" She sat up, but kept hold of his hand.

"Yeah. Being the hero, being needed, being the guy all the woman want—that's what I need and want."

She nodded. "I think that's true on some level. But then again, you've never been asked what *you* want, right?"

He frowned. "What do you mean?"

"Women make you pancakes, but you don't ask them to."

"I love pancakes."

"But they don't actually know that because they never ask."

"Pancakes are a lot like sex—they're pretty damned good even when they're not so good."

"But why don't you deserve to have cinnamon rolls once in a while?" Gabby asked.

He knew exactly where this was going. "Once in a while I run into a girl who likes cinnamon rolls more than pancakes." Once in a while he ran into a girl who liked sex the way he liked it—hot and spontaneous on a poker table, for instance.

"But it's a coincidence then. Still not because she's making you cinnamon rolls because that's what you want."

"Look, even blueberry muffins are good when they're made with warmth and affection." That was really the bottom line for him. He liked women who liked him. And he liked making women who liked him happy. Which sometimes meant eating blueberry muffins…or having vanilla sex in bed with the lights off. It wasn't like he really thought anyone would feel sorry for him.

Gabby rolled her eyes. "You don't like blueberry muffins?"

"There are a lot of better things."

"You shouldn't have to have blueberry muffins if you don't want them, Conner."

"I can't ask every woman I meet if she likes cinnamon rolls," he said. He never would have thought of using breakfast foods as euphemisms for sex, but it worked.

"You need to find a woman who will eat cinnamon rolls once in a while because *you* like them. Shouldn't *always* matter what she likes."

"Gabby, you know what happens when I eat blueberry muffins?"

"What?"

"I get full and happy. Same thing happens with cinnamon rolls."

"Not the point."

He sighed and sat up. He knew that shutting her up with a kiss would only move the conversation to another time. "What's the point?"

"Just that you deserve to have someone who likes *you*."

He chuckled. "Women like me, Gabby."

"They don't," she said. "They think they do, of course. They like how you look and the things you say and the way you make them feel. Because that's the focus, right? You focus on *them*. What makes them smile, what makes them giggle, what makes them blush, what makes them coo and follow you around."

"Coo?" But she was very close to the truth. He loved when women smiled and giggled and blushed and…cooed.

He felt like a fucking king when he could evoke those responses.

And knew *exactly* where it came from.

When his dad died, his mother and sisters had been, rightly, devastated. His mom had lost her one true love and Conner would never forget the look on her face as his dad's coffin was lowered into the ground at the cemetery. A piece of her had died too. She was never quite the same. But Conner couldn't accept that. He did everything he could think of to make her smile, to make her feel special, to make her happy again. Even if it was for just a little while.

He'd taken up his father's torch, making sure the Dixon women knew they were valued and special and deserved respect from the men they interacted with—from teachers to bosses to boyfriends.

And he'd extended his actions to other women. He felt very rewarded when he could make a woman feel important, valued, special.

"Yes, coo," Gabby said. "But they don't really know you. Otherwise they'd know that you'd prefer cinnamon rolls and they'd like you enough to give them to you."

Yeah, she definitely needed to be doing something other than talking.

"Do you like me, Gabby?"

That seemed to take her back for a moment. "Of course I do."

"Then let's go to bed."

She tipped her head. "And what are you going to do in there?"

"Make you scream."

She looked at him for several seconds. Finally she said, "What do you want me to do to *you*, Conner?"

He reached for her. "Anything you want, G."

She moved back. "I want to know what *you* want."

He sighed and dropped his hand. "I *want* to make you crazy."

"I want to make *you* crazy," she said.

"Making you crazy will make me crazy." He was getting a headache.

"I want you to demand something from me."

She was still naked, but somehow managed to look fierce anyway.

"No." The cock-sucking comment was as close to that as he was going to get and he'd said it mostly because he knew it would turn her on.

"Look, Conner, I'm not going to go crazy. I'm not the type of girl to go crazy. That's going to frustrate the hell out of you. Why not let me concentrate on *you* for a change?"

"So generous of you," he muttered. Christ. He wasn't the type, had never been the type, to put himself ahead of someone else, even in bed. He was sure some psychologist could have a great time with *that*. But he was no saint either. And his entire body was screaming for him to take her up on her offer.

She grinned. "It really is, huh? But it'll be good. Like…charity."

He scowled at her. "Excuse me?"

She nodded. "You're a good guy. You take care of your sisters and your mom, you're a great friend, a fantastic paramedic—you're all about everyone else. Now I'm here, not the type to like being fawned over...but you want me. So I can do some of the fawning over *you*. It'll go along with your retirement plan. The kicking back in the hammock with the piña colada... Just add a cabana girl to the picture."

And of course his imagination easily put Gabby in a coconut bra and grass skirt. Then out of them. Serving him, jumping when he snapped his fingers, doing his bidding...

"No." He pushed the fantasy to the back of his mind.

"Then I guess we're done here." She pushed to her feet and gathered her clothes.

"We're not even close to done," he growled, reaching for her.

She dodged his hand.

"Night, Conner. See you tomorrow."

He watched her walk away, stunned. She was almost to the hallway when he said, *"What?"*

She looked over her shoulder. "Until you're ready to be a little selfish in bed, no more sex for you."

"You *want* me to be selfish in bed?"

"Yes."

He wasn't sure he could that.

"You're kidding, right?"

"Sleep well, Conner." And she disappeared down the hallway.

Well, fuck.

Conner got to his feet, looked at the broken table and knew he couldn't deal with that tonight. He turned off the lights on his way to his bedroom.

But not without glancing at her bedroom door and realizing that he'd managed to have mind-blowing sex *and* was getting his bed all to himself in the same night.

That should have sounded like heaven.

It didn't.

The one woman he *wanted* to sleep wrapped around was the *one* who could easily walk away.

Wasn't that just perfect?

He climbed into bed more sure than ever of one important fact—women were trouble. Always.

GABBY WALKED into the break room at St. Anthony's for
their shift at six forty-five the next morning. Conner could leave
the apartment before she made it to the kitchen, but she was
curious how he thought he was going to avoid her for the next
twelve hours of work.

That was exactly why, previously, she'd felt very strongly
that she should *not* get involved with a coworker. There was no
room for awkward mornings after.

"There's my girl!" Mac Gordon stepped in front of Gabby
and gathered her and her backpack all up into a huge bear hug.

Her feet dangling a good four inches off the floor and all of
her air squeezed out, the only thing Gabby could do was
hang on.

A few seconds later, Mac put her back on her feet.

She staggered back. "What was that for?" she asked, her
hand splayed on her chest as her lungs sucked in oxygen.

"I've always liked you, Evans," Mac said with a huge grin.
"Ever since you won that hot-dog-eating contest at the annual
picnic, I knew you were special. But you are now my new

favorite person in the entire world," Mac announced. "I swear, I want to…buy you a car."

"I don't need a car. What are you talking about?"

"You're the new Sara," Mac said. "Thank God."

"What?"

"This might help."

Gabby looked over at Dooley Miller, another of the paramedics on the overnight crew. He was holding up a box wrapped in shiny red paper with a big white bow.

"What's that?"

"For you. From Conner. Along with these." Dooley held up a plate of what looked like cookies.

"And this." Sam Bradford was holding up a hot-pink envelope.

Suspicious, Gabby moved closer. The cookies were round and frosted to look like poker chips.

She stared. Stunned.

"What's in the box?" she asked.

"I didn't open it," Dooley said, offended.

"But you peeled off the tape on the end, looked and then retaped it, right?" Gabby asked.

Dooley's mouth dropped open.

"So what is it?" Gabby asked.

"A Crock-Pot."

"A Crock-Pot?" she repeated. It had to be one of the smaller ones. Like for hors d'oeuvres. Or dips.

She took a deep breath. "And the envelope?"

"We didn't look at *that*," Dooley said firmly.

"He couldn't figure out how to open it without it being obvious," Sam said with a grin, holding it out.

Gabby took it with trepidation. Just what was Conner up to?

Inside the envelope was a gift card to Tease, the lingerie and adult-toy store downtown, and a note that said, *You deserve the good stuff.*

Uh-huh.

"Oh good, you're here."

She spun at the sound of Conner's voice. The voice that made her tingle. Damn.

"What the hell are you doing?" she asked.

"Making you crazy," he said simply, crossing to the coffeepot.

Well, that was about right. And that was *before* the poker-chip cookies. Walking away from him last night had been the hardest thing she'd done in a long time. And that included intubating a clown at a kid's birthday party last month.

"And if he's running all over Omaha before dawn getting poker-chip cookies for *you*, he won't be doing anything asinine for *my wife*," Mac said, looking quite pleased.

"Crazy like I'm-so-gonna-make-you-pay-for-embarrassing-me-at-work crazy?" Gabby said, tucking the envelope into her back pocket before any of the other paramedics could see it.

She was so using that. Conner hadn't seen crazy yet.

"How is a Crock-Pot embarrassing?" Conner asked, filling his coffee cup and turning to face her. "It's sweet. It's a meaningful gift." He sipped. "It's called *fawning* over someone, I believe."

"*I'm* supposed to be fawning over *you*, remember?" she asked, crossing her arms.

"I did it first. I win." He sipped again.

She raised both eyebrows. "You win? This is a contest? Because I can so outfawn you, Dixon."

"Doubt it. You don't have the experience I have."

"Or the connections. I don't know anyone else who can call someone at five a.m. and have poker-chip cookies by six," Dooley said, taking one of the cookies and popping it into his mouth.

She narrowed her eyes and studied Conner. Something Mac had said sank in and she felt a slow smile stretch her lips. "Oh, I get it. I'm the new Sara, huh?"

"I don't know what you mean," Conner said, leaning against the counter in the kitchen area.

He so knew what she meant.

"Sure," she said, nodding and walking toward him. "I'm leaving in two months, I'm adamant about staying unattached, so I'm safe, right? You can be all romantic and crazy and…"

"Doting," Conner supplied. "I like the word *doting*."

She rolled her eyes. "Doting. And now you'll get even more attention because this is new. This will shake things up. There's a girl *besides* Sara Gordon getting all your ridiculous gifts."

"The Crock-Pot is not ridiculous. It's top of the line. Very practical, actually," Conner said, "considering it's how you get all the men in your family to do what you want them to do."

She stopped in front of him, vaguely aware that the break room was full of some of the loudest and most obnoxious people she knew—and they were all completely silent.

She smiled at Conner. "It won't work. I know it's all BS, remember?"

He met her gaze directly and nodded. "I know. I can't get to you, can I?" He lifted a hand and stroked his thumb over her cheek. "You know me. You know that I keep up the façade of Mr. Romance so that I can stroke my ego and never let anyone know that deep down I'm scared."

She felt her smile die and she had to take a deep breath. Damn, the guy was good. Those deep-green eyes, that scratchy voice, the blond stubble on his chin that she wanted to feel rasping against her inner thigh…

"I'm scared of letting someone close and then disappointing her," he went on, his voice lower. "Of not being everything she wants and needs, not being able to *truly* make her happy. So I keep it all on the surface."

Gabby lifted her hand to his wrist and squeezed. "Conner…"

"Yeah, G?" he said earnestly.

"Really good try."

He blinked for a moment, then slowly his lips curled into a grin. "Damn."

"Yeah." She stepped back and he dropped his hand. *"I'm doing the fawning."*

"We'll see."

"You're not giving up?"

"Doting on you while you're trying to one-up me by being all sweet and caring and romantic? That, Gabby girl, is what they call a win-win situation."

"Why so intent on doting on me?" she asked. "Just to prove you can get to any girl?"

He shrugged and she got caught up in the sincerity in his eyes. "Because you haven't been doted on enough."

She frowned. "How do you know that?"

"I've worked with you for two years, and I've never seen a boyfriend show up around here, never seen a bouquet of roses delivered, never seen you sneak off to take a private phone call," he said. "And I met some of the main men in your life. They don't dote."

Conner had noticed her. Details about her. She wasn't sure how she felt about that. "I don't like doting."

"That's because you've never had good doting."

"Good doting?"

"Yeah, I don't see your family as being very good doters."

Gabby was pretty sure they were making up words at this point. "And you're a good doter?"

"One of the best."

"Uh-huh."

"You'll see." He seemed incredibly smug. He took his cup and sauntered toward the front of the ER, no doubt to make sure the girls in Admissions knew about the gifts he'd given Gabby.

The guys from the night crew all grabbed cookies and headed for the locker room.

"So you're sleeping together?"

This came from Ryan as the break room door shut behind Mac.

She swallowed hard and turned. "He doesn't just dote on the

women he sleeps with," she pointed out. Sara Gordon being the prime example.

"But *you* are sleeping together?" Ryan asked.

"Um…"

"Please tell me you're sleeping together," Ryan said. "His flirting with Sara never gave us any hope because she was married, but *you're* not. This could be awesome."

Gabby's eyes got wide. "Us sleeping together would give you *hope*?"

"Yes."

"That's a…strange word to use."

Ryan nodded. "Hope." He pulled out his phone, typing in a quick text.

"How?"

"Conner went with Amanda to do the cake tasting the other day."

Gabby shook her head. "I don't know what that means."

"For the wedding cakes. She needed to go to the bakery and do a tasting to decide which to get. Conner went with her."

"They picked out a horrible cake?" Gabby asked.

"No. It's amazing. Perfect even," Ryan said. He punched in a couple of numbers on his phone and lifted it to his ear.

"And *this* is a bad thing?" She did not know what was going on.

"He got Isabelle a spa day too," Ryan said. "Shane said she wouldn't shut up about how great it was and how sweet he was to do it."

Gabby just raised an eyebrow.

"Hey," Ryan said into his phone. "Gabby is sleeping with Conner."

He held the phone away from his ear and Gabby could hear the "fuck yeah!" from the other end.

"Who is that?"

"Cody," Ryan told her. "Tell Gabby why you need Conner to

be involved with someone," he said to Cody, then held the phone out to her with the speaker function on.

"Nobody said *involved*," she said to the phone.

"Olivia wanted to see the new chick flick that was out," Cody said. "I was working so she asked Conner. He went along and bought all the popcorn."

Nate, who was apparently already at the hospital that morning, strode into the room. "Conner bought Emma the new fancy car seat she wanted for the baby."

Gabby sighed. These guys were nuts. "So?"

"So I wanted to buy that for her," Nate said.

"You're mad that her brother did something nice for her?" Gabby asked.

"He's stealing our thunder!" Cody declared.

She snorted. "What?"

"Seriously. He doesn't have to *worry* about the girls anymore, so he is becoming the fun one. The one to buy them stuff and do stuff with them."

Gabby looked from Ryan to Nate.

"I still don't get it," she said. "Shouldn't you be happy that he's adjusted so well to you all being with the girls?"

"He's making us look bad," Ryan said.

Gabby shook her head. "You've got to be kidding."

"No," Cody said. "He's right. Conner loves being the bigshot, sweet guy that all the girls are so crazy about. He's good at it. He can get women wrapped around his finger in two seconds. And now he's doing it to his sisters."

"Instead of getting on Isabelle about eating better or lecturing Emma about getting enough sleep at night with the pregnancy, he's buying them things and having a good time with them," Nate added.

"You guys are being ridiculous. This is a *good* thing," Gabby insisted. In fact, she thought it was pretty damned sweet. She was on to him, but that didn't mean it didn't kind of work.

Seeing what Conner was capable of, even if it wasn't directed at her, made Gabby a little fonder of him, she could admit.

"See, now *we* have to be the ones to worry about if they're eating right or exercising. We're the ones who they might get frustrated with. We're the ones that they get irritated with when we can't go to a cake tasting or a movie," Cody said.

"He's pampering them and making them happy because that's all he has to worry about now," Ryan said.

Gabby shook her head. "Listen to yourselves. He's being sweet to his *sisters*. He's getting involved in the things that matter to them—the wedding, the baby, all that stuff. And yes, you're in relationships. It's not all sex and roses now."

She wanted sex and roses from Conner.

The thought hit her out of the blue. The sex thing made sense, of course. But roses? She wasn't a roses kind of girl.

Roses from Conner though…

Dammit. Gabby shook her head. He was sucking her in. Like all the other girls. The doting, the sweetness. It was making her want to boost him up on that pedestal. And he'd barely gotten started on *her*. This was all about him doting on other women. His *sisters*, for God's sake.

But it also made her want all the other stuff too—the making sure she was eating right and listening to her rant when she was upset and…she wanted to go to movies with him.

She frowned. He hadn't even sent her roses yet. He was getting to her with the *idea* of roses?

Pathetic.

"We're good with all that stuff," Cody said from the speaker-phone. "That's not it. We're all in it for the long haul. And I believe that he's having a good time doing this stuff for the girls, but…"

"But what?"

"He's doing it on purpose."

Gabby chuckled. Of course Conner knew that not only would all of this get him on the girls' good sides, but it would frustrate the hell out of his buddies. His buddies who had *insisted* on having relationships with Conner's sisters in spite of Conner being against it.

Oh yeah, he was totally doing it on purpose.

"So you think I'll be a distraction for Conner so you can all have some over-the-top romantic weekend with your girls?" she asked.

"We need to be rid of him for a lot more than a weekend," Nate said.

She looked at him. "I don't know any hit men, if that's what you're asking."

"There's only one solution," Cody said.

Ryan and Nate nodded.

This should be good. Gabby crossed her arms.

Ryan took the lead. "We need him to be in a long-term relationship. Not a hookup, not a one-night stand. A relationship. He needs someone to give all of this attention to, someone who will take up his time, someone who he can shower all this sweet bullshit on, who will keep him interested in his own life rather than everyone else's."

"And *that's* why it's great that you're sleeping with him," Cody concluded.

She chuckled, but her stomach twisted. Conner did need those things. He needed someone to give his attention to, someone to give *him* attention. But someone who'd be there long term. He deserved a relationship like all of his sisters and friends were finding. "I think you might be overestimating my importance."

Nate chuckled. "I don't think so."

"No, really—"

"This is perfect. You're perfect for this," Cody said.

"But I'm not—"

"Honestly," Ryan said, "this is awesome."

Yeah, he'd mentioned that.

Thankfully, it was only twenty minutes later that their first call of the shift came in.

They pulled up next to an old warehouse outside of the Old Market District downtown.

"Thought you said there had been a fall with injuries?" Ryan asked as they bailed out.

Conner nodded, shouldering the big supply bag. "That's what they said."

"This is where Eddie and his buddies hang out," Ryan said.

Eddie was the leader of a small band of homeless guys who were allowed to sleep in the warehouse as long as that's all they did there. It was a strange relationship the four men had established with the warehouse owner, Henry. They never drank or did drugs in the warehouse, they never brought anyone else to the warehouse and they always cleaned up after themselves, including refolding the blankets and stacking the pillows Henry left for them.

They'd been sleeping in the warehouse—with Henry's knowledge—for over a year.

Gabby and the crew were the only other people that knew they were there and were allowed in. The guys routinely needed detoxing, stitching up, IV fluids, antibiotics or even just antibacterial soap.

The crew visited the guys about once a month.

Eddie didn't like Ryan or Conner. He did like Sierra. He loved Gabby.

So when Eddie needed attention, it was always Gabby who took care of it.

"Who called?"

"Eddie."

Gabby nodded. The other guys didn't talk much. "Well, let's go see what we've got."

The warehouse was a typical warehouse. There wasn't much

to climb and fall off of, other than stacks of crates, an old car that didn't run and some high ceiling beams. But Eddie and the guys didn't screw around when they were here. For one, the youngest of them was easily fifty and not exactly spry. For another, they appreciated the shelter. They wouldn't dare risk pissing Henry off.

One of them needing medical attention and being seen in the warehouse was one thing. One of them actually getting hurt *at* the warehouse was something else. Henry wouldn't like that.

They'd pulled up without lights or sirens at the door where they always met the guys.

Conner and Ryan didn't get smiles and greetings, but there was no way they'd stay back in the rig and send Gabby and Sierra in alone.

Gabby appreciated that. She was a highly trained paramedic, had excelled at her crisis-situation courses and psych classes and prided herself on being able to de-escalate nearly any situation, but she couldn't lie—she liked having the guys behind her.

"Eddie?" she called, sliding the door open. "It's Gabby. And the ambulance."

There was no answer for a moment. Gabby stepped in through the door. The interior of the warehouse was dim, the sunlight not potent enough to penetrate the years of dust and dirt on the high window.

"Eddie?"

"Over here." Eddie had a distinctive low, rough voice.

Gabby called out, "We're all coming in."

The four of them headed to the left, Gabby leading the way with Sierra right behind her.

Eddie was kneeling on the floor on a pile of blankets. "I think she's dying," he said, lifting his head when Gabby stepped around a stack of wooden crates.

Gabby approached slowly. Eddie had never done anything threatening to her, but he was often agitated, and the first time they'd met he'd grabbed her arm unexpectedly. She wanted to help the man and had no reason to expect him to do anything aggressive, but she wasn't stupid—Eddie lived on the streets and had some mental illness. They'd never found drugs in his system, but alcohol was a regular part of his bloodstream. She needed to be careful.

"Who's dying, Eddie?" Gabby had never heard the man refer to a female companion.

"Lady."

Gabby stopped about eight feet from the pile of blankets. "Lady? Lady is dying?"

Eddie nodded, clearly upset. "I think so."

Gabby glanced at Sierra. Sierra shrugged.

"Did you call us about Lady?" Gabby asked.

"Yeah."

"Do you know where Lady is now?"

"Yeah."

"Okay, Eddie, we'll do whatever we can to help her. Can you tell us where she is?"

"Right here." Eddie moved out of the way and Gabby saw a dog lying on the blankets. She was on her side, her breathing was shallow. She barely lifted her head.

"Oh." Damn. It was a dog.

Gabby looked at her team.

Conner nodded toward the animal, silently communicating that she should get closer.

"Eddie, can I come check on Lady?" Gabby asked.

He nodded and stood.

"Did you find her?" Gabby asked, approaching the animal slowly. Just like the man, the animal lived on the streets. She'd be wary of people, especially strangers.

"She found me," Eddie said.

Oh, that was nice. She gave the man a smile. "Are you okay?"

"Okay," he said with a shrug. "Do you have any soup?"

Gabby glanced at Ryan, who was already handing a small plastic bag of supplies over to Eddie. They'd become accustomed to carrying nonperishable food items in the rig since meeting Eddie and his friends. They passed the food out to other homeless as well. The four of them had all shown up the day after their first trip to the warehouse with food. They'd simply smiled at one another and stored the stuff in a plastic bin. Ever since, they all helped keep it stocked.

Gabby felt something tap her arm. She glanced to find a pair of heavy work gloves in Sierra's hand. She gave her friend a smile. The gloves might not fully prevent a dog bite, but they'd lessen the chances of deep penetration. She pulled the gloves on as she knelt by the animal.

"Hey, Lady," she crooned, reaching out slowly and letting the dog sniff her as she visually scanned the big body. Lady looked like a golden lab mixed with…something else.

"So, why Lady?" she asked Eddie. She had to know.

"You seen the movie *Lady and the Tramp*?"

"Yeah."

"That might be my favorite Disney movie."

Gabby must have shown her surprise because Eddie added, "They show movies at the shelter sometimes."

Okay, the homeless guy knew Disney movies.

Gabby smiled at him. "You're right. Naming her after the dog from your favorite movie is special."

"She's dying," Eddie said again, sounding sad.

Well, Gabby didn't know about that. But she didn't know much about dogs. She did, however, have an uncle who was a veterinarian.

"Why do you think she's dying, Ed?" Conner asked, moving in closer.

"Because she's sick," Eddie said with a frown. He really didn't like Conner.

Gabby gave Conner a back-off look, which he fully understood because he shook his head no.

She sighed.

"Tell me how she's been acting," Gabby said to Eddie, still

running her hand over the dog, simultaneously working to soothe and examine the animal.

"Sick."

Right.

The dog whimpered as Gabby stroked toward her back leg. Gabby frowned and did it again slowly. Lady pulled her leg away and gave a soft growl this time.

"Back left leg," she said to Conner.

Conner knelt at the dog's head. "Hey girl," he crooned, stroking her head. "You're a beauty, huh?"

Gabby watched him for a moment. God, that voice. Even when he was talking to a dog.

"She doesn't like that," Eddie said, frowning at Conner.

Lady hadn't gotten the memo about not liking Conner, however. She lifted her head for him to better access her neck and looked up at him adoringly.

"See, girls always look at you like that," she said, turning her attention back to Lady's leg.

"Except you," he reminded her.

She smiled but kept her eyes on Lady. "Right, except me."

He chuckled softly.

The examination of Lady pulled her focus from Conner a moment later though. "Eddie, did Lady fall?" She remembered Ryan saying the call had reported a fall with injuries.

"She was up there." Eddie pointed toward the corner of the warehouse.

There was a narrow metal staircase leading to a loft area with a walled-in room that might have been used as an office at one time.

Ryan and Sierra were already moving in that direction.

"She was comin' down the steps and fell," Eddie said.

Gabby was fairly certain the poor animal was dehydrated, possibly starving...and she'd just had puppies. Not to mention broken her leg in her fall.

Her uncle was going to have to take a look at this.

"Eddie, my uncle is a veterinarian. I'm going to take Lady to see him, okay?"

"No!" Eddie took two steps forward. "Lady's mine."

"I know," Gabby said gently. "I just want to make her better."

"She stays here," Eddie said firmly.

"Dude," Conner said, keeping his voice calm and continuing to pet the dog's head, "if you care about Lady, you need to let Gabby help her."

"Help her here," Eddie said. He frowned at Conner. "Gabby can help her here."

"I don't think so, Eddie," Gabby said. "She needs a dog doctor."

"Um, so do these three," Ryan said as he came across the floor. He held three puppies in his arms.

Eddie looked stunned. "Those are Lady's?"

"Yes," Gabby said, stretching to her feet.

The puppies whined and Lady's head came up.

"Easy, girl," Conner said.

But Lady was focused on Ryan. She growled in the back of her throat.

"She doesn't like you," Eddie informed Conner.

Lady wasn't even looking at Conner.

"She's just worried about her puppies," Gabby said, stepping toward Eddie. "We need to take care of all of them. You trust me, right?"

Eddie looked at the dog, his face taut with anxiety. "I don't know. I don't know."

"I promise she'll be okay. But if we don't take her, she won't get better," Gabby said, stepping closer again.

Eddie started shaking his head and reached behind him, pulling a knife from his waistband.

Whoa. Gabby came up short, hands up. "Hey now, it's okay."

"Put the knife away, Eddie," Conner said firmly.

He also got to his feet and stepped in close to Gabby. He

seemed calm, but as his shoulder contacted hers, it was as if she could feel tension humming in him.

"No. You can't take my dog."

"She's hurt. We're going to help her," Conner said.

Gabby felt his hands on her upper arms. He squeezed her, then quickly shifted her back behind him.

Hey.

"Eddie, you called us for help."

Eddie's eyes darted from Conner to Gabby and back. "I called Gabby."

She started to move around Conner to calm Eddie, but Conner stepped in her way, blocking her from the other man.

"You know we all come," Conner said. "We're Gabby's friends. We come to help her."

"I just want Gabby," Eddie said, his voice rising. He still held the knife out in front of him.

Conner spread his arms wide, hands up in surrender. "Dude, I know. I get it. She's awesome. But you have to let her do her job and you can't pull knives out or we're not going to let her come back to see you."

Eddie's eyes narrowed. "You can't do that. She has to come if I call."

"Nope," Conner said. "Next time you'll just get me and Ryan."

"I want to see Gabby," Eddie insisted.

"I know. I don't blame you. I like seeing her too."

Gabby rested her hands on Conner's waist, then pinched him and tried to shove him out of the way.

He held firm. In fact, he started backing up, pushing her with him. She tried to dig in and resist, but he was bigger—and more determined—than she was.

What the hell was he doing? He knew she could talk Eddie down. She'd done it before.

"Conner," she hissed. "Knock it off."

"No way," he said back.

"Hey, you can't leave," Eddie said, realizing they were moving. He started forward.

Gabby felt a rumble from Conner, almost a growl.

"Put the damned knife down and we'll stay and help," Conner said, his voice harder now. "Otherwise, we're out of here."

"Lady's still hurt," Eddie said, *not* putting the knife down.

"I know. And I want to help her. Gabby's gonna be pissed if I make her leave without helping Lady—" Conner said.

He was right about that.

"—but we're not staying if you're going to be an asshole," Conner told him.

Gabby gasped. They always talked gently to Eddie. They wanted to help the guy and riling him up was not the way to get him to cooperate. "Dixon—" she started.

"Stop it," he told her firmly, eyes still on Eddie.

Stop it? Seriously? She shoved him harder this time, knocking him enough off balance to get a step around him. But he wrapped an arm around her waist before she could get far and hauled her up against him.

"No," he said in her ear. "I mean it."

He meant it? He was bossing her around? Manhandling her? No way.

She pushed against his arm. "Let go, Dixon."

"No fucking way."

"Dammit—"

"Let her go," Eddie said, raising the knife. "She said she wants you to let go."

"Put the knife down, Eddie," Conner said.

Gabby kicked her heel into Conner's shin, but his hold only tightened around her.

Lady noticed that the man who'd been feeding her was getting worked up. A growl sounded from her throat. The puppies, hearing their mom, started whining louder and squirming in Ryan's arms. Sierra showed up with another one just then, her eyes widening as she took in the sight.

"What the hell's going on?"

Eddie turned toward her voice and Conner lunged, hitting Eddie's arm and sending the knife skittering across the cement floor.

Conner let go of Gabby to grab for the knife, Gabby caught her balance against a short stack of boxes, Lady started barking and Eddie started swearing. The boxes, precariously stacked in the first place, began to tip. Gabby shoved Conner out of the way of the falling crates. His foot hit the knife, sending it sliding, and Eddie dove for it. The boxes hit the cement with loud *crack*s, the dog's barking got louder and Gabby saw Ryan trying to unload three puppies into Sierra's arms.

The next thing she heard was "Son of a bitch!" from Conner.

Conner and Eddie were wrestling on the floor, the knife in Eddie's hand, Conner's hand wrapped tightly around Eddie's wrist.

Gabby went for the supply bag Ryan had dropped. She pulled out a syringe and stalked to where Conner and Eddie were tangled together. Conner saw her and managed to flip Eddie so the man was on top—and his leg was clear for Gabby to jab with the needle containing the sedative medication.

Eddie's fighting slowed and Conner flipped him again, then pushed back off of him.

Eddie's eyes started to close as he passed out.

But not before he took a swipe at Conner with the knife.

The blade punctured Conner's thigh and the six-inch gash immediately began bleeding through his pants.

"Fuck!" Conner swore, flopping back onto the floor.

"Dammit!" Gabby sank to her knees next to him, shucked off the dirty work gloves, and immediately pressed her palms flat against the wound. "Ryan!"

"Yeah, yeah." Ryan had been holding on to Lady. He let go of the dog to scramble for the bag.

The dog got to her feet shakily, growling and looking less impressed with Conner now.

Sierra moved toward the new mother. "It's okay. Take it easy."

"Be careful," Ryan snapped.

"No shit," Sierra shot back. Then she gentled her voice and knelt with the puppies, letting them scramble from her arms to their mom.

That seemed to placate Lady a bit.

Gabby worked on keeping her breathing calm. Having Conner's hard, warm leg under her hands was one thing. Having his warm blood seeping out of that hard leg and onto her hands was something else. Blood, even big amounts, didn't bother her. *Conner's* blood did.

She didn't like it when any of her crewmates got hurt, of course, but it happened. Cuts and bruises and sprains and burns —they were part of the job.

This felt different. And that pissed her off.

"You're an idiot, by the way," she told Conner.

He didn't ask what she was referring to. He didn't argue. He just sighed.

Well, it was better than calling herself an idiot. Which she wanted to do. She'd been living with the guy for two days. She'd slept with him once—okay, kind of twice, but it had been so close together it practically counted as once—and she was already letting it affect her at work.

And she wasn't the only one.

Her unhappiness at having Conner's blood on her hands was overshadowed only by the fact that she was *pissed* at him for getting in between her and Eddie in the first place.

Ryan hauled the bag up to Conner's side. "What the fuck did you do that for?" he asked, digging for supplies.

"Shut up," Conner told him.

Ryan pulled out a pair of scissors and deftly cut Conner's pants away from the wound.

"Dammit," Gabby muttered. It was deep.

"You need stitches man," Ryan said. "A bunch of 'em. Let's go."

"Fuck," Conner swore.

"We're gonna need someone to come for the dogs," Gabby said, pulling her hands away.

She grabbed the cloth that Ryan held out to her, wiping her hands as best she could. She headed for the rig and grabbed a pair of gloves. Typically, those went on *before* the hands-on-blood part, but now she'd use them to keep the blood off of her phone.

She called her uncle and he agreed to send someone out to pick the dog and her puppies up.

"Who do you think he'll send?" Sierra asked when Gabby told the crew. Sierra was sitting next to Lady, the mama dog's head on her knee, two puppies crawling on her lap while the other two nestled next to the big dog.

Gabby shrugged. "One of the guys." It could be any of her cousins or brothers.

"I'll just hang out here, make sure Lady's okay until they get here. They'll give me a ride back, I'm sure," Sierra said.

Gabby rolled her eyes. Sierra found two of Gabby's brothers and several of her cousins hot, funny and sweet.

Gabby didn't see it.

"You sure?" Ryan asked.

"Oh, I'm sure," Sierra said with an eyebrow wiggle.

"You're sure you're okay to stay or you're sure one of them will give you a ride?" Ryan asked, his emphasis on *ride* making the word dirty.

Sierra laughed. "All of the above."

"I'm feeling a little sick," Gabby said, packing up the supply bag and trying not to look worried when she glanced at Conner.

Ryan had a compression bandage on the wound, but the blood was still coming through.

"You'd love to have me as a sister-in-law or cousin-in-law," Sierra told her.

"I would," Gabby agreed. "As long as you promise not to tell me anything about your sex life."

"We tell each other everything about our sex lives," Sierra protested, her glance going to Conner, then back to Gabby.

Gabby frowned at her.

"Ladies, I'd love to hear all the details you've shared with one another over the years," Conner said, "but if all my blood routes south at this point, I might bleed out."

Sierra laughed and Gabby tried to smile. It didn't matter. His eyes were closed.

"You're such a drama queen," she said instead, hoisting the bag onto her shoulder. "Do we need to take Eddie in?"

Ryan looked over at the still drugged man. "He should be out until the dog rescuers can get here. You okay with making sure he wakes up well?" he asked Sierra.

The sedative shouldn't give Eddie any lasting problems but it was always good to be sure a patient was stable afterward.

"No problem."

"You okay if he wakes up early?" Conner asked, pushing himself up to sitting, grimacing in pain as he did it.

"They're on their way," Gabby said. "I'll call and make sure they know Sierra's waiting. They all want to see her as much as she wants to see them." Which was true. Too true.

"Yeah, he'll be out until they get here," Ryan agreed.

"I'm not worried," Sierra said, grinning down at the wriggling puppies. "Eddie likes me almost as much as he likes Gabby."

"And we're taking his fucking knife," Conner said. "In fact, pat him down for anything else," he told Ryan.

"Uh…"

Conner frowned at his friend. "What?"

"Listen, I'm sorry he knifed you," Ryan said. "But he lives on the street, man. I can't take his knife."

Conner started to reply, then apparently thought about it.

"Fuck," he breathed. "Fine, but give the knife to Sierra until the guys get here."

Ryan handed the knife over. Sierra tucked it under her leg.

"Let's go, big shot," Gabby said to Conner. "You need us to carry you?"

"I can think of better ways to get your hands on me," he said, trying to push to his feet.

She clung to the flirting and teasing. "You shouldn't jeopardize those opportunities by getting yourself hurt. You're no good to me like this."

"Babe, I'll be good to you, blood loss or not."

She wrapped an arm around his waist, whether he needed it or not. "I might make you prove that to me."

"Maybe I'll stay back with Sierra," Ryan muttered, taking the bag from Gabby when it was clear that she was handling Conner.

And Conner wasn't protesting. He leaned his weight on her, off of his sore leg.

"No you won't!" Sierra called. "The puppies and the hot Evans guys are all mine!"

"They're not my type anyway," Ryan called back, striding ahead to the rig, leaving Gabby and Conner alone.

"You're in big trouble, you know," Gabby told Conner once they were sort of alone.

"I'm not apologizing."

"I'm shocked to hear that," she said dryly.

She helped him up into the back of the ambulance and started to slam the door, but Conner caught her hand and tugged her up into the rig with him. "Back here with me," he said.

"You're a patient." But she sat down next to him on the gurney.

"This is your best chance to dote on me," he said, still holding her hand. He settled back against the side of the ambulance as Ryan started it up and headed for the hospital.

"You expect me to dote on you *now*?" Gabby asked.

He gave her a half smile. "You know you want to."

"I want to kick your ass," she told him. "What the hell was all of that? You know I could have talked him down."

Conner's smile died and he frowned. "He had a fucking knife."

"He wouldn't have hurt me, Conner."

"You don't know that."

She studied his face for a moment, then glanced up front to where Ryan sat.

"Ryan!"

"Yeah?"

"Turn up the radio."

"Why?"

"Just do it," she told him, focusing back on Conner.

Ryan glanced in the rearview mirror. "I can still see you, even if I can't hear you."

"You're only going to be missing the ass chewing," she said.

"Sure." But he leaned forward and turned the volume dial.

She turned sideways, tucked her foot up underneath her and leaned in toward Conner. "Dixon, you need to get your shit together if we're going to do this."

"This?"

"The sleeping-together-and-working-together thing."

"I don't know what you mean." But he was looking at the oxygen tubes swaying on the other side of the ambulance from where they sat.

"A week ago, this whole scene at the warehouse would have gone very differently," she said. "You never would have stepped between me and Eddie."

Conner frowned. "Yes, I would have."

"No. I've been on the hot end of a gun, I've had a guy grab me in a choke hold...and you let me handle it. You and Ryan both wait for me and Sierra to tell you we need help. You trust us to do that. We know you're there. Escalating a situation like you did today is not cool."

Conner's jaw tightened but he didn't say anything.

"The only thing that's changed is that we've slept together," she went on. "If you're having…feelings for me…you have to lock it down at work."

"I don't want to have…feelings," he muttered after a long silence.

Gabby felt her heart thump in her chest. So there *were* some deeper feelings going on.

She liked that more than she should.

It complicated things. She didn't want things to get complicated. She was trying to *un*complicate her life right now. And, yeah, she hadn't expected some of the things she was feeling where he was concerned either. She'd thought she knew Conner. Discovering there were layers there was a surprise…and very nice.

And complicated.

"I know you don't want these feelings," she said. Conner liked superficial and easy.

That finally drew his eyes to hers. "I'm not complaining."

"Really? Even as your leg is throbbing like a bitch?"

"Ryan shot me up."

Ah, Ryan had given him an injection for pain. That explained why he'd been able to walk to the rig without being carried.

"Then these feelings might be just the effects of the drugs," she said with a shrug.

He leaned toward her. "That's not it, Gabby girl, and you know it."

She wanted to kiss him so bad it hurt. She knew he was going to be fine. They were going to take care of his wound. It was nothing serious, really. But she was feeling some new emotions here too—like feeling that she wanted to hold him and fucking *dote* on him.

"I hate this uniform on you," he said.

"Random thought of the day?" she asked.

"No. I've been thinking about it since I saw you in the break room. I also hate your hair up like that."

"Good. That should be less distracting then."

"You'd think so. But it's *more* distracting because I'm constantly thinking about the contrast between this and how great you look in jeans…and out of your jeans."

Her heart flipped and she felt everything in her body go soft and warm.

"You have to stop that."

"I know."

"And you can't be worrying about me at every scene and jumping in. At other scenes there will be other people who need you and if you distract *me* then I can't do my job either—"

"I know."

"I don't need you to take care of me."

"I fucking know that, Gabby."

He looked incredibly irritated. Well, good.

"Then knock it off. You can't think of me as a girl you're sleeping with when we're at work."

"I don't get stupid about the girls I sleep with," he said, his attention on the swaying oxygen tubes again.

That was…interesting.

"Who do you get stupid over?"

"My sisters."

"I was pretty sure we'd established that I'm not one of your sisters," she said lightly, even as her entire chest felt tight. She didn't want a relationship with Conner. Not a *relationship* anyway. His life was crazy too. If they combined their two crazy lives, and families, she'd be…crazy.

But it felt pretty damned good to hear that he was feeling differently for her than he did for most of the women he slept with.

He'd never done it on a poker table with any of them either.

Of course, now the poker table was broken.

She sighed.

Maybe that was a sign. A metaphor, at least.

"My sisters…and you," he finally said.

She swallowed. "That's probably not good."

"It's very not good."

She was a big girl. She knew what she wanted. She could handle this. Probably. "It's two months, Dixon. Can you handle it or should I sleep on Sierra's couch?"

He was quiet for a moment and Gabby felt her heart in her throat. She didn't want to move out. But she knew she should do just that.

"Well, you've already got your stuff all moved in," he said.

Relief flooded through her. Stupid, complicating relief. "Yeah, that's true."

He grinned at her and she could have easily labeled it goofy. Conner did flirtatious and sexy and over the top, but he didn't do goofy.

She grinned back. Goofily.

Conner reached and cupped the back of her head, pulling her in for a kiss that was hot and sweet and felt completely, totally right.

CHAPTER
EIGHT

"WELL, THAT EXPLAINS IT."

Gabby turned toward the back of the ambulance. Which was now open. With Ryan and Nate standing there looking in. With a bunch of ER staff gathered behind them—as ER staffs were inclined to do when an ambulance pulled in.

She hadn't even noticed that they'd arrived at St. A's.

And dammit if she didn't feel herself blushing.

"Why are you here?" Conner asked Nate with a frown.

"I'm a doctor. You need stitches. And Ryan likes me so he called to be sure I'd be here waiting for you."

"It's a cut. Any intern can handle it. You're a big-shot trauma surgeon. Don't you have real patients to treat?" Conner let go of Gabby and eased himself off the gurney.

"No. And this is far more interesting. I can't wait to tell Emma."

"You can't tell Emma," Conner said quickly.

"Why not?" Nate asked, helping Conner into a waiting wheelchair.

"Because…she'll tell everyone."

"Emma? No," Nate said with an eye-roll.

"My sisters don't even make cereal without asking each other how much milk to use," Conner said.

Nate laughed and started pushing him toward the ER. "Exaggerate much?"

Ryan turned in the direction of the locker room.

Gabby followed Nate and Conner, but hung back slightly.

She had heard the guys interact a thousand times, but honestly, she usually tuned it out. Guys giving each other a hard time was like white noise.

Now, suddenly, she felt like she should pay attention.

"But you don't want them to know about Gabby?" Nate asked Conner.

"No. They like her."

Nate glanced at her over his shoulder. "That's a bad thing?"

"It will be when the two months are up."

Gabby lengthened her strides to be sure to keep up as Nate rolled Conner through the ER waiting area, past the Admissions desk and down the hallway leading to the exam rooms.

"When the two months is up?" Nate asked. "What's that mean?"

"That's when Gabby and I will be done."

He glanced at her again. She tried to keep her face impassive.

"You don't have to be done," Nate said.

Gabby felt her stomach flip at that. Of course they needed to be done then. Very done. I'm-over-this-and-never-want-to-do-it-again done.

Though she was beginning to have some strong suspicions that it might not happen like that.

"We do have to be," Conner insisted.

"Why?"

"She's going to medical school in August."

"So?"

"So she wants to be done then."

Nate didn't answer for a long moment. "*She* wants to be done then."

"Yep."

"Okay. Then stay away from her," Nate said.

Gabby held her breath, waiting for Conner to respond to that.

"I can't do that either," Conner said.

Another much bigger stomach flip.

Now she definitely couldn't make herself turn in the other direction—the direction that would lead her to the locker room where she could clean up.

As they headed for the procedure room where they did stitches and casts, Gabby noticed all the nurses and aides noticing Conner coming through. Not that Nate wasn't fine to look at, but he had never given off any flirtatious vibes. She knew they were all watching Conner. She could practically feel their urges to go in and fuss over him.

She had to hold back from snarling at them all.

Yep, things had changed between her and Conner.

Dammit.

"Your sisters are smart and know you really well," Nate said, rolling him into the procedure room. "I'm not sure you're going to be able to hide that you and Gabby have something going on."

"I have to try."

Gabby hung back now. There was no need for her to be in there. But she wanted to be in there anyway.

Nate, bless him, didn't close the door all the way.

Gabby hovered outside.

"So you're going to, what, date her for two months until she starts med school?" Nate asked.

"Apparently." Conner didn't sound all that thrilled. He sounded resigned, at best.

They were *dating* now? Wasn't that something they should decide together? That seemed much more…complicated. Still she leaned closer.

"And you think after two months with her, *living together*, that you'll be able to just say goodbye and move on?" Nate asked.

She frowned. Nate didn't have to make it sound like such a stupid idea.

There was a long pause with no sound from Conner. Then he said, "I've done it a hundred times before."

"Not for that long."

"Still."

"And not with this girl."

There was another long pause and Gabby held her breath.

She didn't really understand why. She could still hear when she was breathing.

"She's just a girl."

That was what Conner finally said.

She was just a girl.

Ouch.

Gabby pulled back from the door. Well, *that* hadn't been worth eavesdropping on. At all.

"You, my friend, are a complete idiot," Nate finally said. "But I have to admit, watching you go through this is going to be entertaining. Especially once your sisters figure it out."

"You can't—"

"Dix, I'm not going to tell them," Nate interrupted.

"Yeah?"

Nate chuckled. "I'm not going to need to."

Conner blew out an exasperated breath that was loud enough Gabby could hear it from the hallway.

"Be right back," Nate told him. "Don't move and don't you dare try to stitch yourself."

Gabby stepped back quickly as Nate came to the door, pulled it open and stepped out.

He didn't look surprised to see her. He shut the door behind him. "Congrats on med school."

"Thanks." She knew Nate had graduated from the University of Nebraska.

"He didn't mean it, you know."

"The two-month thing? That's my rule."

"The just-a-girl thing."

She shrugged. "Maybe I am."

"Uh-huh. Okay, so you're kind of an idiot too. You're perfect for one another then."

She frowned. "You're not going to tell his sisters then?"

"You don't want me to either?"

"They're a little scary."

Nate laughed. "Yeah, they are. There are four adult, intelligent, professional men who have been turned inside out by them."

Gabby couldn't help her smile. That was nice.

"Like you're doing to Conner."

Her smile died. "Stop it."

"Stop what?"

"Playing matchmaker."

"I don't need to," Nate said, looking like he was quite entertained. "You're right there doing it yourself."

She blew out an exasperated breath of her own. She sympathized with Conner, having all these people with interest in and opinions about his life. "You won't tell his sisters?" They would very likely turn on the matchmaking like crazy and, frankly, Gabby wasn't sure *anyone* could resist the Dixon Divas as a group.

"I won't need to."

"Ryan will?" She'd kick his ass.

Nate pointed over her shoulder. "Ryan won't need to either."

Gabby turned to find a gathering of female Emergency Department staff at the end of the hall.

She faced Nate again. "Maybe they'll think it's all because he got hurt."

"Yeah, sure," Nate agreed. "Maybe. Good thing Conner is the only one acting weird."

His sarcasm was clear.

"What do you mean?"

"You're not really the type to hover outside an exam room, you know."

Damn.

"I've waited around to get reports on patients before."

"You're also not the type to eavesdrop."

Damn again.

"By the way," Nate said, "I managed medical school and a kid on my own."

Everyone who knew Nate, knew that Nate's son, Michael, was his proudest accomplishment. Michael was a great kid.

"You had a nanny," Gabby said. Everyone also knew that Nate came from money.

"I'm saying you find a way."

"I need to find a nanny for Conner? Women who get paid to take care of the needs *he* has are called hookers and they're illegal."

Nate grinned and shook his head. "You find a way to do it all if it's important."

She took a deep breath and dropped the flippant attitude. "It's been two days." There was no way that Conner was something she needed to "find a way" for already.

Nate chuckled. "It's been two years, Gabby. You've both just realized it in the past two days."

Nate stepped around her and headed down the hall.

But the guy had a point.

Double damn.

Nate had kept his promise not to tell his sisters about Gabby—so far. Unfortunately, he *had* told Emma about Conner getting knifed. Which meant they all knew within ten minutes and that meant he'd had to make a stop at his mother's house after he was released from the ER because his sisters had told *her*.

And, of course, they all showed up too.

After reassuring the women in his life that he was fine, letting his mother feed him, catching up on baby and wedding and kitchen-remodeling plans, and plotting how to get revenge on Nate, he finally headed for home. His leg ached, but he was happy. His sisters were happy. That's all he really wanted.

Until he came through the door to his apartment.

Then the list of things he wanted expanded quickly.

He wanted to watch the movie that was on his big screen, he wanted to eat the plate of nachos that was sitting on his coffee table and he wanted the woman who was curled up in the corner of his couch under the fleece blanket with her hair up and makeup off.

She looked up as he came in and smiled. But her smile quickly died.

"No," she said, shaking her head and sitting up straighter, pulling the blanket up to her chin.

"No, what?" He dropped the plastic bag he'd carried in from the car and tossed his keys toward his kitchen table. Or where the kitchen table had once been. Before he and the woman looking at him like he was a serial killer had broken it having sex. His keys landed on the floor.

He didn't care.

He started toward Gabby.

"What you're thinking," she said.

"I'm thinking that this is my favorite movie."

She glanced at *The Replacements* and muttered, "Damn."

"And I love nachos."

"I made these," she said, waving a hand toward the platter that was still half-full. "They're not like Trudy's."

Trudy really did make fantastic nachos. And burgers. And pizzas.

He plopped onto the couch next to her—right next to her—and reached for the plate. He put a chip in his mouth and groaned. She'd used beef and beans, lots of cheese, guacamole and sour cream *and* jalapenos.

He'd eaten meatloaf at his mother's to make her happy, but he was suddenly still hungry.

He ate several more chips, watching Gabby as he did it.

She was concentrating on the movie. Or making it look like she was concentrating on the movie anyway.

"A football movie, huh?" he asked nonchalantly.

Except that it definitely wasn't nonchalant.

"Keanu Reeves is hot," she said.

"Whatever. You like football." She came to every Hawks game.

"I grew up with football. On TV, watching my brothers and cousins play. It's a great game."

"You like Hawks football in particular."

She glanced at him. "I love Hawks football."

"Because they have a hot quarterback?"

She turned slightly toward him with a tiny smile. "Their quarterback leads the league in rushing touchdowns."

"Ah, you appreciate his talent too. That's nice."

"But he only has the *sixth*-best completion percent in passing touchdowns in the league and is third in the league for sacks."

Conner munched on a chip as he watched her grin at him.

"And there are only nine teams in the league," she added as he chewed.

He was aware. "He's number three, huh?"

She laughed. "Being sacked isn't a good thing."

"His offensive line probably sucks."

"They don't," she said. "He takes too long in the pocket."

He really liked her. Most of the women he dated knew that he was a football player and knew that the Hawks won a hell of a lot more than they lost. That was enough for them. And for Conner. He didn't expect to sit and talk football with the women he slept with. He didn't expect to sit and *talk* with the women he slept with.

"Still, he leads the league in rushing touchdowns," he commented.

"He's a ball hog."

He snorted and ate another chip. "These are awesome. You're doing good at the doting thing," he said. In spite of the disparaging remarks about his football skills.

"Doting?" she asked sharply. "I'm not doting."

"Watching one of my favorite movies and making me my favorite food?" He leaned and grabbed her half-full beer bottle, tipping it back. "And my favorite beer?"

She leaned over and took the bottle from him, clutching it to her chest. "This is *my* favorite movie, my favorite food and my favorite beer. This isn't about you."

"Really?"

She looked a little panicked.

Interesting.

"What are you wearing?"

She quirked an eyebrow. "Doesn't matter. That's also not for you."

He reached over and tugged on the throw blanket. It fell to her waist, revealing a long-sleeved, gray T-shirt—a loose one. He pulled again and the blanket slid off of her lap. She was dressed in baggy, black yoga pants. And socks.

He lifted his gaze to hers.

"I think this is very much for me."

"I'm as *unattractive* and *unsexy* as I can get!"

He grinned. "Intentionally."

"No. I mean… Well…fuck," she finally muttered.

"You're trying to tone it down now? After we broke my poker table?" He wasn't about to let a woman who made nachos and knew that he spent too much time in the pocket and…all the other Gabby stuff…tone things down.

She sat, chewing her bottom lip and watching Keanu for a

few minutes. Finally she pointed the remote at the TV and muted it, then turned to face him, tucking her foot up under her.

"I told you not to fall in love with me."

Yes, she had. And there was no chance that had happened. Strangely, though, he didn't feel the urge to immediately deny that it was a possibility.

"You've been here for two days." He couldn't actually be in love with her in two days.

Right?

"I know. But Nate said some stuff at the hospital about me being a matchmaker here. I don't mean to do that."

"I know." He did. He knew that she didn't want anything more than sex from him. Either. Because that's all he wanted from her. Probably.

"This is getting complicated. In two days. That's not good. That's—"

She stopped and tipped her head as she caught his eyes scanning over her hair and focusing on her mouth.

"Conner?"

"Yeah?"

"Is this like the uniform thing?"

"What uniform thing?" God he loved her mouth. Not *her*, but her mouth. For sure. And her laugh. And her sarcasm.

"The uniform is the opposite of sexy. But instead of being a turn-off, now it reminds you of the sexy stuff because it's such a contrast." He also really liked that she could play poker and wore pink lace and drank her coffee black.

"Yeah, that's probably what it is."

"So I should go back to the mall and get some of the lipstick and look like all your other girls."

The thing was, she would never be like all the other girls— lipstick had nothing to do with it.

Damn.

"You don't want to be in love with me either," he pointed out.

"No, I don't," she said firmly.

More firmly than she really needed to, in his opinion.

"Because of medical school?" he asked.

"And because neither of us needs a bigger or crazier family."

He thought about that. They both had families that would always be there and involved. If they got together their family—their impossible-to-ignore, loud, meddling family—would get *a lot* bigger. Then he chuckled. "All those years I was using my sisters as a reason not to have a relationship, and now they're the reason this relationship won't have me."

He heard her suck in a quick breath, saw her frown. "You don't want this relationship to have you."

She said it softly, with something in her eyes he couldn't identify.

It wasn't really a question. But he shook his head. "No. At least, that's what I'm used to thinking and telling myself."

Gabby looked at him, still chewing her bottom lip. After a minute, she reached over and switched the TV off completely, then drew her legs up and wrapped her arms around them. "Why is that?"

Ah, crap. He'd spent the afternoon with his sisters and mother *talking* about himself. He didn't want to do it now.

"My sisters."

She nodded. "I believe that your sisters are part of it." She narrowed her eyes. "But I'm guessing there's another girl in there somewhere."

He shifted and thought about grabbing the beer again. "My sisters were all the girls I could handle."

She shook her head. "Nope, don't believe it. Who was she?"

"Who?"

"The girl who broke your heart and made you so determined to keep things superficial with women."

Dammit. He moved to put the plate back on the coffee table, wiped his hands on one of the napkins and sighed. "If I tell you mine, you have to tell me yours."

"My what?"

"Your heartbreak. Everyone has one."

She nodded. "Okay. You first."

This was Gabby. She'd seen him at a few low points. She'd seen him drunk at Trudy's; she'd seen him being a jerk to his sister Olivia when she'd been acting out; she'd seen him threatening to remove a guy's liver through his ass when Conner found out the guy had been abusing his kids and then telling their boss off when the hospital administration wanted to write him up for it.

But he trusted her to know who he really was. It hit him now as it never had before. In spite of how he acted or how situations affected him, he knew that Gabby knew *him*. She knew that he'd do anything for his family and friends, that he'd risk his own safety to save a victim who needed him, that when he couldn't save one of those victims it hit him hard and that no matter how much he flirted with Sara Gordon, he would never act on any of his big talk.

Gabby knew him. And liked him. He could tell her about Ashley without worrying that it would change her opinion of him.

But, he *really* hated this story.

"Cody and I lived together in college. Our first day on campus was the first day I met him. But we clicked right away. We were playing football, so things were crazy and I didn't get home much. It was great to have a friend."

Gabby rested her chin on her knees, her eyes riveted on him.

"Cody and I lived together and had a ton of fun being big shots on campus. Parties, girls, the whole thing," he went on. "I didn't know for months that he had a girlfriend back home, Ashley. Who he was cheating on regularly, but who he kept hanging on with gifts and promises and just enough contact to keep her from ending it."

Gabby frowned. "Cody? Cody Madsen? The nicest guy I know?"

Conner rolled his eyes. That's what everyone thought of Cody. "Yep." Of course, they weren't wrong. Cody was a nice guy. He had a good heart. And he was loyal to every single person in his life—now. Cody had, of course, grown up and changed over the years and Conner had finally seen it. He really was glad that Olivia had fallen for Cody. He'd take good care of her. But it had been hard on Conner to let her go.

"She was his high school sweetheart," he told Gabby. "They were practically engaged when they went to college. But he didn't expect college to be so...fun. Anyway, one night she called and he wasn't there. I picked up and we started talking. She needed him because her grandmother had died and she was having a hard time."

Conner still remembered how he felt talking to her. He'd instantly gone into protective, knight-in-shining-armor mode. "We talked for almost two hours and I actually got her to laugh."

Gabby gave him a little smile. "And you loved that."

He shrugged. "Of course." He loved making women happy. Period. "When Cody got back I told him, but he wouldn't call her. In fact, he ignored it all for almost a week. But she kept calling *me* to talk. Finally I told him that if he didn't call her, I was going to tell her about all the girls and partying. Actually, I grabbed him by the front of the shirt, pushed him up against the wall and ranted in his face. Then told him to call her."

Gabby was nodding. "Sounds just like you. Defending a woman, even one you barely know."

Conner never had apologized for that. He couldn't. Cody had been in the wrong. The callous way he'd handled Ashley had been Conner's biggest hang-up about Cody and Olivia. Back then, Cody had done everything the easy way, had always taken the path of least resistance. Keeping a long-distance relationship going—keeping *any* relationship going—took effort. So he'd bailed. Except, actually ending things and dealing with that drama would have been *hard*. So he'd just ignored it all and hoped it would go away.

"I was so pissed at him," Conner told Gabby. "I couldn't be in the same room with him. But I kept talking to Ashley. I went to visit her. I…"

"You helped her get over Cody," Gabby filled in.

He nodded. "I tried." And in retrospect he knew that was the primary attraction he'd felt for her.

"Did it work?"

He scratched his jaw. How could he word this so he didn't sound like a pathetic loser?

There was no way to do it.

"She was using me to make Cody jealous. When she realized it wasn't working, she moved on."

Gabby's eyes widened. "She hooked up with you to get back at Cody? When you were there for her?"

He shrugged.

"But you fell for her," Gabby said quietly. "Right?"

He shrugged again. He had. Hard.

"You fell in love with her?" Gabby asked.

"Yeah, I guess I did."

"That bitch," Gabby said softly. "How could she not fall for you right back?"

"She wanted Cody."

"But she never got him back."

"No. In fact, when she realized that was never going to happen, she dropped out of college, slept around and had a big drinking problem for a while."

Gabby didn't say anything for a minute. Then she reached out and took his hand. He let her slide her fingers between his. "And that broke your heart even more, didn't it? Knowing that you'd tried to help her and that it didn't work."

Conner liked making women happy. And he *hated* failing at it.

But Gabby already knew that. "It's better to keep things light and superficial with women. On a level where I can make or keep them happy. At the level where I can meet their needs."

Gabby pressed her lips together, then cleared her throat. "Except with your sisters."

"Well…they're different. I had to worry about the deeper, not-fun stuff with them, especially right after Dad died. Seeing them sad and lost was…horrible." *Horrible* wasn't even the right word. There wasn't a word *horrible* enough to describe how he'd felt watching his sisters deal with their father's death.

Gabby nodded. "You wanting to avoid the serious stuff now makes even more sense. And even more reason why your retirement matters," she said. "Now Ryan, Shane, Nate and Cody have to worry about the deeper, not-as-fun stuff. You can finally do the light, more superficial stuff."

He wasn't embarrassed by that. He'd been there for his sisters, sometimes when they *hadn't* wanted him to be, times when they'd messed up or needed bailing out or chewing out.

It was awesome to be able to go to the movies and cake tastings and buy them fun things now.

He was enjoying it immensely and wasn't going to apologize for that either.

"Exactly."

She nodded. "I completely get it. All of it. Ashley was a stupid bitch and I'm very sorry you fell for her crap, but I get it."

And that was Gabby. Practical. Smart. Sweet—in her own way.

"Now you. Who broke your heart?"

"I told you that I had three long-term relationships. I broke up with two of them. One was amicable, one wasn't, but neither was a heartbreak for me. I guess the closest I've come was Sean. He broke up with me after ten months of dating. I thought things were going well, he thought he wanted to travel through Europe for a year."

"That's it?" Conner asked when it became clear she wasn't going to say any more.

"What do you mean?"

"He wanted to travel for a year and you wouldn't go with him."

"With my family and stuff, I couldn't. He knew that. If he'd wanted to be with me, he would have stayed here."

"But…" Conner trailed off, shaking his head, "…he didn't break your heart."

"Well, I thought it was kind of crappy that seeing the Eiffel Tower was higher on his priority list than I was."

"Did you cry?"

She shrugged. "I don't cry much."

"What did you do when he told you he wanted to go?"

"I told him that it was kind of crappy that seeing the Eiffel Tower was higher on his priority list than I was."

Conner smiled. "And then you told him to get the hell out."

She nodded.

"And not to call or send you postcards and definitely not to show up on your doorstep when he got home from his travels."

"Pretty much."

Conner laughed. "That's not a heartbreak, G."

"Then what is?"

"If not crying, then at least some ranting and raving, maybe a broken plate, getting drunk, something."

"If I broke a plate or got drunk every time a guy in my life pissed me off, I'd have no dishes and no liver."

"Family doesn't count."

She gave him a half smile.

"He didn't break your heart."

"Well, that's good to know. Seems I'm pretty well-adjusted and normal, then."

Conner moved closer on the couch. Yes, there was a real possibility that they were getting in too deep here. There was a chance he was feeling, or was going to feel, more for this woman than he wanted to. There was a chance that he might end up heartbroken for the second time in his life.

But as he'd told Nate, he couldn't leave her alone now.

"You broke a couple of hearts though." He tugged on their entwined hands, pulling her to her knees and then onto his lap, tipping her back and looking down into her eyes.

Her breathing caught but she put an arm around his neck. "Nah, it was all very grown up and reasonable."

"Bullshit. The guys who've had a taste of you haven't walked away unscathed, Gabrielle Evans."

Now her gaze traveled over his hair, over his face, settling on his mouth.

"Then we should stop now. We wouldn't want you scathed," she said softly, putting her other hand against his face. "Again."

"That's what you were trying to do tonight?" he asked, running his hand over her hair and pulling the ponytail holder loose, tossing it over his shoulder. "You were dressing down, being casual, acting like this is friends only, to save me some heartbreak?"

She nodded. "We should just be roommates."

"Too late."

"We can go back. After all, I'm just a girl."

He froze, his hand buried in her hair. He stared into her eyes. "What did you say?"

She met his gaze directly. "I'm just a girl. You've said goodbye a hundred times before."

Ah, dammit.

"You heard that."

"I did."

She didn't try to pull away from him, or push him away. She simply lay still, waiting for him to say…whatever he was going to say.

Should he tell her that the moment he'd said the words *she's just a girl*, the truth had slammed into him and he'd known he'd never said anything more untrue in his life?

No. He was freaked out about it enough. He didn't need to freak her out too. But the words had hurt her, because she was, if nothing else, his friend and his crewmate. Of course she wouldn't want to be lumped with all the other girls in and out of his life.

So he had to say *something*.

"I have said goodbye a hundred times before," he told her. "Easily."

"Then this will be no different. And," she said, "it'll be easier on your furniture if we stop now rather than later."

If only she were just a girl. God, that would make things easier. And how the hell had all of this happened so fast? And what was *this* exactly?

All he knew was she was not just a girl. She was not just one of the guys either. She was…Gabby.

She was the only one he could tell what he needed and wanted. He pulled her upright, straddling his thighs, facing him.

"Gabby, you're just a girl like…Olivia's super-supreme cinnamon rolls are just cinnamon rolls."

"And we're back to the cinnamon rolls."

Yep. They were. Definitely.

"Love cinnamon rolls. And even though I've had more pancakes and blueberry muffins, I've had some pretty great cinnamon rolls in my time."

She snorted. "You're really into breakfast food, huh?"

He ran his hands down her back to her butt and back up. "Pay attention. You started this analogy last night."

"Oh, we're talking about sex? Not actual cinnamon rolls?" she asked, sitting up a little straighter.

He nodded solemnly. "Yes. Sex and cinnamon rolls."

"I'm listening."

"So, I've had some great cinnamon rolls."

Now she frowned. "Wait, we're talking about you having great sex with *other women*?"

He nodded. "But they were *just* cinnamon rolls. You're a super-supreme cinnamon roll."

Her eyes stayed narrow but she asked, "What makes it super-supreme?"

"She frosts them with a sweet cream-cheese frosting. But then there's a cream-cheese filling thing wrapped up inside. And bacon."

"Wow. Bacon?"

"She puts chopped up bacon in the cream cheese filling."

"Holy crap."

"Yeah. It has everything you love about cinnamon rolls. Then inside you find a whole lot more to love."

She tipped her head. "That was pretty smooth."

He laughed and ran his hands back to her ass and squeezed. "There's more."

"Please go on."

"She's only made them twice. So they're rare. And something that once you've had one taste, you'll never forget."

"Oh, *wow*." She chuckled and shook her head. "That's beyond smooth. That's downright cheesy."

"Does it make you want to get naked with me?"

She paused. "You walking in here tonight made we want to get naked with you."

His entire body felt like it had responded to that. "You could have spent the night in my bed. Naked."

"You know why I didn't."

"Yep, I remember. I'm supposed to be selfish in bed. I'm supposed to tell you what *I* want without thinking about what you want."

"Something like that."

"Then let's go." He reached over and snagged the handle of the plastic bag he'd dropped by the couch, grabbed her butt and stood.

"Conner!" She wrapped her legs around his waist and arms around his neck. "What's going on?"

"I want to have the best cinnamon roll I've ever had."

As they passed through the kitchen she laughed. "Oh good, we're still talking about sex."

A moment later he tossed her onto his bed, then stripped off his shirt, kicked off his shoes and unbuttoned his pants.

"Take off your clothes."

"I don't know… I was kind of trying to avoid all of this tonight."

"No, you weren't."

"I was." She pulled at the front of her T-shirt. "The nonsexy, no-makeup look, remember?"

"That's funny. All I see is the woman I want even *more* than I could ever want a cinnamon roll. Even one with bacon."

"Well, that *is* something. The yoga pants aren't cooling you off, huh?"

"You know how you were dirty and covered with blood today?" he asked, stepping to the bottom of the bed.

"Yeah. Your blood."

"I would have stripped you down right there on that warehouse floor if I could have."

She swallowed, then took a deep breath. "Okay, fine. One quick time, lights off, missionary."

He grabbed the bottom of the yoga pants and yanked, pulling them down over her hips. "Uh, hell no."

"Hell no?" she asked, letting her pants slide off. "Seriously?"

"You told me to be more selfish in bed."

"Hmm, I did say that, didn't I?" she asked, pulling her own shirt off and unhooking her bra, tossing them both to the side.

Heat and hunger coursed through him. And a new feeling —greed.

"So this is going to be all about me, got it?"

She smiled. "If I have any fun I'm sure it will be purely accidental."

He stopped. "Hey, G?"

"Yeah?"

"You knew this was going to happen tonight, right?"

She pulled her bottom lip between her teeth, then sighed.

"Yeah," she admitted. "I was sure you'd be able to figure out how to be selfish by tonight."

He tickled the bottom of her feet. She shrieked and pushed away from him, scooting up the bed.

He'd always tamped down any desires that he wasn't sure the woman he was with would welcome. That came from—so many places. Yes, Ashley. He'd wanted a relationship and had gone full steam ahead, only to be brought up short when he realized they were *not* on the same page. But it came from looking out for his sisters too. He couldn't stomach the idea that any man would push something on one of them that they didn't want. Both Amanda and Olivia had been involved with men who had pushed the limits—one had been short term, one night really, and physical, the other had been longer term and more emotional. But both situations had shaken him.

Now, though, looking at Gabby, he realized who she really was —and why she was exactly the woman he needed. She wouldn't let him push. She'd stand her ground and push back if needed. She'd be honest about what she wanted and needed, and if he went too far or not far enough, she'd be in his face about it. He could trust her to get and be exactly what and who she wanted—in bed and out. He could trust her to be happy, to show him how to make her happy.

He was someone she'd trust completely.

And he realized he could also trust himself. He would never do anything to hurt her. He would never be that guy who didn't know when to say when. He'd listen to her and do whatever he could to make her happy. Her pleasure would always go hand in hand with his…no matter how selfish he tried to be.

So with Gabby he could do some things he'd only fantasized about.

"Dixon, you still with me?" she asked.

Conner realized he'd been standing at the foot of the bed staring at her for several moments.

"Yeah. I'm—" he cleared his throat, "—I'm so with you."

"Then tell me what you want."

The words rocked through him. He could tell her what he wanted. That was…a bunch of things he didn't have time for right now.

"I want to spread you out, tie you up and cover you in cinnamon-roll frosting," he told her, stepping forward and running his hand from her ankle to her knee.

Her eyes widened and she blew out a breath. "Damn, Dixon."

"What do you think?" He ran his hand over the silky path again.

"I think…I'm all yours."

Lust almost buckled his knees. "Damn, Evans."

She grinned and lay back to lift her hips and push her panties off.

He reached for the plastic bag he'd brought home, pulling out two black-silk ties.

He held them up.

"Only two?" she asked.

He lifted an eyebrow. "You've done this before?" It didn't matter—this was what he wanted but…

She shook her head. "No. I've read about it."

"You've read about it?" he repeated, putting a knee on the mattress.

She smiled. "More men should read romance novels."

He crawled up to her. "I'm in. You can give me a reading list tomorrow. Start with the ones with the four black ties. I'll get two more on my way home."

"You got it."

She was at the top of the bed now, resting against his pillows. She looked fantastic there.

Then she reached up, grasping two of the wooden spindles in his headboard. The position thrust her breasts up and Conner forgot how to breathe.

"I assume that if you had to buy ties, you haven't done this before either?" she asked.

"Never."

"But it's what you want? Of all the things?"

He looked from her nipples to her face. *She* was what he wanted. Of all the things. "Yes."

"Why haven't you done it before?"

He swallowed and leaned over her to wrap one of the silk ties around her right wrist. "I have a hard time purposefully putting women in vulnerable positions."

She didn't say anything and he looked down at her.

Her eyes were soft. "I don't feel vulnerable."

He paused, his hands at her other wrist. "What do you feel?"

"Like I'm about to be worshipped."

CHAPTER
NINE

SO MANY EMOTIONS swept through him that all he could really identify was that his chest was really tight.

He gave her a little smile, trying not to give away how much that meant to him. He was on the verge of feeling pretty freaking vulnerable himself. "You're going to make this all about you?" He secured the second tie around her left wrist and leaned back to look.

She stretched luxuriously and gave him a sexy smile. "Oh yeah. I'm about to become your favorite food. And all I have to do is lie here and take it."

One of the emotions swirling in him was most definitely lust. He understood that one, so he latched on to it. "You're going to take it all right. However I want to give it to you."

"I just don't know if this is all that selfish of you," she told him as he shucked his pants and underwear. "I mean, I can't reach you. I can't put my mouth anywhere. Yet, I get to lie here and have orgasm after orgasm."

That was the moment he fell fully in love with her.

Not because she looked hot, her hair tousled, her eyes heavy with passion, her body bare and exposed to him, but because she was focusing this on him, letting him be selfish, giving him exactly what he wanted, without hesitation, without letting him have any mixed emotions.

"I'm going to take what I want, Gabby. And I get to hear you beg, hear you tell me how much you *need* me. Because you can't reach your clit. You can't help yourself along. You're going to need me bad."

Her attention was focused on his cock, thick and hard for her.

He needed her to need him. Somehow. Some way. There was very little he could do or give this woman, really. She was strong, independent, smart and surrounded by people who would have her back. And she didn't want him to be there for her.

But he could make her *need* him this way.

She wriggled against the sheets. "Bring it on."

And she, of course, had to make it a challenge.

"Hang on tight." He fished the can of frosting from the bag.

She laughed. "Actual frosting?"

He grinned. "Of course."

"Bacon too?"

He shook his head. "I've got *you* as the best part of this treat."

He pulled the lid off the frosting container and dipped a huge glob out with two fingers. He took his time painting her body, covering her nipples, then both breasts. He swiped a stripe down her belly, frosted out to both hip bones, then down over her thighs.

The sounds she made and the way she moved against his sheets were as delicious as the icing. When he moved between her knees and she spread her legs for him, he looked up at her.

She was panting, her cheeks flushed, her eyes on him.

He lifted the fingers he'd been using and put them in his mouth, sucking them clean.

Then, still watching her, he ran his finger along her cleft to her clit. She was so wet. She moaned his name as he circled the sensitive nub.

He lifted his fingers to his mouth again. "Even sweeter," he told her honestly.

"You having a good time?" she asked, completely breathless.

"I'm having the best time. You?"

"Great. Totally good."

Uh-huh. He could tell that having her hands tied was frustrating to her. "Need anything?"

"No, I'm good. Take your time. Whatever." She even managed a small shrug.

He grinned. "You sure? You look like you're a little uncomfortable."

"No, this is fantastic. Completely comfortable."

"Right. Good to hear." He ran his finger over her clit again, making her hips buck.

He dipped his finger into the frosting again, then covered her clit with the icing.

"Conner," she gasped. Almost accidentally.

"Right here. Not going anywhere. Not for anything."

He swirled his finger through the frosting over both nipples, between her breasts, over her left hip and down to her clit, circling and pressing, then repeated the path.

She was wiggling harder now.

"You're still good?"

"Keep going, Conner," she said, meeting his gaze directly. "I'm yours. Do whatever you want."

Gabby would have never imagined letting a guy tie her hands during sex. She wasn't good at being vulnerable, at turning over power. But she'd meant it when she told Conner that she didn't feel vulnerable with him.

For one, whether or not he thought this was selfish of him, she was having a pretty great time.

He rubbed over her clit again and she amended that to a really great time. Then he slid a finger into her and she changed it to a super great time.

"God, I love putting that look on your face," he muttered, watching her as he pressed a second finger into her.

"I love you putting this look on my face too."

She did feel worshipped. And wanted. Wanted like she'd never been wanted before.

He slid his fingers deep, then out, his thumb circling over her clit. Over and over.

Her body wound tight, heat and electricity swirling through her, lighting every nerve on fire. "Conner."

"Not yet, G. Not yet."

"Please" fell out of her mouth without her thinking.

His smile was huge. "That's better."

"You want me to beg?"

"I want you to admit you need me."

"Only because my hands are tied. With five fingers I'm fine without you. Give me ten and I'm better than fine."

He kept moving his fingers in and out, but his rhythm slowed. "Holy shit, I'd like to see that."

"Untie me."

He reached up...and tugged on the end of one of the ties, tightening it. "This is about me, remember?" He looked down at where he still had two fingers deep. "*You* are all about me right now. Your nipples." He leaned in and licked the frosting from one, then sucked the frosting off the other.

She gasped, then moaned.

"Your lips."

He pressed his lips to hers and she tasted the vanilla cream-cheese flavor on his tongue.

"Your pussy."

He pressed his fingers deep.

"Your clit…"

"Yes, God, Conner. Yes. Please. I need you."

"That's my girl." He grasped a thigh in each hand, pushing up and out, spreading her open. "Oh yeah." He didn't hesitate. He leaned in and took a long, firm lick that made her cry out.

He ate at her—licking, sucking, thrusting, stroking with fingers and tongue—until she was wound tight. "Come for me, Gabby. Come on, babe."

Her orgasm hit hard and hot. She panted his name over and over, the word spilling from her without her control, as he rose to his knees between her legs. He watched her face as he slid on a condom, and the look in his eyes was enough to keep the ripples of pleasure going. He looked—intent, determined and barely contained.

Before she could form a more coherent thought, he took hold of her thighs again and slid home.

They moaned together.

There was something about not having her hands, about being at his mercy, that fired her blood. Conner was trying to be selfish, but even when he was absorbed in what he wanted, he was focused on her. As if *she* were everything he wanted. In that moment, she felt as if he were already, on some level, satisfied. Just being there, in that moment, with her.

That was dumb. This was sex. There was a lot more going on than just *being*.

As if to illustrate, he pulled out and thrust in again.

But even as her orgasm—her second during this all-about-Conner sexathon they were supposed to be having—built, she truly had the feeling that Conner was already good and happy.

And she hadn't done much. She'd lain there and let him worship her.

More or less.

Her orgasm washed over her a minute later and Conner was only a minute behind that.

As they came down from the clouds together, Conner shifted

to the side, freed her hands and then pulled her up against him. And with her head against his chest, his heartbeat strong in her ear, Gabby came to a startling realization.

Everyone in her life believed she was fine, independent, strong. Including Conner. He knew those things. But he also understood that her not *needing* him didn't mean she didn't *want* him. And he wasn't going to let her use that to keep him at arm's length.

She could change her own oil, but that didn't mean it wouldn't be nice for someone else to do it once in a while. She could make her own cookies, but that didn't mean that her mother's care package didn't choke her up.

And she could take care of herself, but that didn't mean that it didn't feel really nice when someone else did it anyway.

Yeah, Conner reminded her of her mother.

Gabby laughed out loud at that, then covered her mouth quickly.

Conner shook his head. "Laughter? Really? You couldn't pretend you needed to go to the bathroom before you started the giggles?"

She felt sticky from head to toe, knew Conner had gotten just as much frosting on him as she had and the sheets were going to be a mess, but she wouldn't have moved for anything.

She ran her hand over his stomach. "You're acting like the girls don't usually laugh after sex."

"The girls *don't* usually laugh after sex."

She lifted her head slightly. "Oh really? Well, don't feel bad. I'm sure they *meant* to laugh."

He rolled to face her, his hand going to her butt—she noticed he seemed to really like it there. Then he pinched her. "Laughing after sex is a good thing?"

"Of course. It helps release all those endorphins and all the crazy hormones that get stirred up. Unless you *don't* get them stirred up. Like maybe with those other girls," she said with a straight face. "But don't worry, you must be getting better. I feel like laughing and laughing."

He swatted her butt this time. "You're trouble, Gabrielle Evans."

She grinned. "How so?"

"You're laughing at me after sex and I still like you. I think I'm in deep."

She forced her mouth to stay smiling, but she felt her heart flip. Dammit.

The three relationships that hadn't broken her heart? Yeah, that was because they'd never had her heart to break.

That was not the case with Conner Dixon.

"So, I think I messed something up."

Twenty minutes later, Gabby was lightly dozing, still wrapped around Conner—and probably permanently stuck to him since the frosting had dried between them.

"I wasn't laughing at you," she said groggily, snuggling close. "Honest. I was teasing about that."

He ran his hand up and down her back. "Not that. I think I might have done something you told me not to do."

She tried to read his tone, but was too sated to decipher if he was teasing or not. And too sated to care. About anything.

"I told you to do whatever you wanted," she said, then yawned. "You're good."

He ran his hand over her butt. "So it's okay that I think I did the falling-in-love thing?"

And just like that she was wide awake. She quickly lifted her head. "*What?*"

"You told me not to fall in love with you."

"Yes, I definitely did." Her heart was pounding so hard she was sure he could feel it. Or maybe even hear it at this point.

"Well, I did it anyway."

"Did…what exactly, Conner?"

"Fell in love with you."

She stared at him, then sighed and slumped onto her back. "Dammit, Dixon."

Complicated. It was all complicated. In three days.

"Three days," she said out loud. "It's been three days."

"We've known each other forever. The big, important stuff, we've known forever."

He was right. Which made this all even more complicated because it was possible that his feelings were real.

Which would mean hers might be too.

"You're just having a sugar rush. All that frosting," she said, pushing up to sit on the edge of the bed.

He didn't say anything at first and finally she looked over at him.

"Yeah, it's not the sugar," he said.

"It's…kind of big," she said.

"Yeah."

"Yeah."

"Okay, I'm going to take a shower," he said, pushing up off the bed and heading for the master bath, unabashedly naked.

She averted her eyes. That was her only hope of not saying something stupid like "let's have sex for the rest of our lives", which Conner would no doubt interpret as "I love you too", which was not a good way to keep things from getting more complicated. Especially since it wasn't that far out of the realm of possibility.

"You can't be in love with me," she said, keeping her eyes off of his tight abdominal muscles and the impressive muscle just south of them.

"Why not?" He grabbed a clean pair of sweatpants from a drawer in his dresser.

"It doesn't happen that quickly. Or that easily."

He chuckled. "I have four friends who would tell you differently."

She opened her mouth to argue, but yeah, Ryan, Amanda, Shane, Isabelle, Nate and Emma had all fallen quickly. It had taken Shane and Isabelle a little longer to get to the happily-ever-after part, but the true-love part had been there from the very beginning. And Cody and Olivia had fought it for almost two years—but it had been there.

"Why do you get to shower first?" she asked, suddenly feeling itchy wherever there was cream-cheese frosting—which was pretty much *everywhere*. She could use some time locked in the bathroom by herself to think and resolutely put cream-cheese frosting on her list of things-to-be-cleaned-out-of-my-life-so-I-won't-go-insane-in-medical-school". The frosting definitely seemed to have a funny effect on her. Like a love potion.

"If I let you go first, you might sneak out while I'm in there. As long as you're covered in frosting, I figure you'll stay." He stepped into the bathroom and closed the door.

She stood up from the bed, then realized he was right and sat back down.

Then realized that there was another bathroom in the apartment. And that Conner hadn't invited her in to share his shower. And that she wanted to get in the shower with him.

She headed for the guest bathroom.

Fifteen minutes later, she stepped into clean panties and determinedly kept her mind on *anything* but the fact that she'd fallen in love with Conner Dixon—how stupid was that?—and that he'd supposedly fallen in love with her—how unbelievable was that?—in the space of three days.

She was pulling a shirt over her head when her phone started ringing. For the first time in a long time she thought *thank God* at the sound.

"Hello?"

"Gabs, we need to talk."

"Grant? Is everything okay?"

"No. Josh screwed up."

Well, that wasn't the first time either of them had said those words. "What's up?"

"Can you meet us at the shop?"

She frowned and glanced at the clock. It was almost ten. That meant it was important. No one else would be at the shop, making it a safe place to talk privately. That meant it was *really* important. "Yeah. Okay. I'll be there in ten minutes."

She pulled her hair up and secured it with a large clip, finished dressing, grabbed her keys and shoes and started for the door.

"Where are you going?"

Conner, only a towel around his waist, was leaning in the doorway to his bedroom.

"Damn, I could get used to that view," she said without thinking.

"Feel free to get used to it."

And he was in love with her. Supposedly. And she was in love with him. Probably.

She shook her head. "I, um…" had to do something—oh yeah, "…I have to meet my brothers."

"At ten at night? Can't it wait until tomorrow?"

She looked at him in surprise. "Excuse me?"

"Ask them to come over here."

"I'm going to meet my *brothers*. I won't be alone."

"Fine, okay. Give me two seconds to get dressed."

She crossed her arms. "Get dressed for what?"

"I'll go with you."

"Don't be ridiculous." Good grief. Not just because this was family business with her brothers and Conner wasn't invited, but because that was…ridiculous. If she wanted to go out, no matter what time it was, she would go. Like she'd always done before she'd moved in with Conner.

"It's no big deal. Just let me get some clothes on."

He started to turn away.

"Conner," she said firmly.

He stopped and looked back.

"I'm going to meet my brothers. Alone. You're not coming."

He sighed. "I know I freaked you out with the love thing."

She sighed back at him. "Yes, you did freak me out. But that's not why I'm saying no. They need to talk to me. Grant just called."

"Then I'll go with you and make sure everything's okay."

"Why wouldn't it be okay?"

"If everything is okay, they wouldn't be calling at ten at night."

"They might. We all have crazy schedules."

"I have some experience with late-at-night, can-you-come-over-here-right-now calls, Gabby."

"These are my brothers, not your sisters." But even as she said it, she realized that he was right—this wasn't going to be just a chat with her brothers. That could have waited. And she realized that neither she nor Conner would ever be completely without these crazy, at-all-hours phone calls. Which was even more reason not to combine their lives and their at-all-hours craziness.

"I'm coming along," he said firmly.

"The minute you go into your bedroom to get dressed, I'm leaving," she told him. "Can we just be up-front about this so you don't feel like I'm sneaking out or mad?"

He narrowed one eye. "I might be able to catch you."

"You'd come running after me?"

"Very likely."

Dammit. She kind of wanted to see that.

"I'm okay on my own," she said anyway.

He sighed. Again. "Fine."

She could tell that was hard for him to say. "I'll be fine. I'm going to see Grant and Josh. It's a ten-minute drive."

"Text me when you get there."

She rolled her eyes. "No."

"Gab—"

"I'm not your little sister."

"I'm very aware of that."

"I don't need your protection." But it felt good. She liked that he was concerned.

Which was unfair. He didn't want to be concerned about people anymore. He didn't want to worry. He was retired from that.

And she didn't *need* him to worry.

"It's a fucking text," he said, clearly irritated. "It will take two seconds."

For God's sake. She should just do it. Then he *wouldn't* worry and she could stop having this conversation. "Fine, I'll text you."

"Text me when you're on your way home too."

She shook her head. "You're annoying me, Dixon."

"You ain't seen nothin' yet," he told her.

"Is that right?"

"If you *don't* text me when you get there and when you're on your way back here, I'm going to do some *really* annoying things."

She put a hand on her hip. "Such as?"

"Go out looking for you. Call all of your relatives. Call Shane."

He'd call a cop? No way would Conner... But seeing the determined look on his face at the moment, she believed him.

"Do you do this with all the women you send home after sex?" she asked.

"No, I don't," he said without hesitation. "You're a special case."

She was not going there.

"I thought Nate was the crazy-overprotective one," she said. She'd never had anyone go out looking for her if she was late getting somewhere. Her family knew she was completely competent and capable and would call for help if needed. No reason to go looking.

Conner wouldn't *really* have a reason either. He'd just want to know where she was and how she was.

Dammit. He was getting to her.

"Nate's an amateur," Conner scoffed. "Michael's one kid, who didn't do anything rebellious until he was eighteen. I had *four* girls, two of whom started misbehaving before they could spell *misbehaving*, and all four gave me gray hair well into their twenties."

And right there was the reason she could not let him be in love with her. He didn't want more women to worry about, he didn't want to be crazy-overprotective anymore. He wanted to be fun and laid-back.

Well, hell, the kind thing to do here was let him come along. If he was with her he wouldn't be worried and wouldn't act crazy.

"You're killing me, Dixon. Fine, let's go. Just stop talking and get moving."

"I'm going?" he asked.

"If you can be dressed and in my car in three minutes."

Four minutes later they were on the way to Gabby's family's shop.

As they neared the shop, Gabby felt her stomach getting tighter. It wasn't like Josh screwing up was new. The youngest of her brothers was a fly-by-the-seat-of-his-pants kind of guy. He was spontaneous and fun. He was laid-back and took things as they came. But he also had a hard time planning ahead and seeing possible consequences. Gabby knew that Grant and Reed cleaned up a lot of Josh's messes without ever telling her. So the call tonight meant it was something big, something only she could help with or something that affected her directly.

She jumped when she felt Conner's hand on her arm.

"You okay?" he asked when she looked over at him.

"Mostly."

"Grant didn't tell you what it was about?"

"Just that it was something Josh needed help with."

Conner didn't say anything. He didn't offer encouraging or soothing words. He didn't say "it will be okay" or "don't worry". He knew how this worked—it might not be okay and she would worry anyway. Instead, he tugged her hand free from the steering wheel and laced their fingers.

And the knot in her stomach loosened a bit.

They pulled into the shop parking lot a minute later.

"Want me to come in or stay out?" Conner asked.

She looked over. In. She wanted him to come in. "I get to pick?" she asked.

"I'm here for you. Tell me where you need me."

She wasn't sure what to do with that. She had lots of people on her side, a lot of people's support. But she didn't have anyone who was all about her.

She couldn't get used to it.

"Two months, Dixon." Calling him by his last name helped her keep some distance.

He didn't ask what she was talking about. He nodded. "I'll take what I can get."

And that seemed liked such bullshit. Conner Dixon didn't want to fall in love, he didn't want to be serious. He wanted to keep things superficial and fun. That was his attraction to her, she knew. She was easy. Not *easy*—well, okay, *easy* too—for *him* anyway. But she knew that her ability to handle anything, to *not* call him in the middle of the night for help, and her general lack of major baggage and hang-ups was all very appealing. So appealing that he thought he could be in love with her.

He was in love with things about her.

She could accept that. And he'd get over it.

"Come on then," she said, getting out of the car.

He met her at the front fender and they walked into the shop together.

Her brothers were in the office. Josh was sitting in their father's creaky, old office chair, a cup of coffee in one hand, looking like hell. Grant was perched with one hip on their Uncle Tim's desk that sat perpendicular to their dad's. Reed was leaning against the counter across from them.

"I see I'm late for the Sunshine Club meeting," Gabby said dryly, trying to ignore that the knot in her stomach had drawn painfully tight.

"You brought company," Reed commented, eyes on Conner.

"Yep. Is there a problem?" Gabby asked him.

"Just family dirty laundry." Reed glanced at Josh.

"I'll wait outside," Conner said, stepping back through the office door and pulling it shut behind him.

Gabby missed his big, comforting presence immediately.

She was losing her mind.

She tucked her hands into her pockets and regarded her brothers. "What's going on?"

"Josh has something to tell you," Grant said.

There was no more mention of Conner or the fact that he'd come along. Conner was a nonissue as far as they were all concerned. Because Gabby said he was a nonissue. The men—and women, for that matter—in her life took her at face value. If she said she was fine, she was fine. They didn't prod or poke or push. Because there were plenty of people and issues in their lives that *did* need their attention. In her family, you had to ask if you wanted something. If you needed help moving a dresser, six people would show up, but you had to tell them you wanted them to show. If you wanted a second helping of potatoes, that bowl wasn't going to get passed to you unless you said something. Loudly.

She would bet good money that Conner's sisters were bombarded with help and attention, whether they wanted it or not.

She almost laughed.

How Conner had thought he could keep his friends and

sisters from falling for one another was beyond her. If you were Conner's friend, you knew his sisters and you were moving dressers and eating potatoes with them from minute one.

"Josh, go," Reed said with a frown at his youngest brother.

Gabby focused on Josh. "What's up?"

"I, um…needed to borrow some money."

She felt her spine tense. "Okay."

"I'll pay you back."

Shit, fuck, dammit.

"How much?"

"Two thousand."

"Two thousand *dollars*?"

"No, two thousand forks."

Grant kicked him. Josh sighed.

"Yes, two thousand dollars."

"He knows you're the only one who has that kind of money saved up," Grant said.

"It's my school money." Gabby frowned at Josh. "How long until you can pay me back?"

"This weekend."

Reed scoffed. "Maybe. And you're not telling her everything."

Gabby frowned. "What's going on?"

"I'm entering a big tournament this weekend."

She knew he was talking about poker. Josh played in big games on nearly a weekly basis. He often entered tournaments. When he won, he won big. And when he didn't win, he usually managed to at least cover his losses, but she, Reed and Grant had begun to suspect that he was getting in over his head.

"No way am I giving you money. That's for school and you know it." She couldn't believe he'd even ask.

"Winner gets thirty K."

Her eyes widened. "Thirty thousand?" That was a big game.

He nodded. "Six tables of five each. Everyone's in for two K. Donovan's not keeping anything for himself."

Grant rolled his eyes. "There's no way you're going to win."

"Second place is twenty, third is ten."

"And nothing after that. You really think you're in the top three that will be playing?"

"I have to be."

Her eyes narrowed. "Why?"

"To cover the two he needs to enter and the five he borrowed from Dad," Reed said.

Gabby looked from Reed to Josh. "You owe Mom and Dad five thousand dollars?"

He shrugged. "I'm not worried."

"Of course you're not. You never worry about anything," Reed said, clearly frustrated. He pushed off the desk. "You have a problem, little brother."

"I'm fine," Josh said with a scowl. "I know what I'm doing."

"You're not already in the game?" Gabby asked. If he didn't have the money to enter, he wasn't officially at a table yet.

She knew that in spite of his application to the fire department, Josh really believed he could make a living playing poker. And some guys did.

But thousands didn't.

"I think you need to sit this one out. We'll help you pay Mom and Dad back," Gabby said, mentally calculating what she had in the bank and what she would need for her first two semesters. Dammit. She didn't want to dip into her savings. She'd worked her butt off and gone without a lot of luxuries—her phone was a piece of crap and she'd gone down to two fancy lattes a week— to get that nest egg together.

"I can do this," Josh said, pushing out of the chair. "I'm good. I can play with these guys."

Josh was a great poker player. He was calm and cool, almost unreadable. But Gabby could beat him. Partly because she knew him well enough to read what tiny hints were there. Partly because she was more careful than Josh was. She took risks but calculated ones. Josh got easily caught up in the drama and excitement and often got carried away.

"You don't have the entry fee," she said. "I'll help you pay Mom and Dad back." What they'd been thinking—loaning him money in the first place—was beyond her. "But I'm not giving you more money to gamble with."

Josh was clearly pissed now. "I have the money. And an invitation. I'm in the game."

"An invitation?" she repeated. "It's a private game?"

"Yeah."

"Who's the guy?"

Josh hesitated. "Uh. Richard Donovan."

Gabby stared at him. Richard Donovan was a bigwig with Omaha National, a Fortune 500 Company. He was one of the richest men in Omaha, even the entire Midwest. He was worth millions. Maybe more.

"So you're in this guy's private game where you think you're going to win ten thousand dollars?" Gabby recounted.

Josh shrugged. "I'd rather win twenty."

"No."

"No, what?"

"I'm not giving you two thousand dollars."

"I already borrowed it."

"The money?" she asked.

"Yeah."

"Okay, so why do you need money from me?"

"It was your money he 'borrowed'," Reed said. "He got it out of your dresser drawer."

She turned to face Josh. He stretched above her by four inches, but she got right up into his face. "What the hell is he talking about?"

"I found the money in your dresser drawer, okay? I'm sorry. I know it was a shitty thing to do, but I was desperate. I have to play in this game. Some of the guys invited are huge. If I impress them, it could mean even bigger invitations."

She wasn't sure which idiotic thing to comment on first. "My dresser burned in a fire a few nights ago, if you recall. I don't have a dresser, not to mention one with money in it."

He frowned. "In your bedroom at Conner's."

Her whole body went ice-cold. "Are you fucking kidding me? You went through drawers at someone else's house?"

"It was *your* dresser."

"You were intentionally trying to *steal* from me?" She couldn't believe it.

"I'm going to pay you back *this weekend*."

"*If* you win. And you know that's a big if, Josh!"

"Well, thanks for the support and believing in me."

She pulled a long, supposedly calming breath in through her nose. He was only twenty-two. And he clearly had an addiction. Besides being an idiot. He wasn't deliberately trying to hurt her.

But it still did.

"I'm so sorry for not believing in my thieving, lying little brother," she snapped, the calming breath not doing a damned thing.

"Well, now you have to let me play because it's the only way for me to get the money back," he said.

Let him. Right. Like she had any say in it. She didn't *want* to have any say in it. She wanted the people around her to make good, logical, safe decisions without needing a flipping baby-sitter. She wanted them to be in control of themselves. Like she was. She knew what she wanted and she was going to go for it, even if it meant sacrificing something else she really wanted.

If she could walk away from Conner for medical school, then Josh could walk away from the fucking poker table for his own well-being.

"There's one other way to get the money," she said, a sense of calm smoothing over her jangled nerves.

"What?" Josh asked.

"I can win it back."

Josh stared at her. "You want to play?"

"Not exactly. But I have a better chance of winning than you do."

"Why would you do that? Just to bail me out?"

"No." She looked up into her little brother's face. "I should let you go down and maybe learn a lesson here, but I can't."

"Why not?" Reed asked. "He stole from you."

"That's why," she said. "He didn't steal from me." She pinned Josh with a serious look. "He stole from Conner. My friend. The guy who let me stay at his place when mine burned down. The one who's been there for me and hasn't asked for anything in return. You took *his* two thousand dollars."

"Fuck," Grant muttered.

"Dammit, Josh," Reed said angrily.

Josh just stared at her. "It wasn't yours?"

"No."

"And you're willing to enter the game to win it back for him?"

"I'm going to win it back for *me*," she told him. "I'll pay Conner back out of my account. Then I'll replace the money in my account...and Mom and Dad's money...with the winnings."

Josh swallowed hard. "This doesn't help me make any contacts in the poker world."

She couldn't believe him. "No, Josh, it doesn't. You're welcome for that too, though I don't expect you to appreciate it right now."

"Gabby—"

"Just don't, okay?" she asked, stopping him. She hated what was happening with Josh, she hated that she hadn't realized how bad it was until now. She hated that it was now dragging Conner into it too. He didn't know, of course. And she'd get to the bank tomorrow first thing and replace the money in his drawer, hopefully *before* he knew about it. But it made her sick to think that he'd let her into his house and welcomed her family in, simply because they were her family—and then this had happened.

It didn't matter that Josh hadn't meant to take Conner's

money. It didn't matter that he meant to pay it back. For all she knew, Conner needed that money tomorrow for something important.

This was a perfect example, though, of how letting someone into your life let everyone in *their* life in too—for better or worse.

Keeping things light and superficial made sense if you didn't want a big, freaking mess. And Conner wasn't the only one who'd like a little less chaos in his life.

"Just give me the details," she said to Josh.

"Are you sure this is a good idea?" Grant asked.

"I have a better chance of winning than Josh does. And I want my money back."

"The tables are all full by now," Josh said smugly.

"Except that someone at one of those tables is going to get sick at the last minute," Reed said, stepping closer to Josh. "Right?"

"If I don't play, I forfeit the money."

"Gabby's going to play in your place. With that money. There won't be any forfeit," Reed said.

"What if I *don't* get 'sick'?" Josh asked

"Then I'll help Conner press charges against you," Reed said flatly.

Gabby stared at her brother. There was something in Reed's eyes that made her think he was completely serious.

Apparently Josh thought so too.

"Okay, okay, geez, calm down," Josh said.

If the warning was enough, that was good with Gabby. Sometimes it was okay to have a brother who was a lawyer. He was a legal aid attorney, so he didn't have money to lend, but still, he could make threats with the best of them.

"So you're sick at the last minute and I'll be ready to fill in," she said to Josh.

"But you can't just waltz in there," he told her stubbornly. "Even if you're replacing me, Donovan has to go for it. This is a private game. You have to have money *and* an invitation."

She thought about that. She had no idea how to make this work. "I'll figure it out." Right now she needed to get Conner back to his apartment without him knowing anything was wrong—or that any of it involved him.

But they had to work tomorrow. She wouldn't be able to get to the bank until Friday.

Dammit.

"I'm leaving now. Unless there's anything else I need to know?" she asked Josh.

"Nothing I'm aware of," he said, sounding very put out.

Right. Because he didn't think she needed to know even as much as she did.

She opened her mouth to reply, then shut it, shook her head and turned away. "Good night."

Conner was pacing right outside.

"You okay?" he asked the moment he saw her.

She looked at him and felt even sicker that Josh had stolen from him. The one bright side was that Conner didn't know about it and she could replace the money. But it made her want to smack her little brother. Conner was a good guy. Hell, Conner might have *given* Josh the money if he'd known Josh needed it. Without question he would have given *her* the money.

But Josh had taken it. While she'd been right there. *Because* she'd been right there.

"I will be," she finally answered Conner honestly. "We're taking care of the problem."

"What can I do?"

And he meant it.

Well, at least when she finally really fell in love it was with a great guy. It was good to know she had good taste.

"Honestly?" she asked.

"Of course."

"I could go for some ice cream."

He looked surprised, then smiled. "I can definitely get you ice cream."

"How about ice cream sandwiches?" she asked, remembering something she'd overheard Conner's sisters talking about at Trudy's.

"Uh…sure," he said.

She smiled. He clearly didn't know about the magic of ice cream sandwiches. That was probably for the best.

And she could tell he wasn't going to push to know what had happened with her brothers, he was going to let it go. He was going to concentrate on her and what she needed right now that he could give her.

She felt some of the tension of the twenty minutes with her brothers melt away. Conner made her feel better. It was new and surprising, but she really liked it. The least she could do was keep it light and easy for him.

"Then more sex. After the ice cream," she said. And if it happened to make her feel *a lot* better in the process, that was a bonus.

There was instant heat in his eyes as he moved in close to run his hand up and down her arm. "Hell, G, I can do them both at the same time."

Yes, that was exactly what she needed. "Well, your sheets are already a mess…"

He grabbed her hand and started for the car. "Right. Might as well make that wash cycle worthwhile."

CHAPTER
TEN

"SO I WAS WONDERING if Nate would know anyone who could get me an invitation to the game?" Gabby asked Ryan.

Sierra was keeping Conner busy restocking supplies in the rig—supplies that Sierra and Gabby had emptied a few minutes before Conner got to work—while Gabby cornered Ryan and told him about the poker game.

Nate Sullivan came from money. He was a talented trauma surgeon but his family had money beyond that and with it came connections.

Ryan shrugged. "Sure. It's possible. I'll ask." He pulled his phone out. "What's the guy's name?"

"Donovan. He'll know who that is."

Gabby chewed on her right thumbnail as she watched Ryan hit Nate's number and wait for it to ring. She hadn't chewed her nails in years. "Oh, and you have to schedule a team get-together for Friday and Saturday."

Ryan glanced at her. "What?"

"You have to keep Conner busy so he doesn't wonder where I am."

"Or you could tell him the truth," Ryan said. Just then, Nate answered and Ryan focused on filling his friend in on the favor they needed.

The door to the break room bumped open and Gabby jumped. She looked over her shoulder guiltily. But it was just Mac and Dooley.

"Hey, Gabby," Mac greeted, grabbing water from the fridge.

"You guys aren't out of here?" she asked.

"Waiting around for Ben to get off so we can go grab some breakfast," Dooley said.

Ben Torres, one of their close friends, was a surgeon at St. A's. He worked side by side with Nate, in fact.

"Nate says he'll try. He doesn't know Donovan personally, but he's sure he knows people who do."

Gabby sighed. That was the best she could do, she supposed. "Okay, thanks for trying."

"Hey, Nate might come through. He'll work on it. He's heading into surgery in a few minutes but later on he'll—"

Gabby shook her head. "It might be too late by then. Josh is supposed to pull out this morning. They'll fill the spot by the time Nate's done."

Dammit. She felt the frustration rising and her throat felt tight. There were other tournaments. She could win the money back. But few around here had such big pots. She'd have to play in a series of games to get that kind of money back quickly. She didn't have the time for that.

"What's going on?" Mac asked, taking in Gabby's expression.

She wasn't surprised that he'd noticed. She was typically even-keeled, calm and cool. She rarely looked frustrated or angry or desperate, and if she did, they were at a scene and things weren't going well.

"Just...nothing," she said, the situation weighing on her, making her tired.

"She's wanting into a big poker game," Ryan said. "Richard Donovan is hosting."

"Hey." She frowned at Ryan, then turned to Mac. "That's kind of a secret. I don't want it getting out."

Mac nodded. "Okay. But…you play poker?"

She shrugged. "I kick ass at poker."

Mac grinned. "Why can't you get in the game?"

"Because about a million other people want in the game too, I don't have a big name on the poker circuit and I don't know Richard Donovan personally."

"I do."

They all swung to look at Dooley. He was on the couch, feet propped on the coffee table, reading a *People* magazine.

"You know Richard Donovan?" Gabby asked.

"Well, Morgan does," Dooley said of his wife. "She hosted a few parties for him when she worked for Britton. I've met him. He's kind of a dick."

Morgan had run the posh Britton Hotel, the best in the city, prior to opening her B&B. It was very easy to believe she'd rubbed elbows with Donovan and multiple other high rollers.

"So she knows him? Like, well enough to call him?" Gabby asked.

She was so not used to asking people for favors. But she had to get Josh and his problems cleaned up before they got in Conner's way.

"I'm sure she does. Morgan has a way of making an impression." Dooley gave Gabby a wink. "So what's the deal?" Dooley fished his phone out of his pocket.

"He's hosting a private game," Gabby said. "I *really* want in that game."

"Got it." Dooley lifted his phone to his ear. "Are you naked?" he asked a moment later when, presumably, his wife answered. He paused and a big grin stretched his face. "Why can't you dust naked?"

He laughed at whatever her response was and Gabby felt herself smile in spite of everything.

"Well, I guess I'll just have to *imagine* you dusting naked then. And I think those low shelves need some extra attention—"

Mac cleared his throat and Dooley glanced up.

"Oh yeah, right. Hey, Morg, do you think you could call Richard Donovan? Or maybe Jonathan could call him."

"It's not Richard Donovan hosting the game," Nate said as he came into the break room.

"I thought you were in surgery," Gabby said.

"I got a call just before I was gowning up. And it's not like they can start without me, right?"

"So this is why physicians never run on time?" Ryan asked.

"Hey, my patient is out cold. He's not feeling anything. And even physicians sometimes need to take care of their friends."

Gabby blinked at Nate and let those words roll around in her head. She was his friend? And he was taking care of her? She wasn't sure what to do with either of those things.

"Wait, what do you mean Richard Donovan isn't the one hosting the game?" she asked, *those* words finally catching up as well.

"Richard Donovan, the president of Omaha National, the millionaire, is not hosting a poker game. His son Ricky is."

Gabby frowned. "His son?"

Nate nodded. "My friend said that Ricky, Richard Donovan's twenty-three-year-old son, is the one who puts these big games together. So, I called Michael to see if he knew anything."

Michael was Nate's eighteen-year-old son. Michael was a down-to-earth-in-spite-of-his-dad-being-rich kid but he likely knew of someone like the younger Donovan.

"Michael knows some kids who have hung out with Ricky so he did some quick computer searching and messaging," Nate went on. "Apparently Ricky brings a bunch of his friends together for a weekend poker game and party every few months. Sometimes he holds them at his dad's place in Vegas. Sometimes in Cabo. Sometimes on a yacht. And sometimes he holds it here when he feels like slumming it in his hometown. His dad's out of town and he's using the family home. The twelve-bedroom house on ten acres where he grew up."

"Holy shit," Mac muttered.

"It's just him and his friends?" Ryan asked.

Nate nodded. "Along with a few people who kiss his ass to get an invitation. He especially likes to invite top local players so that he and his friends can feel superior—they like to beat anyone who's cocky enough to play with them and they like to rub their wealth in people's faces. The parties are over the top, I guess—the best food and booze and music and accommodations. If you get invited, everything's paid for the weekend."

Gabby's head was spinning. But it made more sense that Josh would be hanging out with a twenty-three-year-old kid and his rich, bored buddies than with a guy like Richard Donovan, the millionaire mogul.

"I wonder how Josh met him," Gabby mused. "He can't afford to play in those games at the casino all the time and they don't really run in the same circles, I'm guessing."

"Morgan just called one of the guys she used to work with at the Britton. He confirmed that Ricky's the one who throws these poker parties," Dooley said, stretching up from the couch. "This guy knows him because Ricky used to throw parties at the Britton. He and his friends trashed more than one room at the hotel in his time."

Gabby sighed. "Yep, those sound like the kind of guys Josh would love to hang out with."

"It gets better," Dooley said with a grin. "I guess Rick Junior likes to *really* slum it sometimes. He'll hang out at local bars and taverns incognito and get spontaneous games going. He loves when he finds some random guy who can really challenge him."

Nate's phone rang again and he answered, turning away from them as Dooley went on.

"It's possible that Ricky met Josh at one of the bars downtown," Dooley said.

"Very possible," Gabby agreed. Josh would never pass up a

chance to play some cocky guy who walked into one of his regular hangouts and dared someone.

"Ricky is very interested in meeting you."

They all turned to Nate. He was grinning.

"He's very interested in meeting *me*?" Gabby asked.

"He's very interested in JD Evans's hot sister filling in for him while he's sick."

Gabby stared at Nate. "How does he… Why would he… Hot? JD?"

The guys all laughed. Nate nodded. "Michael tweeted him."

"Michael tweeted Ricky about me?"

"Guess so. He tweeted Ricky to say that Josh was sick, but his hot sister wanted to fill in. Ricky thinks that's awesome. And yeah, I guess they call him JD."

She blinked at him. "Michael called me hot?"

The guys all snorted. She glanced around with a frown, then focused back on Nate.

"Ricky's going to let me play?"

"He thinks it's hilarious that JD, the arrogant asshole—his quote, by the way—can't play for himself. Then Michael sent him a picture of you and he said you're totally in. You can just show up at the house Saturday night. He wants you to wear heels though. Said not enough people he plays poker with wear heels."

Gabby watched Nate for a moment, trying to figure out if he was kidding.

He wasn't kidding. She was in. She felt the flutter in her stomach, even as the tension in her chest loosened.

"Well, awesome," Ryan said. But he didn't sound like he thought it was awesome.

"What's wrong?" Gabby asked.

Nate's phone chimed again. He looked down. "Oh."

"Oh?" Gabby repeated. "What's oh?"

"Ricky wants you to wear your hair down. And he promises

you'll be at his table. And he's offering you one of the rooms in the house Saturday night. Even if you lose."

"What picture did Michael send him?" Mac wanted to know, holding his hand out for Nate's phone.

Gabby frowned. "Even if I lose? What's that supposed to mean? I'm not going to—"

"Oh, I see why he's interested," Mac said. He turned the phone toward Gabby.

It was a photo Michael had clearly lifted off Facebook. Gabby, Sierra and a couple of the nurses from the ER, at a bar downtown, their arms around each other, smiling for the camera. She was dressed up for a girl's night out in a fitted dark-green dress, her hair down, makeup done, laughing and having a great time.

She looked a lot different than she usually did.

"That's the girl that has to show up at the game," Mac said.

"And *that's* what's wrong," Ryan said.

She glanced at him. "I'll be fine."

"You'll take someone with you, though," Ryan said. It wasn't a question.

"Someone like who?" she asked.

"Conner," Nate replied evenly.

"No."

"One of your brothers," Ryan suggested.

Dooley laughed. "She can't take a brother. She needs a boyfriend."

Gabby turned to him. "What?"

"You need a boyfriend," Dooley repeated. "Someone to be all over you so Ricky doesn't get any ideas."

"He's a twenty-three-year-old kid with too much time and money on his hands. I'm not worried," she told them.

"If you don't show up with a boyfriend, you're going to be fending him off the whole time...and pissing him off," Ryan said.

"I don't care if he's pissed off."

"He could throw you out before you have a chance to win anything."

"But—" Dammit. He had a point. It was a private game, invitation only, at Ricky's house. He could make the rules and call the shots.

She did not want to deal with being the object of a spoiled, cocky rich kid's crush. She wanted to play—and win—at poker.

"Can you beat him?" Mac wanted to know.

"I can give him a run for his money," she said confidently.

"Well, then he's going to be ticked enough to find out that you can actually play and win. Not a good idea to ruin his Casanova dreams too."

"So I need to show up with a boyfriend."

"And you'll have to *act* like he's actually a boyfriend. One of your cousins or brothers can't fill in," Nate pointed out.

She sighed. This was getting complicated. She was really, really trying to keep that from happening.

"I'm not taking Conner. I'm not telling Conner about any of this. And you," she said, pointing to Ryan, "need to help keep him distracted so he doesn't wonder what I'm doing, so you can't come with me either."

"Conner would wonder what you're doing?" Mac asked.

She felt her cheeks heat. "Um, yeah."

"She's living with him," Dooley said, nudging Mac. "Didn't you know that?"

"I've been a little distracted, what with having a new baby at home and all," Mac said, regarding Gabby with renewed interest.

"Well, my wife's pregnant and sending me to the store for Pop-Tarts every other day, telling me I have to quit swearing around the house because the baby will hear and…" Dooley's grin got huge, "…wanting sex *constantly*. And I still knew Gabby and Conner were shacking up."

"Morgan is pregnant?" Gabby exclaimed. She hadn't known

that. And she'd do anything to take Mac's attention off of her. "That's awesome, Dooley. Congrats."

"Thanks." The man did have a distinct proud glow about him.

"Have you been trying for a while?" she asked.

"Got it on the first try," he said. "We've been practicing for a while."

"How long have you been living with Conner?" Mac asked.

Apparently he already knew about Morgan and Dooley. Crap.

"Just a few days," she said. "It's…no big deal."

Possibly the biggest lie she'd ever told. Living with Conner was turning her life upside down.

"And he would care where you were spending Saturday night?"

"I don't know that he would *care* exactly," Gabby hedged. "He would *notice*. Probably."

Another not-so-tiny lie. He'd notice. He'd care. And that was exactly why he couldn't know.

"And why you don't want him to know that you're playing poker with Ricky Donovan?" Mac pressed.

"I just…" It was very hard to explain. She supposed she could tell Conner that she was playing poker without telling him why the pot was so important to her—and him. But she had a definite gut feeling that he wouldn't like it. And if she told him she needed him there to fend off a bunch of twenty-something party boys…well, he definitely wouldn't like that part.

This was her family's mess, *her* problem. Not Conner's.

Mac chuckled. "Uh-huh. I get it."

She scowled at him. "You do?"

"Sure. And I'll be the one taking you to the party," Mac said.

Her eyes went wide. "Excuse me?"

"You need a fake boyfriend. A big, intimidating fake boyfriend. Someone the obnoxious rich kids won't mess with," Mac said. "You can't take a relative because you're going to have to act lovey-dovey with them. It might require some touching which would be gross with a relative. You can't take Ryan or any of those guys because they need to be with Conner. You can't take some random guy because he might get the wrong idea—that you want a real boyfriend. I'm the perfect choice."

Gabby knew her mouth was open as she stared at him.

"And this would have nothing to do with you getting to flirt and act lovey-dovey over Conner's girl?" Ryan asked.

Conner's girl? "I'm not—"

Mac laughed. "Payback is a bitch."

Gabby couldn't help but smile at that. Conner had acted lovey-dovey over Sara for a long time. But…"I'm not—"

"Conner's not even going to know about it," Nate pointed out. "That's not quite as satisfying, is it?"

Mac gave Gabby a once-over. "I think Saturday is going to be very interesting."

She raised an eyebrow at him. "Sara won't mind?"

"Sara is going to get a huge kick out of this," Mac told her. "She knows that I've just been waiting for the day when Conner finally fell."

"But Conner hasn't—" She stopped. Conner *thought* he had. That might be good enough for Mac.

And now that she thought about it, having someone with her at the overgrown frat party wasn't a bad idea. Mac would definitely work to squelch any romantic notions Ricky Donovan might have toward her and that would help her concentrate on the game. And kick his ass.

"Fine. You can come with me," she told the big guy.

"Yeah, that's what I said," Mac said, as if there had never been any question, or need for discussion.

"Thanks for all your help, guys," Gabby said, turning to Ryan, Nate and Dooley.

Nate and Dooley were both typing into their phones. They looked up.

"Thank *you*. This is gonna to be fun to watch," Dooley said.

"Fun to watch?" Gabby said. "What do you mean?"

"I'm having Morgan work on getting us into the party. I want to see this game."

"Michael says that Ricky always invites extra guests," Nate said. "He loves showing off."

Gabby sighed. "You're all going to be there?"

"Well..."

Nate and Dooley looked at one another, then back to her.

"Yeah," they said in unison.

Great.

"How the hell do we go through that amount of gauze in a week's time?" Conner asked, coming in through the door with Sierra right behind him.

She gave Gabby a look and Gabby gave her a nod to tell her it was okay.

Conner crossed to the coffeepot, and Gabby shot keep-your-mouths-shut looks around the room.

"What are you doing down here?" Conner asked Nate. "Heard you were in surgery."

"What? Oh yeah, right. I am." Nate started for the door. "See you all later."

"And what are you guys still doing here?" Conner asked Mac and Dooley, turning with a full cup in hand. "Ben was looking for you."

Dooley and Mac grabbed their bags. "Good, I'm starving," Dooley said. "It's been fun. See you soon."

"What's been fun?" Conner asked.

They ignored him.

Unfortunately, Mac didn't ignore Gabby. "Bye, Gabby," Mac said with a grin. He rarely singled her out.

She sighed, knowing he wasn't going to pass up *any* opportunity to annoy Conner. "Bye, Mac."

"You should wear that body spray more often, by the way. You smell delicious."

Great. Really subtle. "Thanks." She didn't smile.

She did, however, notice that Conner straightened away from the counter and frowned at Mac.

"You smell delicious?" Conner asked her.

She shrugged.

Mac shouldered his bag. "You haven't noticed?" he asked Conner.

"I have actually," Conner said. "But why have *you* noticed? Don't you have your own girl to smell?"

"I do," Mac said with a nod. "But any woman who smells as good as Gabby deserves to be sniffed as much as possible."

She had to press her lips together to keep from smiling. No one could rile Mac like Conner could, and it looked like the same was true the other way around. It was, indeed, time for some payback.

She also couldn't ignore that being the reason for Conner getting riled up kind of made her heart beat faster.

"Gabby doesn't need anyone else sniffing her," Conner said firmly.

Mac started for the door. "I don't know, Dixon, Gabby is very sniffable. And I'm guessing there are some other *a-b-l-e* words that apply to her too."

Gabby felt like she was choking as she tried not to gasp or laugh at the same time.

"Huggable, unforgettable," Mac went on.

"Kissable, lickable," Dooley called from the outer hallway as the door shut on him.

"Just keep walkin'." Conner raised his voice over both of them. "Keep walkin' back to those sweet wives of yours. Wives that might be very interested in you using 'able' words with other women."

Mac chuckled and pulled the door open, clearly unconcerned about anyone telling Sara on him.

"Sniff you later, Gabs," Mac said as the door shut behind him.

"I don't like him calling you Gabs," Conner said, dumping his coffee out.

"Yeah, *that's* what you don't like him doing," Ryan said with a grin.

Gabby decided that she should probably check Conner and Sierra's stocking job and headed for the rig. And away from the man who was making things more complicated than even her brother was making them.

She was stalling coming home.

Conner knew that was why Gabby still wasn't back at the apartment with him three hours after their shift ended. But he'd spooked her. That was the only reason he wasn't calling her mother. Or her grandmother. Her grandmother would definitely know how to find her. Or would at least have access to people who could. He was not, however, confident she, or anyone, would know exactly what Gabby was thinking. And that was what he was most interested in.

He made himself go through his usual routine. He trusted that Gabby would come home. If she wasn't going to, she would tell him. She was honest and up-front.

She wasn't Ashley.

That's what he kept repeating as he went for a run, showered, made dinner.

But he was holding himself back from calling her grandmother and seeing if the woman had a GPS tracking device on each of her grandkids.

"Gabby is not Ashley," he said out loud as he washed his dishes. "She didn't say she loved you too because she wants to be sure. That's better than having her say it and not mean it."

Ashley had said plenty that she hadn't meant—that she needed him, that he was saving her.

Getting Gabby to say something like that would be like pulling teeth.

That was a *good* thing. That meant the things she did say, he could trust.

But while Gabby was definitely not Ashley, Conner was acting very Ashleyish.

Not like Ashley had acted, but how he had acted with Ashley.

He'd jumped ahead there too, rushed things, pushed.

He'd told Gabby he was in love with her after three days. He'd told Ashley he was in love with her after their third date. They'd talked on the phone until well past midnight almost every night and e-mailed constantly, but they had been on separate campuses and they'd only seen each other on weekends, so it had taken him almost a month to say it to her.

And he hadn't said it once since. Until Gabby.

"Don't push. Don't pressure her," he told himself.

He knew that there had been a lot going on with Ashley and that telling her he was in love too soon wasn't the biggest problem they'd had—and maybe hadn't made a damned bit of difference in how things turned out anyway—but he'd never been able to shake the idea that if he'd taken it slower, given her more time, it would have had a different outcome.

He wanted a different outcome with Gabby.

"Be cool. Just be cool. Be patient. Don't scare her off."

"Talking to yourself? Are you still smelling cinnamon too?"

He swung around to find Gabby had finally come home.

"Uh…"

If she'd heard him, she knew what—who—he was talking about.

"No cinnamon. Spaghetti sauce. You hungry?"

She had her hands tucked in the front pockets of her jeans and was standing a good ten feet away. She shook her head. "I ate at my mom's."

So that's where she'd been. And apparently not ready to introduce him to her mom and dad…

Conner shut that thought down. Damn. Of course she wasn't ready for that. Four days ago she was single and thinking that the start of medical school had to be the end of everything else. Actually, she was still thinking that last part.

And maybe the first part.

He was the one in love here.

Well, he had two months to convince her she wanted this too. Somehow. Maybe.

Ashley had been hurt and lost and unsure of herself. He'd been able to sweep in like a hero. Getting her attention and time had been no problem.

Gabby wasn't lost or hurt or unsure. She knew exactly who she was and what she wanted. She didn't need a hero.

He waited for her to say something more because he sure as hell didn't know what to say.

"I'm going to head over to Sierra's tonight."

Conner was proud that he didn't react with his first instinct of *hell no*.

"Why? Everything okay?"

She gave him a smile—that he didn't believe for a second. "Yeah. I just need some girl time."

Girl time. Right. Gabby Evans needed girl time.

"You're going to do each other's hair and talk about boys?"

Her smile at that was more genuine. "I'm guessing you will come up in the conversation, if you must know."

He relaxed a little. "Be sure you tell her *every* detail."

Gabby rolled her eyes but her smile grew. "Promise."

"How about we go out to a nice dinner tomorrow night then?"

Her eyebrows went up. "A nice dinner?"

"You've heard of them? With silverware, napkins, wine?"

She swallowed. "Like a date?"

"Not *like* a date," he said with a slight frown. "An actual date."

"I...can't."

His frown was more than slight now. "You can't? What does that mean?"

"I'm going to be staying with Sierra for a few days."

She was running, pulling away. He'd spooked her with the I-love-you stuff. She was putting distance between them figuratively and literally.

And *he* was panicking.

Calm the fuck down, Dixon. She's not moving to England. She's not marrying some other guy. You can figure this out. Doting. You need more doting.

"Okay, how about this weekend then? Or we can stay in. I'll cook."

She looked at him for several seconds. "I can't do this weekend either."

He consciously relaxed his spine. It felt as if someone had shoved a metal rod up his back. "You'll be at Sierra's all weekend?"

He could send roses over. Or stop by with her favorite bagels.

"Yeah. At least. Maybe longer. I just... I'll let you know when I'll be back."

Or he could just leave her the fuck alone since that was clearly what she wanted him to do.

He gritted his teeth, then purposefully unclenched them and sighed. "Gabby, what's going on?"

"Nothing. It's...nothing."

Yeah. He believed that as much as he believed she and Sierra were going to do each other's hair. The talking-about-boys thing was likely going to happen though.

But now he was afraid of what she might say about him, especially if she really did include every detail.

Maybe he should send the roses to Sierra as a bribe to tell him what the hell was going on with Gabby.

Might as well get the issue out in the open. "I know it feels like things are going fast between us—"

She held both hands up. "Conner, I can't do this right now."

"I think we need to talk about it. I don't want you to feel—"

"Seriously. Please. I need to take care of some things before I can deal with anything else."

"Let me help."

"No. It's fine. It's…nothing."

"Gabby—"

"Conner, it's not about *you*."

He scowled. "It doesn't have to be about me for me to want to help."

"It's always about you." Her frustration was clear. "Helping makes you feel good. That's about you."

"I'm trying to be your friend here."

"You're trying to be my *boyfriend* here," she argued. "And I don't have time for that!"

He stopped. She sighed. Several seconds of silence ticked by.

"I'm sorry. That sounded bitchy," she finally said.

She'd sounded bitchy because she was exasperated. Because he was pushing. Dammit.

"It's fine." That sounded a lot more stilted than he'd meant it to. It was fine. Or it should be fine. He got that.

She took a deep breath. "Conner, I…" she trailed off and shook her head, "…I'll call you in a couple of days."

He wondered what she'd been about to say first. He knew there was something more there.

He took a moment before replying, squelching the urge to protest about not hearing from her for a vague "couple of days". Finally he said simply, "Fine."

It wasn't fine at all.

She nodded. "Fine." She started for the bedroom, clearly to gather her stuff.

He hated the idea of going into the guest bathroom and not seeing her stuff all over the place.

Ironic that the things he'd felt would be in his way were the things that now made him smile when he saw them.

She emerged a few minutes later with her bag. He hadn't moved.

"See you soon," she said, barely hesitating on her way to the door.

"Sure. Okay." He forced himself to stay where he was.

He'd told her he loved her and she was now on her way out the door.

Déjà-fricking-vu.

The door shut behind her.

And there was one more reason for keeping things superficial and happy with women.

Falling in love sucked.

Conner lay on his back, blinking at the sky.

Dammit, that hurt. Even more than it had the first three times.

"Dixon? You getting back up?" Shane asked. A moment later his big friend—and almost brother-in-law—moved into his line of sight.

"I'm having some deep realizations down here, actually."

"Hey, Coach, we need a break!" Shane shouted across the football field.

The next thing Conner saw was Nate, Cody and Ryan gathered around with Shane, all leaning over him.

"Isn't it your job to keep him from ending up on the ground on his back?" Ryan asked Shane.

Shane was one of the best offensive linemen in the league.

"Hey, I can only do so much. He's hanging out in the pocket for like a year."

And there Conner was, thinking about Gabby again. Which

was exactly why he was spending most of the practice on his back.

"It does make *my* job more fulfilling if you, you know, throw the fucking ball once in a while," Ryan—one of the best receivers in the league—said dryly. He held out his hand.

Conner sighed and let Ryan—also an almost brother-in-law—pull him up to a sitting position.

He looked around. All of these men were almost brothers-in-law. They'd fallen, one by one, for Conner's sisters.

In spite of his protests.

"Tell me more about these deep insights you've had while on your ass today," Shane said. "'Cause it's been a lot. You should be a fricking genius by now."

Conner looked at each of the guys. "You were thinking about the girls when you had your head-up-your-ass practices."

The guys looked at him, then each other, then they sat. The rest of the team wandered off, leaving the five men, the core of the team, alone.

"Head-up-your-ass practices?" Shane asked.

"You each had one. I remember them specifically. Suddenly the best players in the league were acting like they'd never seen a football."

"You think that had something to do with your sisters?" Nate asked.

"Uh, yeah."

"You really just now figured that out?" Ryan asked with a grin.

Conner ran a hand over his face. "How long until it goes away?"

The guys all looked at one another.

"The love thing? I'm hoping never," Nate said.

They all nodded.

"I mean the shitty practices," Conner said.

Cody chuckled. "It gets better once you tell her how you feel."

Conner groaned and flopped back onto the grass, his arm over his eyes. "I already did that."

"You told Gabby that you're *in love* with her?" Ryan asked.

"Yeah."

"How long has she been living with you again?" Cody asked.

"Three days," Conner admitted.

"You're in love with her after three days?" Shane asked. "You sure?"

Conner moved his hand, staring up at the clouds overhead. "Turns out, Gabby's sort of…very lovable."

Ryan snorted. "That's one of the 'able' words Mac left out."

"Fuck Mac," Conner said shortly. It was stupid to have felt jealous over the other man flirting with Gabby. But he had anyway. Sharply jealous. She was his. And even though Mac had been kidding around—clearly having figured out how Conner felt about her—Conner had wanted to punch him. Hard.

He had a sudden, new appreciation for how patient Mac had been with him all this time.

The flirting he'd done with Sara had been obnoxious and he probably owed the other guy an apology. Not that he'd ever get it. But Conner probably owed it to him.

"So I'm going to assume that Gabby was less than enthusiastic about your declaration of love?" Shane asked.

"Why do you assume that? Multiple women have been trying to get me to fall in love with them for years," Conner said.

Shane laughed. "Because you're having a head-up-your-ass practice."

Conner sighed. "Yeah." He definitely was.

Ryan lay back on the grass beside him. "I am completely impressed that you fell for Gabby, Conner," he said. "Gabby's awesome. You deserve a girl like her."

"But?" Conner asked, his gut tight.

"But are you sure you *want* a girl like her?"

"I deserve her, but I might not want her?"

Cody lay back on the grass on his other side. "You deserve a girl who challenges you, a girl who you don't have to put on an act for. But Gabby won't let you always be the hero. She won't let you get away with keeping everything superficial and happy all the time."

"I don't do that." But he did. And the fact that she wouldn't let him be her hero was weighing on him like he was carrying a lineman across the line of scrimmage.

"Of course you do. You like happy women."

"Doesn't everyone?"

"I don't know," Shane said, thoughtfully. "There's something kind of cool about being the person someone wants around when things aren't happy too."

Yeah, there probably was. Not that he would know. Gabby didn't want him around for whatever was going on with her. He was around for less-than-happy stuff with his sisters, but that was something he *had* to do. *Choosing* to be there for the tough stuff was different.

It was something all of these men were doing with his sisters.

And that was supposed to making Conner's life easier.

He did *not* feel like these guys were easing any of his burdens at the moment. "You tell yourself that," Conner said. "But I know you'd rather have been the one who bought Iz the spa package."

Shane looked at him for a long, uncomfortable moment.

"What?" Conner asked with a frown.

"I'm just thinking that deep down you'd like to be the one pushing her to go to the pool and then hanging out in the hot tub when she's not feeling well."

Conner took a deep breath. God, he hated thinking about Isabelle being sick. It made him feel helpless and, frankly, pissed off. "Does the pool and hot tub make her better?"

"Sometimes. Sometimes not."

"Exactly. The fibro is complicated," Conner said. "I've done some reading, but it affects everyone differently. And I don't want to bring it up with her because I don't know if she really wants to talk about it." In fact, the more he read, the more frustrated he became. He'd do anything to help Isabelle, but there was nothing concrete, nothing specific. Even for each individual patient, what they needed could vary day to day. So he stuck with the things that he knew would make her smile. Pedicures, for instance.

Shane nodded, but he looked…disappointed. Or something. Conner rubbed his head, feeling the tension of an oncoming headache.

"You do the same thing with Emma. Instead of talking to her about how she's a little freaked out by the whole baby thing, you buy her elaborate gifts," Nate said.

Yes, he most certainly did. He didn't have a clue how to reassure her about the pregnancy and labor and delivery and motherhood. He didn't know anything about the pregnant female body or babies. But she'd been all smiles when she'd seen the car seat. "You're just pissed that I got that car seat for her before you did."

"Yeah, that's annoying as hell," Nate admitted. "And we know that's part of why you're doing it. But that's not all of it."

His friends were insightful now? Was this a side effect of falling in love? Because it was extremely irritating.

"That's right, I also do it because I'm retired."

Shane snorted. "Retired from what?"

"Being worried, being the hard-ass, pacing the floor and cleaning up messes."

Which meant he shouldn't care that Gabby was leaving him out. He should be *happy* and *grateful*. He didn't fucking feel happy or grateful. He felt like biting someone's head off.

"Dammit, Conner."

He looked at Ryan in surprise. His friend sounded pissed. "What?"

"You make it sound like your sisters are incapable of taking care of anything on their own or making any decisions without you."

"I know you guys are there for them now. That makes me really happy," he told them sincerely.

"Your sisters do great on their own," Ryan said. "All of them. And they have each other. We're all lucky they *let* us into their lives. They don't *need* us."

Well, that was all very nice. Conner was glad these men realized the wonderful women they had. But they didn't know everything. They hadn't been there with the girls growing up.

"My sisters are amazing women. But there have been times —" Conner started.

"That they've let you help them out," Ryan said.

Conner frowned. "What?"

"When they were younger, I'm sure they needed you. But now…your sisters don't tell you everything," Ryan told him.

Conner looked at Shane, then Nate, then Cody. They all nodded.

"What the hell are you talking about?"

Shane seemed hesitant but he said, "Isabelle doesn't tell you much about her fibro."

"Just yesterday she told me about this new vitamin she had tried that really helped but that she couldn't find it locally anymore," Conner said, his gut churning.

"Because that's something you can help her with. But she doesn't tell you about all the problems they've had with her pain pills. Because that's something you can't do anything about."

Conner felt the twist in his gut tighten. Fuck.

Isabelle had a chronic condition. It wasn't going to go away. He knew it, but he also liked to ignore it. There was nothing he could do—he couldn't fix this.

He rubbed his hand over his face again. Ignoring it wasn't right. He knew that. He just didn't have a better idea.

Well, except a spa package here and there. Yeah. Big deal. It wasn't like that was going to make any fucking difference. It had made *him* feel better and she'd gone along with it so that he could feel like he'd done something.

"That's bullshit," he said. But he knew it wasn't.

"Sorry, man," Cody said. "But it's true. They know you want them to be happy, so they keep a lot of the stuff you can't control away from you."

Conner looked from one friend to another. They were all looking at him with a combination of sympathy and frustration.

"And they give me bullshit easy stuff that I can do to placate me and keep *me* happy," he said, knowing as he said it that it was true. All this time he'd thought he was taking care of his sisters and really they'd been taking care of him.

Fuck.

"Sorry, Conner," Nate said, confirming it all without confirming it.

"I'm not," Ryan said bluntly. "Amanda's been the one protecting you the most. She takes care of the girls so you don't have to."

Again, the truth of it hit Conner. Amanda, the oldest of the girls, was the responsible one. She'd been protecting him. He knew it in his heart before his mind accepted it.

"And you're pissed at me?" Conner asked Ryan.

"Not pissed, just..." Ryan blew out a breath. "Yeah, okay, a little. You think you're the big hero, you think you keep everyone happy and fix everything, but you don't always. The girls pull themselves and each other through a lot."

Conner felt the sharp twist in his gut move up to his heart. He pushed himself to his feet. "Fuck you, Kaye."

Ryan grabbed his arm. "You need to hear it so you don't—"

Conner yanked his arm away. "So I don't what? Think I'm a good brother? Think I'm actually making a fucking difference?"

"So you don't fuck it up with Gabby."

Conner grabbed his helmet and stomped toward the bench. "Yeah, well, Gabby doesn't have any big issues." Or so she kept saying. "She's totally capable and independent. She doesn't need a damned thing that I can't deliver. I can just focus on keeping her happy." If she ever came back to his apartment and let him.

"Don't be a dumbass," Shane said, following. "Everyone needs someone sometime."

"You gonna start singing too?" Conner asked, swiping up a bottle of water.

"Don't let her convince you she's always fine," Ryan said.

Conner took a huge drink then turned to face his friends. "What's that mean?"

Ryan looked at Nate and Conner scowled. What the fuck?

"Just that I think Gabby…" Ryan sighed. "Gabby thinks she is fine. She tries really hard to be fine. Maybe because there aren't a lot of people who will be there if she's not fine. Or maybe she's like your sisters. She doesn't want the people she cares about to *fail* to help her because *they'll* feel bad."

The frustration and worry and anger—at himself and everyone else—welled up and he grabbed Ryan by the front of his jersey. "What the fuck are you talking about? You know something about Gabby that I need to know?"

Ryan scowled and shoved him. "Knock it off. You're not pissed at me."

Conner shoved Ryan back for good measure, but his friend was right. "What do I need to know about all of this?"

"With Gabby?" Ryan asked.

"And the girls."

"You need to know that you don't have to have all the answers. You don't have to fix everything. Just be there. They will still love you and come to you, even if you can't solve *every* problem. Being there and loving them when things are bad is more important than struggling to keep everything good all the time. Anyone can love them when things are good. It takes *real* love to love them when things aren't good."

Conner felt like Ryan had shoved him again and knocked him on his ass. Had he really been afraid that the girls wouldn't *love* him if he couldn't solve their problems? Or that if he didn't have an answer or botched something they'd stop coming to him?

Yeah. He really had been afraid of that.

Conner blinked at Ryan stupidly as the realization sank in.

He hadn't been able to fix Ashley's problems and she hadn't loved him.

Whether or not that made sense, or if the two things were even actually related, he'd never know. But in that moment he did know that he'd subconsciously believed they were connected for a long time.

And with Gabby? Yeah, he wanted to slay her dragons and defeat her enemies. Yeah, he wanted her gazing up at him adoringly.

But she wasn't the gazing type. She'd said so herself. So if she wanted to slay her own dragons? He still wanted to be there. To watch, to cheer her on, to maybe nurse the burns and cuts she'd probably get in the process. Definitely to hold her afterward if the slaying didn't go so well.

But she didn't want him there. She wasn't telling him about her dragon problem. Just like his sisters had been keeping their battles—the big ones anyway—away from him.

It had happened just as he'd subconsciously feared—he hadn't been able to solve everything, so they'd stopped coming to him.

Gabby hadn't even *started* coming to him.

Conner threw his water bottle down. "You know what? Screw it. I've been there for my sisters for fifteen years. Willing to do anything, anytime. I wasn't perfect, but I tried. And they still kept stuff from me, they still figured it out for themselves and found other people to help them. So maybe Gabby does have problems, maybe she does need people. Maybe it's just not me." He jammed his helmet back on his head. "Let's go play football. I think it's time for someone else to spend some time on his ass."

And if anyone thought it was strange that their quarterback made most of the tackles for the rest of practice, they didn't say anything.

Being a girl was so much *work*.

Gabby stood in front of Sierra's closet and closed her eyes, blocking the sight of the dresses and skirts Sierra had told her to help herself to.

There were too many choices. Some were too fancy, some were too casual, some were too sexy, some weren't sexy enough. She felt like frickin' Goldilocks, but she had yet to find something she'd label as just right.

Then there were the colors—black, red, white, blue, green, silver.

And then there was the fact that she never played poker dressed like this. Jeans with bling on the back pockets were about as dressy as she got and even that was very rare. Her typical attire was shorts and a T-shirt.

She definitely never had to worry about walking in heels at a poker game.

What if that threw off her game? What if the dress's tight fit was distracting? What if she was constantly worried about the front dipping too low and showing more than she intended?

She couldn't do this.

Gabby turned away from the closet and headed for the kitchen. And the RumChata she'd brought.

Even before Sierra had told her that she wouldn't be home for a couple of hours but to help herself to anything in her closet or makeup drawer, Gabby had known she'd be drinking.

She could do girlie. But a girl's night out or a friend's wedding or something was not the same thing. Then she could look nice, but she wasn't the center of attention.

The poker game was different. Ricky Donovan was expecting the sexy, fun-loving girl from the Facebook photo. The girl Gabby was maybe ten percent of the time. If that. She was also going to be the only woman sitting at a poker table. Michael had confirmed that fact when Ricky had tweeted the names of the final players.

So, yeah, there would be a few eyes on her.

She really didn't need this extra pressure.

She needed to concentrate and play well. Worrying about, and being pissed at, her brother was already messing with her mojo, along with the fact that Conner had wanted to push things and been clearly frustrated that Gabby was at Sierra's tonight.

She knew he'd wanted to talk, but she'd been honest when she said she couldn't handle that right now on top of what was going on with Josh and this poker game. It wasn't fair to Conner to have a deep talk about their feelings and relationship when her mind wasn't all there. She'd so wanted to tell him all about this—the game, Ricky's stupid crush, the pressure to get the money back for him and her parents, her urge to punch her brother in the face. But none of this was Conner's problem.

She'd done one of the things that drove him crazy about girls —she'd filled his guest bathroom with *girl stuff*. Though most of it was in her bag now and she'd apparently convinced him that girl stuff could be tolerated, after all, with her little speech the other night. But she was trying to avoid doing the other two things that made him crazy.

She didn't want to be one of the girls who brought drama to his life—and her family was full of drama. She also didn't want to be one of the girls who got her feelings hurt easily. So she was keeping the poker game a secret. She'd also hightailed it out of the apartment before he could see that she was a little hurt that he hadn't tried to hug or kiss her and hadn't said "I love you" as she was leaving.

Yes, those three words had complicated things immensely. No, she hadn't been giving off hug-and-kiss-me vibes. He still should have grabbed her and laid a big, hot, sweet kiss on her. She could have definitely used that. An "I love you, Gabby" as she was leaving would have been nice.

But she'd been trying to discourage the I-love-you thinking. And the kissing would have just muddled things.

She sighed. She hated feeling confused and second-guessing herself.

Falling in love kind of sucked.

With a full glass of RumChata and root beer—okay, a little more liquor than root beer—she headed for the living room. She was going to watch a movie and relax before she tried to figure the closet out again.

Never mind the makeup. That had never been her strong suit.

Maybe Sierra would be home by then.

She'd just settled onto the couch when the doorbell rang.

Dammit.

She took a swig of her drink and paused the movie on a big-screen shot of Ryan Reynolds before heading for the door.

The moment she pulled it open, she had to resist the urge to slam it shut.

Emma, Isabelle and Olivia Dixon stood on Sierra's front step.

"We're here to help."

Oh crap.

"Ladies," she greeted, trying to keep calm. "What are you doing here?"

"Okay, we know they shouldn't have," Emma said, stepping into the house without invitation.

Gabby barely got out of the way as the girls swept in, each carrying several hangers and bags.

"But the guys filled us in on what's going on," Emma finished as she deposited her supplies on Sierra's dining room table.

"The guys?"

"Ryan, Nate, Shane and Cody."

Oh *crap*.

"Look, girls, I know that this is a lot to ask, but you can't tell Conner anything—"

Isabelle laughed. "Don't worry. We have a lot of experience in keeping things from Conner."

Gabby took a deep breath. "Okay." Then she frowned. "So what are you doing here?"

"Helping you," Isabelle said.

"Helping me what?"

"Get ready for tonight," Olivia said.

"You are?" She looked from one girl to the next and the next.

"It's poker, right? Poker's all about who can keep their cool the best," Emma said with a big grin.

"You're going to help me keep my cool?" Gabby asked.

"Better," Emma said. "We're going to help you keep them from being cool."

Oh boy. "What do you mean?"

"They're all guys, right?" Olivia asked.

"The other players? Yeah."

"Then it's gonna be easy," Isabelle said, holding up a short red dress.

Oh.

Gabby looked at Conner's sisters. She'd been around long enough to know that if these girls set their minds to something—especially their collective mind—there was very little anyone could do to stop them.

So she was their new project.

It wasn't a horrible idea.

Letting these girls dress her up would certainly cut down on her frustration—and RumChata consumption.

"What are you thinking?" she asked.

"That no matter how great you are at poker, it's a good idea to use every asset that you have," Olivia said. "Your smarts, your confidence—"

"Your boobs," Emma inserted.

Isabelle shrugged. "Well, yeah. Kind of. Remind them constantly that you're a woman," she said. "And that they all have chivalrous tendencies, deep down. If you're one of the guys, they'll try to beat you. But if you make it impossible to forget that you're a woman, they might take it easy."

"I don't need them to take it easy," Gabby protested.

Emma met her eyes. "Maybe not. But in this game you need to use any advantage. Whatever it takes."

"Whatever it takes," Gabby repeated. Emma was right. This wasn't like playing with her family. She had to swallow her pride here.

"I'm not saying play dumb," Emma went on. "But you need to tone down the kick-ass girl stuff."

Gabby looked at her in surprise. "Kick-ass girl stuff?"

Olivia laughed. "Gabby, you pull people out of mashed-up cars, you see people bleeding and dying and you stop it, you're going to medical school, you handle a whole family of guys, you can fix your car's transmission—" she paused and said seriously, "—you've turned Conner inside out. You're definitely kick-ass."

Gabby didn't know what to say to that. She was trying to process that Conner had apparently been talking about her—to his sisters or Cody and the guys or both—but she was too hung up on Olivia's words about her turning Conner inside out. She liked that. A lot.

"I agree," Isabelle said, having evidently considered her sister's words. "You are kick-ass and if you walk into the game like that, it's going to put up all their defenses. These guys are egomaniacs, they love to show off. You can't make them look bad. You have to let them make themselves look bad."

These girls were definitely completely filled in on what was going on tonight. Gabby didn't know what to think about that. But she looked at them, their eyes and smiles bright—their clothes and hair perfect—and decided she wasn't stupid enough to send them away.

"Okay, how do I do that?"

Emma held up a tiny hot-pink dress. "Distract them."

They were debating about if she should wear her hair up or down when there was another knock on the door.

Grateful for a moment to escape talk of twists and braids, Gabby headed for the front.

She knew it was stupid to hope it was pizza, considering no one had ordered pizza, but a pizza would be really awesome right now.

She pulled the door open to yet another crowd of people.

"We have the best news," Michael Sullivan announced with a big grin.

She stared at him. He was holding hands with the young girl next to him, presumably his girlfriend, Shannon. Nate and Shane and Cody were behind them.

"Does the news involve pizza?" she asked.

Michael looked behind him, then back to Gabby. "You want pizza?"

"In my experience, pizza helps with a lot of things."

"We can do that." Shane pulled his phone out.

"But we have news about poker too," Michael said.

Gabby sighed. If she never heard the word *poker* again, it would be fine with her. She stepped back to let them all in.

They filed in as the Divas came from the bedroom.

Everyone started talking at once.

"Ricky is really excited to meet you," Michael said. "He tweeted about it—and you—specifically."

"Which dress is more distracting?" Isabelle asked, holding up the pink and the black to the men.

"Pizza will be about thirty-five minutes," Shane announced.

Gabby loved him best at the moment.

"Who wants a beer?" Cody asked, holding up the twelve-pack he'd carried in.

Gabby changed her mind to loving *him* best.

"Then Ricky checked up on you," Michael went on as if there weren't six other people talking. "He tweeted that article about you from the paper. From the big car accident on the interstate a few months ago. The one with the picture of you carrying that little boy and girl."

Gabby groaned as Cody handed her a beer. She'd gotten so much attention from that article. She understood that it was a great story. Gabby had coached the kid and his sister how to hold their hands on their mother's abdominal wound while the firefighters worked to get into the car. Their efforts had saved their mother's life. But the photo and quotes from the kids was an over-the-top attempt to sell papers, in her opinion. An attempt that had expanded to the local news stations and eventually Facebook, where it spread like crazy.

"His tweet was something about getting to play poker with a hot kick-ass girl and how he was a little intimidated but that he couldn't wait."

Gabby glanced at Olivia who just grinned and mouthed *kick-ass*.

Everyone moved toward the couches and love seat in the living area. Nate grabbed two chairs from the dining room table and Shannon and Michael settled on the floor.

They were all still talking.

"I don't think Gabby should take Mac with her," Isabelle was saying.

"Yeah, Ricky's got this crush on Gabby. She should milk that. Get him to let his guard down, distract him a little," Emma said.

Shane was shaking his head. "She can't go all alone."

"We'll be there," Emma said, pointing to her and Nate. "Nate's invited."

"So are we," Michael said. "Ricky loves me for tweeting him about Gabby."

"But I still feel like she needs someone really *with* her," Shane said. "A boyfriend is perfect."

"Explain to me why Conner's not going with her?" Michael asked.

Everyone looked at one another, then over at Gabby.

She sighed and took another drink of her beer.

She didn't want to involve him. This wasn't his problem. But mostly she wasn't going to ask him to go to the poker game with her because…he wasn't here with all of them.

She was shocked that it hurt so much. She hadn't even known *they* were all going to be here. How could she be disappointed that he wasn't? Especially when *she'd* left *him*.

They'd argued, she'd more or less told him to butt out, and…he had.

That wasn't like Conner.

That was what hurt.

His sisters had told him to butt out numerous times, but he hadn't listened. His friends had told him to mind his own business—especially when they were seducing and falling in love with his sisters—but he hadn't listened. *She'd* told him not to worry about her after her apartment fire, but he hadn't listened.

But now maybe he really was tired of it all. Maybe it had sunk in that she came with some baggage. Maybe he had realized he was glad to have his space back, now that her stuff was out of his apartment. Maybe common sense had returned, now that the boobs he'd finally realized were under her uniform were out of sight.

He had his girl-free zone back.

Maybe he'd missed that more than he would miss her. "It's Gabby's decision," Olivia finally said. "And I agree with Shane. I think Mac needs to be there."

"Okay, Mac will go. But he has to hang back some of the time and give her a chance to flirt," Emma said. "She'll have to stroke Ricky's ego. Maybe even make him think that she and Mac are on the verge of a breakup." Her face lit up as she plotted. "Oh, I've got it. Michael, you can tip him off that she's wanting to break up with Mac. That would be another distraction for Ricky —he'll be watching Mac and gauging how things are between Gabby and him, maybe worrying about showing Mac up."

"I can do that," Michael agreed.

The plotting and planning continued around her until the pizza delivery showed up.

And after.

Long after.

The plotting turned to teaching. Michael, the computer genius, had pulled information about every player attending the party.

Part of poker was the cards and luck, part of poker was having nerves of steel, and part of poker was reading your opponent.

The more she knew about each of the other players, the better chance she had of figuring them out.

The group grilled her until she knew several bits of trivial information about each player, knew her and Mac's backstory, knew enough about Ricky Donovan to write his biography, and knew which dress and heels she'd be wearing.

She also knew that she would trust Shane to order pizza anytime, but that she'd stay away from Cody's beer in the future.

She looked around the room at the people gathered and it suddenly hit her.

None of these people were people she would have called friends yesterday. Conner, Ryan and Sierra weren't here. None of the others worked with her or were related to her. In fact, she wouldn't know any of them if it weren't for Ryan and Conner.

"Why are you doing this?" she asked.

The group stopped talking and looked at her.

"What do you mean?" Emma asked.

"Why are you all here doing this? We're not coworkers or friends or family." Yeah, so she'd had three of Cody's crappy beers and it was making her blunt.

"Because you're important to Conner," Olivia said with a shrug.

"And Ryan," Shane added.

"And you're doing it for your brother," Isabelle added. "We understand family."

"And for me there's the added bonus of seeing that cocky

asshole, Ricky Donovan, get his butt beat in poker by a girl," Michael said.

Shannon elbowed him. "It's important that she's a girl?"

Michael grinned. "It will be to him."

Gabby didn't know what to say. Except, "Well, now I have even more incentive to kick his butt."

Michael grinned.

Gabby's phone chimed with a text message. From Mac. *Can't wait to smell you.*

She smiled and glanced at the clock. The butterflies kicked up a ruckus in her stomach when she saw that it was ten.

"Okay, ladies," Gabby said to Conner's sisters, "it's showtime."

CHAPTER
ELEVEN

THE KNOCK at the door made Conner's heart thump.

Coming home to an empty apartment had sucked. It had been three days and he was already used to Gabby being there.

But he'd told himself it was for the best that she was at Sierra's. If she didn't want to lean on him, then fine. He could watch some TV and kick back, worry-free.

Besides, he was still worked up from practice and all the truths the guys had shared about his sisters and them keeping things from him and taking care of themselves. He'd wanted to be alone. He'd been thrilled to have his girl-free zone back.

For about twenty minutes.

Then he'd missed her.

He crossed the room in five strides and pulled the door open…and tried not to look disappointed when Amanda was on the other side.

"You okay?" he asked, automatically shifting into big-brother mode in spite of being irritated with his sisters. He stepped back to let her in.

"I'm okay." His sister entered and turned to face him. "How about you?"

"Fine. Why?" He wasn't fine at all.

"I understand that you're in love."

Conner groaned and swung the door shut. He shouldn't be surprised *that* news had spread quickly. "Ryan has a huge mouth."

"Shane told us, actually."

"Us?" But he knew exactly who she meant. "He told all of you?"

"The guys already knew."

Yeah, he'd spilled his guts to them all at once. "I know."

"Why didn't *you* tell us?"

"I just…kind of…found out myself," he said honestly. "Like a day ago."

Amanda nodded. "But it's real? For sure?"

Conner sighed. "Well, like loving the other four beautiful, independent, strong-willed women in my life, I'm sure it's going to make me old before my time and give me an even bigger ulcer but…yeah. It's real. For sure." He smiled at his sister, then frowned and peered closer. "Are you *crying*?"

"I'm just really happy for you, Conner. I've wanted you to fall in love so badly, but I didn't know if you'd ever let yourself."

He shook his head. "I'm not sure I really *let* myself."

"But you are in love."

He nodded. "With a stubborn, independent woman who doesn't need me at all."

Amanda sniffed and smiled. "I think that's great."

"That I'm feeling worthless and unnecessary?" he asked. "Which brings up something I'd like to talk to *you* about, sis, and all the stuff you girls have been keeping from me all these years."

"You're hardly worthless and unnecessary, Conner," Amanda said, looking truly offended.

"Apparently there's all kinds of stuff about Isabelle that I don't know."

Amanda crossed her arms and narrowed her eyes. "Uh-huh."

"And Emma's freaked out about the pregnancy."

"A little."

"I had to go to *her* to even talk about her being pregnant in the first place," Conner pointed out.

Amanda uncrossed her arms and put her hands on her hips. "Why do you think you should always be the first one to know things?"

"Because I'm…the brother." It sounded stupid, even to him.

Her eyes narrowed further. "That sounds so stupid."

"It's not even that I should be first," he said. "There are apparently things I don't know at all."

"Conner, there are things *I* don't know about Isabelle's fibro."

"What about Emma's pregnancy?"

"I know that she's a little freaked out. But she tells Isabelle more than she tells me."

"Tell me something about one of the girls that you know that I don't."

"You don't really want me to do that."

"I do."

"You don't."

"Amanda."

"You sure?"

"Yes."

"Okay, Olivia has filled up two punch cards at Tease in the time it's taken me *and* Emma *and* Isabelle to fill up one."

He stared at her, letting the words begin to sink in. Then he adamantly shut the thoughts down. "There have to be a million *other* things you could have told me."

"I was making a point." She looked pleased.

"And what's that?"

"It's not your job to make us happy. In fact, it's first and foremost *our* job to make ourselves happy."

He grimaced. "We're talking about sex toys? Really?"

She laughed. "You asked. But no, not sex toys. Well, not *just* sex toys."

"Then what?"

"We should all be in charge of making ourselves happy first."

"But…"

She gave him a soft smile. "But what?"

"Then what am I supposed to do?"

"Use all of this crazy energy and creativity to make yourself happy."

That sounded suspiciously like something Gabby would say. Of course, she'd use sex and breakfast food to illustrate that he deserved to have what he wanted and to be happy too.

"So you're happy?" he asked.

"Very."

"Without any help from me." A lot like Gabby.

"Dammit, Conner," Amanda exclaimed. "No. Not without any help from you."

"But you don't come to me."

"Conner, you taught us—by example—how to be there for the people we love and how to support them. We've formed a huge support system including each other and friends and boyfriends and coworkers to tell things to and to ask things of. We're a *family*. Not just your younger sisters."

He looked into her eyes. Okay, that made him feel a little better. She was right. But… "So you've never intentionally kept anything from me?"

"Sure I have. Because you're someone I love too, and some-times keeping stuff from you is protecting *you*."

"Amanda," he said warningly.

She sighed. "Okay, yes, I have kept things from you. Yes, to protect you, but also sometimes to protect *me* or one of the girls because I didn't want you to be mad or disappointed or regret-ful. But for a long time I felt like everything weighed on you and like if you had any chance for a normal life of your own, then you needed some help."

He swallowed. Clearly he hadn't done a great job of *happily* being there for his sisters if Amanda felt the need to protect him.

"But you've changed in the past few months," she went on. "You took things seriously when you—and we—were younger. And I can admit that you probably needed to. But you've lightened up over the past few months. Do you know why?"

He absolutely did. "Because the guys are there for you now."

She looked surprised that he'd realized it. "Yes, you finally understand that you don't have to do it all."

"It's because I finally realized that there are people who can love you as much as I do."

She teared up again and Conner sighed.

"I also realized I don't have to be the one always figuring out why it makes you cry when I say nice things."

She sniffed, but smiled. "And they're the guys that you didn't want getting involved with us," she had to point out.

He rolled his eyes. "I know. Makes you wonder about my judgment, huh?"

Amanda didn't say anything for a moment, but gave him a look that said it all.

"You are questioning my judgment?" he asked.

"In relationships, maybe a little," she admitted.

"And this has to do with Gabby?"

"It does."

"Ryan thinks I'm going to mess it up too."

She nodded.

Of course they'd talked about it. There had been a time when the thought of his friends having sex with his sisters was the thing that felt weirdest. That still felt weird. But the idea that his friends and sisters were sitting around talking about him felt a little weirder.

"How do I keep from messing it up?" Because two things

were becoming very clear—he wanted Gabby and he didn't know as much about women as he'd thought.

"Just be there. Stop thinking you have to *do* things and fix things and have all the answers and be fully and completely in charge of her happiness," Amanda said.

"Just be there?" he said. "I have no idea what that means."

She nodded again. "I know. Because you've never done it. You do stuff and buy stuff and think up the perfect thing to say. Like with Iz and Shane—you helped him pick out the ring. With Emma and Nate—you went over there and had all this great advice. With Olivia and Cody you actually went and *proposed* to her for him."

Conner stared at her. He had done all of those things. When he'd realized what was going on with all of them, he'd jumped in and gotten involved. But Amanda had left someone off of the list.

"I never did that with you, did I?" he asked, thinking about it. "I never did or said anything specific about you and Ryan."

Her eyes were bright with tears again, but she forced a smile as she shook her head. "No, you didn't."

"I went to the cake tasting with you," he said, but he knew it wasn't enough.

"Yeah," she nodded. "That was fun."

Right. But it wasn't enough.

"I'm happy about you and Ryan, Amanda," he said. "Ryan is good for you. And vice versa."

"I know."

And it was clear she did. Even without Conner's blessing. Which should tell him something right there.

"I'm sorry I've never said it before."

"You can make it up to me."

"Anything."

"Give me away at my wedding."

Emotions, numerous and sharp, hit him in the chest. And

damned if *his* eyes didn't tear up a little. But he shook his head. "No way."

Her eyes went wide. *"What?"*

"I'm not giving you away, Amanda. Not ever. But," he said as she started to respond, "I will absolutely walk you down the aisle so you can make one of my best friends the luckiest guy in the world. Well, one of the luckiest, anyway."

Amanda's tears fell this time as she threw her arms around his neck. "I love you, Conner."

He squeezed her, sniffing. "I love you too."

She stepped back and smiled at him, wiping her cheeks. "And you love Gabby, right?"

"Yes." But he was, in fact, fucking that up too. Evidenced by the fact that, the day after he'd told her he loved her, she was staying with someone else.

"Okay, then I'm going to tell you Ryan and Shane and Nate and Cody's secret to keeping us happy."

"I'm all ears."

"Sometimes they do stuff, sometimes they buy us stuff, sometimes they give the perfect speech—usually with some practice—but a lot of the time they just hold our hands, hug us and tell us they love us, that they believe in us, that they'll be there even when we're bitchy and tired and feel like crap."

He blew out a breath. "That's really enough?"

"A lot of the time it is," she said. "Most of the time it really is."

"What about the rest of the time?"

She shrugged. "The rest of the time you'll fix it or buy it or say the right thing."

He gave a short laugh. "I'm not so sure about that."

"Okay, in those rare instances when you can't do it, you have a whole bunch of people who can. Sisters who can help her pick the right outfit, friends who can say the right thing, friends that can do favors or call in favors or…" Amanda trailed off.

Conner frowned. That was…nice. It was a strange way to put

it, but it was nice. "So I need to tell her that even though medical school will be demanding, I want to be there."

"Yes. Medical school. Too."

"Too?"

"There's something I'm not supposed to tell you, but Ryan and I think you need to know."

He could tell he wasn't going to like this.

Twenty minutes later, it turned out he was right.

Conner was dressed and ready to go in record time.

"You're going *to* the game?" Amanda asked, coming off the couch.

"If that's where Gabby is, then yeah, I'm going."

"It's a private game, isn't it? You need an invitation."

Conner held out his phone.

Amanda read out loud, "Hot dam, @HawksQB is playin too #pokerparty." She looked up at him. "Who is this?"

"Ricky Donovan."

"And you're at Hawks QB?"

He grinned. "Of course."

"He spelled *damn* wrong."

"I don't care." Conner grabbed his keys.

"You just tweeted Ricky Donovan?"

"Yep."

"How did you know he'd invite you?"

"He's one of my biggest fans. He tweets to and about me all the time."

Amanda looked amazed. "You tweet? All the time?"

"The Hawks PR department likes us to be active on social media. I leave Facebook to Shane and Nate—though we all know Michael does most of it—but I can tweet."

Amanda shook her head. "Wow." She pulled out her phone and started swiping her finger over the screen.

"What are you doing?"

"Following you on Twitter."

He sighed and started for the door. "You coming?"

"I can come?"

"You're my guest."

"I wouldn't miss it." She tucked her phone away and ran to catch up with him.

"Call Ryan first. I'll call Shane."

"What are we calling them for?"

He stopped and smiled, feeling purpose and pleasure flow through him. And maybe a touch of deviousness. "I'm about to show Gabrielle Evans doting like she's never imagined."

"Ooh, doting," Amanda said. "Can't wait."

As he pulled the door shut behind them, she said, "Oh, by the way, there's something about Mac Gordon you should know too."

"Act like you're crazy about me."

"Instead of like I'm going to puke from nerves?" Gabby forced a smile.

Mac grinned back. "Since I'm trying to look lovey-dovey here, yes. Looking like you are going to puke is hard on my ego."

Her smile was more genuine now. "You're just hoping I don't actually puke with how close you're standing."

She was leaning against the wall in the foyer of Ricky Donovan's huge house, Mac next to her, his hand braced on the wall near her ear. They stood close enough that anyone looking would assume they were a couple, exactly as planned. So far it had worked. They'd shown up together, Mac's hand resting possessively on the back of her neck, his bright smile the smile of a man in love and when she'd introduced him to Ricky as her boyfriend, Ricky had told him he was a lucky man.

But he'd given Gabby a wink behind Mac's back.

"You need to calm down," Mac said, taking her hand and squeezing. "You're here to play poker. It's just a game. Just do it, get it over with."

"The total winnings tonight will be sixty thousand dollars. It's kind of a big deal."

"Yeah, okay. The money is a big deal. But you're thinking about it way too hard."

"I—" She started to protest but then she frowned. "How do you know that?"

He chuckled. "I've known you for a while now, Gabby. You're a gut-instinct girl. You don't overthink—which is a wonderful trait, by the way—you just *do*. Whatever needs done. You think on your feet, you face stuff head on, you react and adjust. That's all you have to do tonight."

She nodded. "Yeah, you're right. I'm feeling the pressure with the game, the money, my brother, all of you guys helping me, Conner not..." She trailed off and literally bit her tongue. That wasn't fair—Conner wasn't here because she hadn't told him about it and because she'd sworn everyone else to secrecy.

He would be here if she'd asked.

Conner Dixon would show up when someone needed him, but once he figured out that she was going to complicate things in his life, she wasn't so sure he'd keep showing up.

Apparently something changed in her expression because Mac moved in front of her, blocking her from the other people enjoying cocktails and conversation in the foyer before the start of the game.

"Conner not being here?" Mac asked.

She shook her head. "It doesn't matter."

"He doesn't know about the game."

She shook her head again.

"But there's some reason that you think he wouldn't be here if he did?"

She felt her throat tighten.

He noticed that too.

"Whoa." Mac glanced around and lifted his hand to her head, drawing it down over her hair, a lover's touch. "Take it easy."

She took in the people milling in the foyer, glancing in their direction. She ran her hand up over his chest, trying to sell the crazy-about-him vibe. "Conner would be here. But he wouldn't want to be. I could drag him into this because…he thinks he's in love with me."

Mac's eyes got wide. "Okay, first, Conner's in *love*?"

She shrugged. "He thinks so."

Mac's expression softened. "Gabby, you're not the kind of girl that a guy just thinks he's in love with. When a guy meets a girl like you, he either fights it because he knows he'll never be good enough, or he jumps in with both feet and revels in it."

She looked at him thoughtfully. "Which were you with Sara?"

"The first. Absolutely."

She would have never guessed that, based on the times she'd seen Sara and Mac together. "But then you jumped in."

He laughed. "She dragged me in."

"You didn't want in? You didn't want to be in love?"

"Nope. I was sure I'd mess it up."

"But you're glad to be there now?" She knew he was. A person couldn't spend five minutes around Mac and Sara and not know that he was truly and fully in love.

"I'm reveling now," he said with a nod.

She sighed.

"Well, I know Conner's not fighting it," Mac said. "I was there for his scene with the poker-chip cookies and everything the other day."

"Right. Um, no. Conner's not fighting it."

He looked at her as if waiting for her to go on. "You're the one fighting it?"

She nodded. "I guess so. Kind of. It's just that relationships can screw up otherwise perfectly laid plans."

A prime example was her standing in Donovan's foyer pretending to be in love with Mac while waiting to play poker to bail her brother out.

But she wasn't sure she wanted to fight it anymore.

She always put the people in her life first, did what she needed to do to make them happy, no matter what the sacrifice would cost her. Even medical school. She knew it could happen again. She knew that the chances of keeping her life uncomplicated for the next six years were a billion to one.

Conner should get all of that. He was the same way.

He'd be here for her if she'd asked him. He'd be there for her in the future if she told him she needed him. But it would mess up his plans—his plans to enjoy life and be worry-free for a change.

Mac laughed at that. "Well, that's for sure. Then again, not all carefully laid plans are good ones."

But how could medical school not be a good plan? How could Conner having his own normal, quiet life without the drama and chaos of worrying about and cleaning up after a bunch of other people not be a good plan?

"Well, it doesn't matter," she said. "He's not *really* in love. He thinks he is because I don't need him. I can take care of myself. I'll let him romance me, he can do things to make me happy or cheer me up, but he doesn't have to actually fix anything for me. I don't have demons, I don't have major baggage. He loves me because I'm okay, I'm well-adjusted, he can't screw me up. And I'm rational and calm and intelligent. I know men. I know he's going to say stupid things sometimes or forget to do things sometimes, but I won't freak out. I don't freak out."

"You don't freak out at all? Ever?" Mac asked dryly.

Okay, so her voice had risen a little and she'd talked really fast there. Some might even call it a rant. But she did *not* freak out.

"That is right," she said adamantly. "I don't go crazy, so he can be with me and relax and be himself and not worry about me dropping out of college and developing a drinking problem."

"Are you absolutely *sure* that you don't go crazy about things?" Mac asked.

"No. I mean *yes*. I'm talking about this girl, Ashley, who he…" She stopped and took a deep breath. "Never mind."

Mac nodded. "Sounds good." He leaned back a little, but took her hand, in case anyone was paying attention. "I think you need to call Conner. Tell him where you are. Ask him to come. He'd want to be here, Gabby. He's in love with you. He will want to help."

She shook her head, feeling tears clogging her throat. "That's just it. He's in love with me in part because I *don't* need him. I can take care of myself, and my family, on my own. He can trust me to be okay. *That's* a huge part of his attraction here. I'm different from the other girls."

Mac leaned back. He blew out a frustrated breath and ran a hand over his head. "Fine. Okay. But let me say one more thing. Life happens and the more people in your life, the more things happen. No matter what other plans you have. But without all those people in your life…you'll be without all those people in your life. You know?"

She nodded. She wouldn't trade any of her family members for peace and quiet. Most days. Probably. "I'll be there for my family. But I don't know if I can take more people on who might need me."

"Well, the thing is about people who need you…sometimes you need them too." He pointed to something over her shoulder.

She turned to see Nate and Emma talking to Ricky and one of his friends. Emma caught her eye and gave her a wink. A few feet behind them, Michael and Shannon were sampling the hors d'oeuvres. Michael toasted her with a shrimp puff. Dooley and Morgan Miller were playing blackjack at the could-be-in-Vegas table set up across the room.

"Everybody needs a cheering section once in a while," Mac said in her ear.

Instantly, Gabby teared up.

They'd been there for her. They were here for her now. As was everyone who'd crowded into Sierra's apartment. She knew she could call any of them and they'd come, no questions asked and do whatever they could for her.

Yeah, maybe having people in your life didn't always mean having to do stuff for them.

"Hey, you'll ruin your mascara," Mac teased, lifting a finger to her cheek and swiping at a tear that had escaped.

"Then knock that shit off," she said, pushing his hand away.

She dug in her purse and pulled out her phone. She didn't need Conner to be here, she didn't even need him to know about the game, the money or her dumb brother. But she did, suddenly, need to talk to him.

He hadn't said "I love you" as she left. But she hadn't said it at all.

And she did. She loved him.

It was stupid, it was going to be hard at times and it was most definitely going to be complicated. But she loved him and, yeah, it felt weird to have all these people here for her except him.

Mac gave her a knowing grin as she dialed. She rolled her eyes at him.

Conner answered on the first ring. "Hey."

His voice made her smile and she felt the tension in her muscles release. "Hey."

"You okay?"

"I just…" her throat tightened and she felt Mac squeeze her hand, "…I just wanted to hear your voice."

Cheesy. Really cheesy.

Then she heard him clear his throat and thought maybe cheesy was good.

"My charming and witty joke-telling voice, my charming and rugged phone-sex voice or my I-love-you voice?"

Her eyes stung. "Your I-love-you voice isn't charming?"

"It's just my voice, no additives needed," he said.

The stinging grew stronger. "I have to tell you something."

"Anything."

"I love you too."

There was a long silence on the other end of the phone. Mac gave her a big grin.

Finally she asked, "Conner? You there?"

He cleared his throat again. "I thought you were going to tell me about the poker game."

Now the surprised silence was on her end of the line. He knew? She looked from Mac, to Nate, to Michael, to Dooley, then down at her dress and heels, and thought about all of the people who knew about tonight.

Of course he knew.

She sighed. This was one of the things that was going to come from combining the people in their lives—even more meddling and big mouths and fewer secrets or private moments.

Well, she could think of worse things. Like *not* combining the people in their lives.

"The game is going to start in a few minutes. I'll…come over as soon as it's done."

"I'm on the front porch."

"What front porch?"

But he'd hung up.

She frowned at the phone, then looked up at Mac. "He hung up on me."

Mac's attention was on something over her shoulder. "Uh, hey, you know how we were talking about you thinking about the game too hard?"

Well, she definitely hadn't been thinking about the game in the last few minutes. "Yeah."

"I'm guessing you usually play with a lot of distractions around, right?"

She laughed. "My family is definitely distracting." If it wasn't the antics and ribbing from the people at the poker table, it was the family watching and coaching, or the family in the kitchen arguing about how much Tabasco to put on the wings, or the family in the living room telling everyone to shut up so they could hear the TV.

"Then you should play great tonight with distractions, right?" Mac asked.

She nodded. "Probably."

"Good. Because I think things are about to get very distracting."

And Mac's hand settled on her left butt cheek.

The first thing Conner saw as he stepped into Ricky Donovan's front foyer was Mac Gordon standing way too close to Gabby—with his hand on her ass.

Of course.

Conner absolutely owed the man an apology for flirting with Sara. And he was absolutely never going to give that apology.

And then the ass itself truly registered. Conner felt like someone had kicked him in the gut. Gabby was all woman. There was no question in his mind, of course. But seeing her now…damn.

The crimson dress covered her only from beneath her arms to midthigh. It molded to her breasts, hips and the firm butt that Mac was still touching. Her long, toned legs seemed to stretch for miles before ending in three-inch heels. Her hair was swept up, sparkly earrings dangling from her ears, her necklace catching the light and drawing his eye to her long, graceful neck and her smooth, bare shoulders.

Gabby hadn't seen him yet, but he knew Mac had noticed him by the huge-ass, smug grin on the big guy's face.

Conner greeted him. With one finger. Then started in that direction.

That woman loved him. Really loved him. There was no way he was going to be able to wait to…

"Conner-effing-Dixon!"

Ricky Donovan stepped in front of Conner, blocking his way to Gabby.

Ricky Donovan. Poker game. *Not* being the barge-in-here-and-save-the-day hero.

Right.

He was here for Gabby. And if Gabby needed to pretend Mac was her boyfriend then…fine. Kind of. For now.

Ricky grabbed Conner's hand in a half-shake, half-slap thing.

"Hey, Donovan. Thanks for the invite," Conner said, plastering on his biggest charming smile.

It didn't just work on women.

"No problem at all. Thrilled you're here. No promises not to kick your butt at the tables, but still thrilled," Ricky said.

"Thanks, man." Conner knew the younger man was a knowledgeable and enthusiastic fan. Specifically of Conner's, but also of the team as a whole. He was known for his live tweeting during Hawks games and his ranting on blogs that ripped on the organization or specific players. He was a staunch supporter and Conner appreciated him. He was going to use Ricky's enthusiasm to help Gabby win a bunch of money off of Ricky's friends, but he appreciated him.

"We're about to get started," Ricky told him, steering him in the direction opposite from Gabby.

Conner glanced back. That was okay. For now.

"Gabby Evans looks great in red, huh?" he asked Ricky.

He'd seen Donovan's tweets. Even without Amanda filling him in, he could tell Ricky had a little crush.

Ricky grinned. "Hey, that's right, you probably know her. You're both paramedics."

"Yeah, I know her. She's awesome." And she loved *him*. Conner felt a big rush of I-can't-fucking-believe-it-hell-yeah.

"She is. She's with the big guy tonight, but I think I'm going to put him at another table for poker. Then I can flirt with her without him staring me down."

Conner nodded and tried to contain the brightness of his smile. "I think putting Mac at another table is a hell of an idea."

Ricky glanced up at him. Then groaned. "You're going to flirt with her too? Man, I don't stand a chance."

Damn right. Conner clapped Ricky on the shoulder. "Ricky, do you believe the old saying 'all's fair in love and poker'?"

Ricky gave him a grin. "Yeah, man, I do."

They strolled through a large room where the buffet and bar were set up, then stepped into a huge room that Conner supposed would have been called the ballroom in old-fashioned mansions. He wasn't sure what Richard Donovan used the enormous room for exactly, but his son had turned it into a Vegas look-alike casino.

There were even six slot machines around the perimeter, a blackjack table and a roulette wheel. Guests were milling about, playing, laughing and drinking.

But the centerpiece was the poker setup. Ten tables with seats for five each clustered in the middle of the room. Each had a dealer and a waitress standing ready to serve the players through the hours ahead.

"Wow."

Ricky nodded. "Thanks." He looked at Conner, clearly proud. "I can't throw a football but I can sure as hell throw a party."

Conner couldn't disagree. "Let the games begin."

"You'll be at my table," Ricky said, pointing to the first table near the arched doorway that led from the dining room. "Gabby will be too and a couple of my buddies."

"Sounds good." It sounded perfect. Conner could hold his

own at poker with his friends, but Gabby's family had proved that he wasn't a serious player. He couldn't win here with these high-level players. But he didn't need to. Gabby didn't need him to win the game. She just needed him to be here.

"I'm going to go announce the start of the game," Ricky said. "Make yourself comfortable."

Conner ordered a rum and coke from the waitress and took the chair to the left of the dealer.

He only had to wait five minutes for Ricky to escort Gabby into the room, with Mac right on their heels. Mac spotted Conner first and started in his direction, but Ricky said something that brought the big man up short. Ricky pointed to something across the room and Mac followed his finger, his eyes narrow. He glanced over at Conner, frowned, then started in the direction of the table he'd been assigned. As far from Ricky's table as possible.

Conner hid his grin behind his drink.

Gabby was at the table when she finally noticed him.

Her eyes grew round and her mouth dropped open.

"Hi, Gabby," he greeted. He kept his seat. Somehow. Everything in him screamed to grab her and kiss her and never let go. He wanted to demand that she tell him she loved him—now, in person, loudly and repeatedly. He wanted to strip her down. He wanted to propose.

But he stayed seated, smiling casually, watching every move she made.

She was looking at him with a combination of emotions—surprise, of course, but there was an instant look of affection, that he loved, and a look of relief. She gave him a quizzical look and a smile as she took a seat in the chair Ricky had pulled out for her.

"I didn't think about the fact that you would know each other," Ricky said as two more men joined the table. "But this is great. I get to hang out with the most beautiful woman I've met in a long time and my football hero in the same night. This is awesome."

"I didn't realize you knew Conner," Gabby said, still looking at Conner.

"I'm a huge fan," Ricky assured her. "I can't believe he's here."

"Well, that's great," she said. "It's that kind of flattery that keeps his custom-made helmet fitting his big head."

Conner gave her a wink.

Ricky chuckled. "This is going to be fun."

It was.

As long as Gabby quit looking at him like she was. It seemed she was also fighting the urge to round the table and grab him. If she kept watching him with the love and heat in her eyes, he wasn't going to last an hour.

Ricky turned to talk to their dealer and a man in a suit who had approached with a question. He seemed to be in charge of something.

Conner took the opportunity to mouth to Gabby, *"Win big."*

She smiled and nodded. Then mouthed back, *"I love you."*

He groaned. He hadn't touched her since she'd said it. He hadn't been able to kiss her. Hell, he hadn't even said it back. Sure, he'd said it first, but she had surprised him so much with her declaration on the phone that he hadn't really responded appropriately.

"Sorry about that," Ricky said, turning back to them. "That's Stan. He's in charge of security tonight."

"Security?" Conner asked. "Really?"

Ricky shrugged. "It's a game and I hope everyone has fun, but there's some big money at stake and some of these people take it too seriously."

"Better safe than sorry, I guess," Conner said. "But no worries at this table, right? Everyone's friends here."

He knew Gabby could handle herself, even if the other players did take it seriously, but he was hoping that his presence would distract Ricky and that if their host felt he was truly playing with friends—or at least people he wanted to be friends with—he'd be more relaxed and less cutthroat about the game. Ricky was well-known as a card shark. After all, practice made perfect and Ricky got a lot of practice. It wasn't like he had a lot of other pressing obligations to attend to. Every advantage Conner could give Gabby, he would.

"Definitely friends," Ricky agreed, clearly pleased. "So I'm taking the night off."

"The night off?" Gabby repeated.

Conner picked up on the note of concern in her voice, but she covered her reaction with a smile.

"How does the host take a night off?" she asked, her tone smoother.

"With you two here?" Ricky asked. "I don't want to play hard. I want to enjoy. We'll just play for fun."

"Fun?" Gabby asked, as if she'd never heard the word.

"You don't have to take it easy on me, Donovan," Conner said smoothly, wishing he could reach for Gabby and squeeze her hand—or kick her in the shin. She needed to be cool.

"Me either," Gabby said, too enthusiastically. "I'm here to play."

"We'll play," Ricky told her. "Just not for money or anything. Just fun."

"We're not going to play for money?" Gabby asked, her tone definitely concerned now.

Conner tried to catch her eye but she was staring at Ricky.

Ricky chuckled. "You are JD's sister. That kid is intense."

Having met Josh, Conner wasn't sure he'd agree with the word *intense*, but he'd looked Josh up on Twitter on their way over and he knew the kid was pissed about not playing tonight.

"We take poker seriously in my family," Gabby said.

"Well, I take charming the ladies seriously," Ricky said, turning a grin on her. "And beating their pants off in cards isn't the way I like to end up with their panties on my floor."

Gabby stared at him as if trying to compute what he was telling her.

Conner thought fast. Okay, they were here playing poker, but it seemed clear that Ricky didn't want to have to concentrate on a serious card game *and* seduction at the same time. Apparently he didn't multitask well. But Gabby needed to play for the high stakes.

There was no way Ricky was going to let her sit at another table.

And it was his house. His rules. If he wanted his table to sit out of the tournament, he could do that.

Good thing that being a good Knight in Shining Armor meant having a backup plan.

Conner slid his phone from his pocket and texted *Go* to Shane, Cody and Ryan, then turned up the volume.

"If you're worried about Conner's ego, he can take losing," Gabby said. She looked at him as if waiting for him to reassure Ricky of the same thing.

"Oh, honey, I'm not worried about Conner," Ricky said, leaning in closer. "But I was thinking this game could be about something more *interesting* than money."

Conner's eyes narrowed.

"More interesting than money?" she asked.

"Yeah, like I would bid a weekend stay at my dad's cabin in Cabo."

Gabby raised an eyebrow. "I don't have a weekend vacation home to counter with."

Ricky's grin grew. "Right, so you'd have to bid something comparable. Like a weekend at the Britton."

"A weekend at the Britton is comparable to a weekend in Cabo?" Gabby asked.

"If the weekend's with you, I'm sure it would be," Ricky said, running his hand up her arm.

Suddenly a shout came from across the room. "Peanuts? Fucking peanuts! I need my EpiPen!"

They all turned. Mac was out of his chair, pulling at his tie and yelling.

"Gabby, where's my pen?" he shouted.

Mac Gordon was a big guy and when he started throwing his elbows around and hollering, people noticed.

"I'm gonna die! I'm gonna die!" He pulled his tie off and shrugged out of his jacket, throwing it to the floor. His eyes were crazy.

Gabby and Conner looked at one another. Mac didn't have a peanut allergy. Conner was sure of it.

But no one other than Gabby knew that.

They both shoved their chairs back and sprang into action. Or fake action anyway.

They were paramedics. If someone was having an allergic reaction to peanuts, they knew exactly what to do. They could fake this, no problem. There had to be a reason for this.

Gabby pretended to dig in her purse for the imaginary EpiPen as they jogged toward Mac.

"Lie down," Conner ordered him as they got closer.

"Oh honey! What happened?" Gabby asked, as she knelt next to Mac.

"We're going to need some space here," Conner said to the crowd, motioning them all back.

"Do you need an ambulance?" someone called out.

"I'm a doctor!" someone else shouted.

Gabby and Conner looked at one another again, then at Mac. He was on his back on the floor on the other side of the table from most of the room. He shrugged.

Gabby grinned, then called, "No, we're fine. He'll be fine. I've got the pen right here."

Conner knelt on his other side.

She jabbed him in the leg with the ballpoint pen she'd pulled from her purse.

"Hey," Mac protested.

She stifled a laugh.

Conner grinned. "Okay, what's going on?" he asked quietly. "You eat peanut butter cookies all the time."

"Just needed a diversion and a way of getting you both in a powwow," Mac said. "What's the plan here tonight? Do *I* need to win the big money while Ricky feels Gabby up and Conner fights the urge to kill him, or what?"

"So far *you've* touched her more inappropriately than he has," Conner told him.

Mac grinned. "She smells really good tonight."

"Give me that pen, G," Conner said, scowling at Mac.

But he didn't mean it and he knew Mac knew it.

Gabby stuck the pen back in her purse. "I don't know what to do. I need to play for money, but maybe I should say I need to take Mac home. I'll enter a different tournament." She glanced over her should with a frown. "A *real* tournament. I don't want to play for romantic weekends with Ricky, that's for sure."

"Maybe *I'll* win," Conner told her. "We could take the weekend in Cabo."

She looked at him. "Conner, I love you. But there's no way you could win in poker against Ricky Donovan."

Hearing those three words from her in person made everything in him shout *yes!*

He started to lean across Mac, but the big man put a hand on his chest. "I don't think so."

Conner looked down at him. "What?"

"You kiss her, leaning over my poor, sick body, how's that gonna look for *me*?"

"Seriously?" Conner asked.

"Seriously."

He blew out a breath. "Fuck. Fine."

Gabby sighed. "Okay, let's get you home," she said to Mac. She started to stand. "At least this way I can get to bed earlier." This she directed at Conner.

And he knew exactly whose bed she was talking about—and his plan B went to plan C. Or so. The new plan B included writing her a check for the money she needed, shaking some sense into her brother and then keeping her naked for the next week or so.

He could do that. It would fix everything.

But there was something just as important as getting this fixed…and that was proving to Gabby that she had *lots* of people who would help her when she needed it.

So instead of, *Here's a check, let's get you out of that dress*, he said, "I have an idea."

She dropped back to her knees. "You do?"

"I don't want to step in here, though," he said. "I'm honestly just here tonight for you. To cheer you on, or comfort you if it doesn't go well, take you home early…" he was still pretty in favor of that one, "…or whatever."

She stared at him for a long moment. "But you have an idea about how to salvage all of this?"

"I do." Two ideas, actually. His checkbook was out in the car.

She didn't say anything for a moment. "Conner?"

"Yeah?"

"What is your idea?"

"You sure? I'll do whatever you want—"

"Conner," she said between her teeth, "tell me."

"I don't want you to think—"

She reached out and grabbed the front of his shirt. "I need you, okay? I'm thrilled you're here. Seeing you sitting at that table took my breath away and made me love you even more. But right now I need your help and if you don't tell me your idea I'm going to…" she glanced down at Mac, "…French kiss Gordon for the next five minutes and tell everyone it was CPR."

Conner looked at Mac, who grinned, then stretched his arms up, linked his fingers and put his hands behind his head—the picture of absolute arrogance.

"You had me at 'I need you'," Conner told her. "I'm on it."

She let go of his shirt and sat back, taking a deep breath.

"Damn." Mac sat up. "Well, it was a nice idea."

"Follow my lead," Conner told them both.

"Everything okay?" the physician in the room asked as they all got to their feet.

"Wasn't a peanut after all," Mac told him. "Garbanzo bean."

Conner heard Gabby's soft snort.

"Okay." The doctor looked at each of them. "Well, good. Let me know if you need anything."

Yeah, like help for the side effects of an accidental injection of norepinephrine. But Conner kept his mouth shut. Maybe the guy was a podiatrist or something and wouldn't know that giving an EpiPen injection when it wasn't needed was kind of a bad idea.

"Will do," Mac told him. "Thanks."

Mac reclaimed his seat at the table and picked up the hand of cards he'd been holding prior to his emergency, as if nothing had happened, apparently choosing to ignore the strange looks from the other players.

Conner steered Gabby back to their table with a hand on her lower back.

That was all the touching he could do.

It was killing him.

"So…" she said quietly.

"Yes, I am going to save your pretty butt," he told her. "And no, no one else is going to be touching it but me."

She smiled up at him. "You really love that you're getting to be the hero here, don't you?"

He stopped several feet from the table. "I meant what I said, G. I don't need to be the hero here. If you—"

She stopped him. "I want your hands all over me. I want to pull you into the coat closet and not let you out until you…" she glanced around to see if anyone was listening—they weren't, but she lowered her voice anyway, "…until you can't stand up."

Heat hit him low and hard and he glanced around for the nearest coat closet.

He never had gotten that blow job.

"But most of all I want you to be my hero, Conner," she said, pulling his attention back to her—and away from the blow job. For now.

"Walking up to the table, my heart pounding, not knowing if I could actually pull this off or not, and then seeing you sitting there…it was like everything else dropped away. I knew it didn't matter how the game turned out, that everything would be okay anyway. Knowing that you were there, no matter what happened, meant something. A lot. More than I ever realized. And now, knowing that when I'm out of ideas you'll be there, that I can lean on you…" She put her hand against his cheek. "Save me, Conner."

HE WAS A STRONG PERSON. He could keep his focus when his entire football team was counting on him to make the last-second-it's-our-only-hope play work, when victims were bleeding faster than he could bandage, when one of his sisters was going on and on about why the dented fender wasn't her fault. But at the moment, it was taking everything he had not to throw Gabby over his shoulder and carry her straight out the front door.

She could get out of this herself. She'd come up with something.

But she wanted his help.

And suddenly the original plan B seemed like a lot of fun.

Sure, writing a check would work and be easy but...it was like the difference between watching the Times Square New Year's celebration on TV or being there in person. Sometimes, being in the middle of the chaos was the perfect place to be.

"Okay," he told her. "But to warn you, things might get a little crazy."

She grinned. "I wouldn't have it any other way."

Conner resisted grabbing her hand as they started for their poker table again. Ricky was slouched in his chair, checking his phone.

"Hey, Dixon, have you seen Twitter?" he asked.

Conner glanced over to where Mac was playing poker. Had Ricky noticed the whole saving someone's life thing he'd just been involved in?

"Uh, not lately. Why? What's up?"

Gabby reclaimed her seat and Ricky gave her a grin before looking at Conner. "A bunch of your buds are looking for you."

"Oh yeah?" Conner didn't smile as he pulled his phone out, but it looked like plan B was in motion.

Ryan, otherwise known as @Hawks81, had tweeted him, Shane and Cody, *@HawksQB @Hawks63 @Hawks25, what's up tonight?*

Shane, @Hawks63, had replied, *@HawksQB owes me a rematch. @Hawks25 @Hawks81.*

Cody had tweeted, *Let's do it! Tonight! @HawksQB @Hawks81 @Hawks63.*

"A rematch at what?" Ricky asked, looking up.

"Oh, they're just talking about how I killed Shane in Call of Duty the other day," Conner said. "I'd better tweet them that I'm busy with you."

"You and your buddies play Call of Duty?" Ricky asked.

Conner fought his grin. They did. Once in a while when things were slow at work. And not well. Ricky and his friends, on the other hand, were big gamers. He supposed that guys who had nothing else to do could only play so much poker.

"Yeah. We're not great, but we have fun."

"Oh man," Ricky said. "We should so get your friends and mine together for a Call of Duty tourney. You should see my game room. Fully equipped. It's awesome. A big game would be epic."

Epic. That's what Conner was hoping for. "Well, it is *tough* to get all those guys together," he said. "It used to happen all the time, but now they've all got girlfriends and work and stuff."

"But they're all free tonight," Ricky pointed out.

"Yeah, my sisters have some shower thing going on tonight." They didn't. They were probably sitting there telling the guys what to tweet. Conner looked around the room. "Too bad we couldn't do it tonight. They'd love your house."

"You're saying that the Hawks would come over here and play Call of Duty with me and my friends tonight?" Ricky asked. "Seriously?"

Conner nodded. "Sure, why not? You have a good setup?"

"My game room is amazing," Ricky promised.

"Too bad about the poker thing though," Conner said.

Ricky looked around. "Yeah, I guess. But damn, we play poker all the time. Call of Duty with the Hawks… That's…epic."

Conner glanced at Gabby. She was watching him, clearly amused. She lifted an eyebrow. He nodded. Yep, this was his idea.

"Well, if you can tear your friends away from the cards, I can get the guys over here," Conner said.

Ricky blew out a breath. "My friends won't care, but it will leave the tables short."

Conner looked at Gabby. She looked back. He raised both eyebrows. She frowned and shook her head. He widened his eyes and nodded. She glanced at Ricky, then back to Conner.

"Oh."

She finally caught on.

Ricky looked at her. "Oh?"

"Oh, I just know some people who would love to come fill in at the tables."

He looked at her thoughtfully. "I thought JD was sick."

"He is. But I have two other brothers. And a bunch of cousins. They all play."

"Are they as good as JD? I don't want to bring pros in here

but I don't want to bring in a bunch of hacks. That would insult my other guests."

She chuckled. "They're okay. They can play."

"They can be here in a half hour or so?"

Gabby glanced at Conner. He gave her a nod.

"I'm sure," she told Ricky. "I doubt they're doing much."

Ricky started nodding slowly. "Okay. This might work."

"Want me to call them?" Gabby asked.

"Dixon, you want to call your buddies first?"

Conner held up his phone. "I just tweeted them. They're on board."

Ricky glanced down and read the newest tweets, his smile growing. "Okay. This is awesome." He looked at Gabby. "Yeah, call them."

Ricky and his two friends at the table got up and headed for the other tables to inform the rest of his gang of the agenda change.

Gabby leaned across the table, her eyes sparkling with excitement. "Now what?"

"The guys and I are going to keep Ricky and his buddies busy in the other room playing video games. You and your relatives are going to spread out so there's one of you at each of the poker tables. That way your odds of winning are multiplied."

"I do need to call them?"

"Actually, they're on their way." He'd talked to her brother Reed on the way over as well and had it set up that Shane would let him know when the plan was a go.

"But they don't—"

He cut off her protest. "They want to."

"They're all playing for me?"

He smiled at her, love and lust and satisfaction and hunger all warring for his attention. "All you had to do was ask."

She pressed her lips together. "Are you mad?"

"That you didn't come to me when you had a problem? That

you went to my friends instead? That you didn't trust me to take care of you? Yes."

"I know. I just—"

"Need to realize that your problems are mine because I love you. I know I said that I wanted to retire, but I was wrong. This is who I am. I take care of people. So you're just going to have to get used to that idea."

She nodded. "I think I can do that."

Whatever else he would have said was cut off by a loud commotion in the foyer that quickly spilled into the poker room.

"The cavalry's here," he told her with a grin.

"*Already?*"

"They were all waiting a few minutes away."

Gabby's eyes were wide—as were the eyes of the rest of the room—as Shane Kelley, Cody Madsen and Ryan Kaye strode into the room followed by Reed and Grant Evans and a handful of guys Conner assumed were cousins.

"Oh my God." Ricky came up beside Conner as he stretched to his feet. "I can't believe those guys are all here."

"This is going to be a good time," Conner said, putting an arm around Ricky's shoulders.

This was a win-win. Ricky was getting to meet some of his favorite players, the guys' egos were getting stroked, they were all going to get to play Call of Duty…and Gabby was going to get everything she needed.

"Ricky Donovan, these are my friends and teammates Shane Kelley, Cody Madsen and Ryan Kaye."

"Yeah, yeah, I know." Ricky took each of their hands, pumping them enthusiastically. "I can't believe this." He turned to the room. "Fifteen-minute break!" he called out.

Chairs scraped and conversation swelled immediately as people stood and headed for the bar and buffet again.

"Let me show you the game room," Ricky said.

Shane, Cody and Ryan started after him.

"How do I get into the Hawks Call of Duty game?" Nate Sullivan asked, coming up on the group.

"I don't know, Sullivan," Conner said, looking at Ricky. "It's up to our host here."

Ricky nodded. "Yeah, of course. Sure, if you want to play. Sure."

Nate grinned. "Can't let these guys have all the fun."

Emma watched them go. "What's he doing? He sucks at Call of Duty."

Conner laughed. "You want to go play? Show them how it's done?"

"Kind of." Then she ran a hand over her belly. "But the buffet is amazing. I'll be okay out here."

"The girls should be here any minute," Conner told her.

"They're coming?"

"The girls?" Gabby asked at the same time.

Conner nodded. "Amanda went to pick Isabelle and Olivia up. They wanted to come check the mansion out."

"Damn," Emma said. "You know they're going to drink in front of me and tell me how great it all is."

Conner nodded. "Probably." He hugged Emma up against his side. "I know it's because of the baby, but whatever the reason, I have to be honest and tell you how much I love that *you're* the one abstaining."

Emma had always been the wild one of his sisters. It was amazing to watch her as a mother-to-be, in love and enjoying life more than she ever had.

"Yeah, yeah," she said. But she hugged him back before extricating herself. "I'm hitting the dessert table again before they get here. Amanda keeps lecturing me about blood sugar and stuff."

He watched her go then turned to Gabby.

She was looking at him with tears in her eyes.

"Wow" was all she said.

With Ricky out of the room, Conner quickly moved around the table and pulled her to her feet. He took her face in both hands and lowered his mouth, kissing her with all the love and desire and hope that he felt.

When he finally lifted his head, she said again, softly, "Wow."

"And I do understand that sometimes you don't need me to do anything," he told her. "Sometimes you just need me to listen. Or be there. And I can do that too. Well," he said with a shrug, "I'll learn how to do that too. But I think you need to prepare to be doted upon. Starting with—this circus."

"Circus?"

"My friends and family with yours. All here, being loud, creating distractions, playing poker, eating and drinking Ricky out of house and home. It's a circus, but it's our circus, Gabby."

She went up on tiptoe and kissed him again. When she pulled back she said, "I'm going to medical school in two months, Conner."

He felt like his heart was going to beat out of his chest. "I know. I'm behind you one hundred percent."

"It's going to be demanding."

"I know. But I want to be there. Even on the bad days, the stressful days. If I'm in the way, you can tell me to get lost. If you need absolute silence, I'll make sure it happens—"

"And I don't think there's any way I could do it without you. And all of them."

Her words stopped him. He stared at her. "Seriously? You think they can be helpful?"

"If I ever need some comedic relief or a study group or a cheering section or…anything," she said. Her eyes were bright and she gave him a funny smile. "I know they'll be there. All of them. Any of them. Anytime. That's worth a few headaches and a few more gray hairs and a few late nights."

Conner took a full, deep breath. Happiness. That's what he was feeling—pure, unadulterated happiness.

"I've realized that without all of that with the girls I wouldn't be enjoying the fun times with them now as much. If I'd always just been the big brother who could buy them cool stuff and take them fun places, it wouldn't mean as much now."

Gabby put her hand against his cheek. "I love you so much."

"I love you too." He took her hand and kissed the palm.

"I just might end up being the biggest problem you've ever had," she cautioned.

"I'm fully aware of that," he said sincerely.

She laughed and swatted his arm.

"But it's strange isn't it," he went on, "how your biggest problem can also be your perfect solution? How the thing that makes you craziest can also be what grounds you and keeps you sane?"

She looked at him, then around at the people who had gathered for them tonight. "Yep, that's absolutely the best strangest thing ever."

His heart was still pounding, but now it was with hope and excitement. "So, no more talk about things being over in two months?"

She stepped in and wrapped her arms around his neck. "Only talk about things beginning."

He kissed her. Or she kissed him. In any case, their lips ended up on one another's again and things got hot fast. He was walking her backward, intent on getting her against the wall where he could make things *really* good, when someone new barged into the room.

"Gabby!"

They pulled apart and spun.

It was Josh.

"Josh, what are you doing?" Gabby met him before he could take more than a few steps.

"I got the money. You don't have to play. Or, you don't have to win, anyway." Josh's eyes were bright with excitement.

"What are you talking about?" Gabby asked him.

She reached for Conner's hand without looking and he linked their fingers, letting her know he was right there.

"I have ten thousand. I can pay everybody back." He thrust a stack of bills at Conner. "Here's your two."

Conner blinked at the money. "*My* two?"

"I'll tell you later," Gabby told him. She grabbed the money from her brother and tucked it into the bodice of her dress. "Do I want to know how you got this money?" she asked Josh.

"I sold some stuff on eBay." He looked very proud of himself.

Gabby frowned. "What kind of stuff?"

He rolled his eyes. "Legal stuff, Gab. Sports memorabilia mostly."

"Where did you get sports memorabilia that's worth twenty grand?" she demanded.

"I…won it in games."

She groaned. "You have a problem, Josh. Don't you see that?"

He nodded. "I do. I know. A…friend helped me see that. And helped me figure out how to make this right with selling that stuff and coming over here."

"A friend?" Gabby asked. "Josh, some of your friends might be part of this problem."

"Sierra is not part of this problem."

Conner felt Gabby's hand tighten on his in surprise. "Sierra?" she repeated. "My Sierra?"

Josh nodded. "She's been very supportive."

That was…interesting.

"But," Gabby said, "you need counseling, Josh. Or a support group. Or something."

"Gabby," Conner said, pulling her against his side and sliding an arm around her, "breathe."

She sighed. "Okay, fine. Great. I'm glad that she's been supportive and that you figured out how to fix this."

Josh pushed his hands into his pockets. "Thanks and…I'm sorry."

Gabby nodded. Josh nodded. They stood awkwardly looking at one another.

Conner nudged her with his elbow.

Finally, she took a big step forward and wrapped her arms around her brother. "I love you, Josh."

Josh hesitated for a moment, his eyes wide, then enfolded his sister in a big hug. "Love you, Gabs."

Conner felt someone slap a big, heavy hand on his shoulder. He sighed and turned to look up at Mac.

"I've always liked you, Dixon," he said.

Conner snorted.

"And it's great to see you becoming less of a dumbass."

Conner laughed. "You're just glad I'll be leaving your wife alone."

"That doesn't hurt my feelings," Mac agreed.

"Thanks for helping Gabby out tonight."

Mac nodded, his eyes on Gabby. "That's what friends are for."

"I'm glad you're her friend," Conner said honestly. There were a lot worse people to have on her side than Mac Gordon.

"I was talking about you." Mac bumped him with his elbow, then he headed for the door.

Conner was still staring after him dumbly when Gabby slipped her arm through his. "So, I don't have to play tonight."

He focused on her. "Yeah, guess not."

"And my family can go home."

"Guess mine can too."

"Yeah."

"And we can get to bed earlier."

"*Yeah.*"

They didn't say anything else for a moment.

"Of course, everyone was so great to show up to help," Gabby said.

"Yeah, everyone's already here."

They heard a shout and cheering coming from a back room. Conner assumed the game room. He looked in that direction. He did love a good game of Call of Duty.

"I mean, I don't *need* to win tonight now," Gabby said. "But it might be nice to play against players who can hold their own with me."

He chuckled. "Yeah, and I promised Ricky this Call of Duty matchup. He'll be crushed if we leave now."

She grinned. "And heck, we're already up by ten thousand."

Conner looked from her to where Amanda, Olivia and Isabelle were sampling the chocolate fountain with Emma, then down into the eyes of the fifth beautiful, smart, amazing woman in his life.

"You know," he said. "You can keep the ten K. I'm up by five…and holding."

Five months later

"How can the ulnar nerve innervate the gastroc muscle?" Ryan asked Shane. "It's an *arm* nerve."

"*I* don't have to know the answer," Shane told him. "She does."

He pointed at Gabby.

"But it's your turn to answer." Ryan pointed at the board lying on the table in front of them. The board was from an old Candy Land game, the game pieces were from Monopoly and they were using Uno cards in the made-up anatomy review game that Ryan, Michael and Dooley had created. It was to help Gabby study, but they all liked to play and even hearing their questions and answers—right or wrong—helped her review the material.

"What motion is the gastroc responsible for?" Ryan asked.

Shane shrugged. "If I shot someone in it, woould they stop running?"

Ryan snorted. "Definitely."

"So it's probably a leg muscle."

Gabby shook her head. Strangely these study sessions were effective.

"But what does it *do*?" Ryan insisted.

"Helps with running."

If she didn't have an A in her anatomy class to prove it, she wouldn't believe it herself.

The gang was gathered around the coffee table in the break room at work.

It felt great to be here, she had to admit.

It had been two months since she'd left the crew for medical school. She'd ended up staying at work almost a month and a half longer than she'd intended, but it turned out that she'd needed less transition time than she'd thought. She was living with Conner and nothing in her family, or his, had really changed that much. She'd realized after the big poker game— where she'd been able to add ten thousand dollars to her medical school fund—that she didn't want her life to change. She was going to add school to it, but the people in it were the same and she wouldn't have it any other way.

She'd already had one anatomy exam and had done very well, thanks to the crazy study sessions. She was now preparing for her second, but she'd agreed to fill in tonight for Sam Bradford who had sick twin girls at home.

But even if she wasn't working, this had turned into a great place to study. The guys loved to quiz her, which helped her a lot, and there were long periods of downtime for the guys during a shift and this was a unique way of killing an hour or two.

"Name two major vessels supplying the lower leg," Shane read from one of the index cards.

"The femoral artery," Ryan replied.

Shane shook his head. "Sorry."

"Yes it is," Ryan protested.

"Not what the card says."

"Well, it is."

"Anterior tibial artery and popliteal artery," Shane read from the card.

"Well, they branch off of the femoral."

"But they're not *called* the femoral artery down there."

Gabby sighed. She had to pull a card that would get them out of the Peppermint Stick Forest—that was where all the questions about the nerves and vessels were.

She appreciated these guys though. Ryan was filling in tonight too and Shane had come over with pizza after his shift ended to help for a while. Apparently Isabelle and Amanda were helping Cody and Olivia frost something like fourteen-dozen cupcakes for something.

She hoped they didn't show up later with the leftovers. Conner's sisters were also very supportive, but Olivia's you-can-do-it encouragement baking was already to blame for Gabby's five-pound weight gain and Emma thought that Gabby needed a lot of study breaks—complete with trips to the masseuse or nail salon.

Though Gabby didn't argue too hard once she was face-down on the table and they were digging into her tight shoulders.

Her family, too, was on board. Poker had gone to once a month—at least games that included Gabby—Conner played more often than that. And she no longer had to make dip. Olivia made it for her. She and Conner attended a family dinner twice a month and she called her mom every other day. Things were good. Everyone seemed to be surviving.

Even Josh had straightened up. Somehow, Gabby had the suspicion that it had to do with Sierra being more than a friend to him, but she didn't want to know. She completely understood where Conner had been coming from all this time regarding his sisters and his friends.

She drew a six and moved her top hat.

"Name two ligaments of the ankle," Shane read.

"Anterior talofibular ligament and the posterior talofibular ligament."

"And if you shot someone in those, they wouldn't be able to

run either," Shane said, sticking the card on the bottom of the pile.

"Should we be concerned that everything is revolving around people getting shot tonight?" Ryan asked.

Shane shook his head. "Rookie shot a guy in the arm last night. He was still able to run. And got away."

"Got it," Ryan said with a chuckle.

She smiled as Dooley and Mac came into the room, arguing about something. Dooley spotted the game and immediately dropped onto the love seat next to Gabby. "I want to play."

"You have to start at the beginning," Shane said. "And Gabby's already to the Lollipop Woods."

"Yeah, but the Molasses Swamp is all the neuroanatomy... that'll slow her down," Dooley said, giving Gabby a wink.

He was right. She hated neuroanatomy.

Dooley leaned in. "And let me guess, you're the thimble."

Shane frowned. "Yeah. So?"

"You're still at the Peppermint Stick Forest. I can so pass you." Dooley drew a seven from the deck.

Shane plunked a game piece down for Dooley. "Fine. Name the nerves that come off of the brachial plexus."

Dooley smirked at him. "The musculocutaneous, the axillary, the median, the radial and the ulnar nerves."

Shane sighed and Dooley moved his piece seven squares and slid across the Rainbow Trail, moving ahead of Shane.

"So where is the female anatomy section?" Dooley asked. "I'll kick ass at that."

"Up by Queen Frostine, of course," Ryan said.

"Ah, got it. Well, I'm ready. Studied up just last night," Dooley said.

"You really think you can do better on female anatomy than *I* can?" Shane asked, sitting up taller.

Dooley nodded sincerely. "I do."

Shane scoffed. "We're going to skip ahead to the Ice Cream Sea," he told Gabby and Ryan.

"Oh brother," Ryan muttered.

"What? I have to defend my knowledge base here," Shane said.

"I'm going to beat you both anyway," Ryan said, moving all the game pieces.

Gabby laughed at that. They all looked at her.

"Really? I *have* female anatomy," she said. "You think you can beat me?"

Shane grinned and Dooley nodded, "It's more important to us."

She shook her head, grinning. "Okay, let's go."

She should have known this was going to happen. But she did need to be able to pass this section of the test.

They correctly identified the labia majora and minora, the clitoris—"Morgan's favorite body part," Dooley added.

"It's every woman's favorite body part," Gabby informed them.

They got the Fallopian tubes, the uterus and the vagina right. But then they stumbled.

They didn't know that fimbriae were part of the Fallopian tubes and they didn't know Bartholin's glands secreted fluid during sexual arousal—and could get inflamed and painful. But Gabby did.

"On to male reproductive anatomy," she announced, drawing a five from the deck.

"But we didn't even get to talk about orgasms or nipples," Dooley protested.

"Orgasms are more physiology than anatomy," Gabby told him with a smile. "Somebody ask me a question about the male sex organs."

Ryan grinned and she groaned.

"An *appropriate* question," she added.

"Well, that leaves me out," Dooley said.

"And I don't want to talk about anything that gets inflamed and painful in the male sexual system," Shane added.

"I don't understand why you need to know the fancy names for all this stuff," Dooley said, picking up a question card.

"Yeah, knowing how it works is the important part," Shane said.

"But when you're talking about it with someone, you need to use the proper terms so you know you're talking about the same thing," Gabby said.

"I have never spoken the term *vas deferens* in my life and the people I talk to about this stuff know exactly what I'm talking about," Dooley said.

Gabby couldn't help her grin. She was going to kick butt on this anatomy test. And likely most of her tests from here on out if she had these guys on her side.

The door to the break room banged open and Cody came in carrying a huge tray of cupcakes.

Olivia, Amanda and Isabelle were behind him.

"We had leftovers," Olivia announced happily. "Carrot and lemon."

Gabby groaned. Olivia Dixon's carrot cupcakes? No way could she say no to that.

"No chocolate?" Dooley asked, getting to his feet.

"Not tonight."

"Cupcakes should always be chocolate," he told her, choosing a lemon and taking a huge bite.

"You should leave these alone then," Olivia said, holding the platter out of his reach.

Ryan grabbed them from behind her and handed Dooley another lemon, taking two carrot for himself.

"What are we studying tonight?" Cody asked, moving toward the board.

"Anatomy. Specifically sexual anatomy," Shane told him.

"Are you the thimble?" Cody asked.

Shane scowled at him. "Yeah, so?"

"You're behind everyone else."

Shane gave him a growl. "So?"

"So whether you're talking female or male sexual anatomy, I feel sorry for Isabelle."

"He's just fine," Isabelle said, sliding onto her fiancé's lap. "It doesn't matter if he knows what to call it, just how it all works."

Gabby sat back, a huge dumb grin on her face and stupidly feeling like crying at the same time.

Things were crazy, chaotic and loud. Just like always.

In other words, completely perfect.

Conner rounded the corner, headed for the break room…and ran smack into someone.

Someone small by the feel of it, but he couldn't see around his armful to who it was.

"*Oof*" was all he'd heard from them so far.

But he knew who it was.

The floor was now littered with peanut butter, chocolate star cookies.

He peeked at Sara Gordon around the giant stuffed duck he was carrying.

"Nice duck," she told him dryly.

"Were those for me?" he asked of the cookies. "I don't know how many times I can tell you—I'm in love with someone else now."

She grinned as she dropped to her knees to gather the cookies. He set the duck aside and knelt to help.

"I'm thrilled about the being-in-love-with-someone-else thing," Sara told him, putting the cookies back on the plate—that was thankfully plastic.

"Was I really such a creepy stalker?" he asked, stretching to his feet.

"No. You were sweet and charming and always made me smile. But," she added as he was about to say something cocky, "it bugged me that you were wasting it on me. I'm thrilled you have someone to dote on now."

Conner grinned. "My favorite word, *dote*."

"Well, you're good at it."

He picked the duck back up. "I do believe I've given you the last pink bunny of our relationship, though, Mrs. Gordon."

"I understand. Though it makes me strangely nostalgic to think you're now taking enormous stuffed animals to someone else."

He patted the duck's bill. "I know what you're thinking. That this will turn Gabby to mush, but this is actually for my sister and my new niece."

Sara's eyes widened. "Emma had her baby?"

He nodded, feeling a strange surge of pride that he didn't fully understand. Little Miss Lucy Sullivan was his niece, not his daughter. But he felt like he was glowing.

It was about Emma, he knew. His little sister was a mom now. It was bizarre and wonderful.

"Last night. Gabby's working for Sam tonight, so I thought I'd swing through and take her up to visit with me if they've got some downtime."

Sara fell into step beside him as they turned for the break room. "I understand there's a big test the day after tomorrow."

Surprised, Conner looked down at her. "How'd you know?"

"Mac was going over the bones of the wrist and ankle last night. Said that he was determined to get to the Lollipop Woods tonight before Dooley."

Conner laughed as he pushed the break room door open.

Chaos.

That's what met him as he stepped into the room.

Everyone was there. Or nearly everyone. They had the Candy Land-Anatomy Review game spread out on the coffee table, there was a crazy amount of cupcakes being passed around and everyone was talking at once.

Except Gabby.

He zeroed in on her right away. She was sitting on the love seat, her feet up on the coffee table, a sweet smile on her face as she observed the crowd.

She met his eyes across the room and her smile grew even warmer.

Damn, he loved her.

"Nice duck, Dixon," Mac observed.

"I'm on my way to being Lucy's favorite uncle," Conner told him, setting the duck on a chair at the kitchen table.

"Aren't you Lucy's only uncle?" Ryan asked.

"Well, that helps too," Conner admitted with a smile.

He headed for Gabby. She scooted over on the love seat, then snuggled up against him once he was seated.

"I saw you walk in with Sara."

"Yeah, she's trying to win me back with my favorite cookies."

"We have the same favorite cookie, Dixon," Mac said.

Ah, he'd heard that. Good.

"Did you notice the heels she's wearing?" Conner asked Gabby. "I think she's realized that I like tall women and she's trying to compete."

"She's always worn high heels," Mac said from behind them.

Conner chuckled. "And did you hear that she tried to dye her hair dark once she realized I like brunettes?"

"That was an accident with some paint at the youth center, you jackass," Mac said. "And it was one streak in her hair."

Conner loved this.

"You know it's true that you don't know what you've got until it's gone," Conner said to Gabby. "Poor Sara."

"Oh God," Gabby groaned, getting to her feet and pulling him up as well. "How about you and I go for a little while and we'll see if anyone misses you."

"Not a chance in hell," Mac called out.

Conner gave him a grin as he grabbed the duck and headed for the elevators with Gabby's hand in his.

"Studying going well?" he asked as they stepped onto the elevator.

"Strangely, yes." She went up on tiptoe and gave him a quick, sweet kiss. "Thanks."

"For what?"

"For bringing all of these people into my life."

That caught him in the heart and he had to clear his throat. "I brought you into theirs too. I deserve a lot of thanks."

"Well, I don't know about everyone else, but I have the perfect way to show my appreciation," she said as the elevator arrived on Emma's floor.

"Does it involve a coat closet? 'Cause we still haven't done that and I know a lot of closets around this place." He followed her off the elevator.

"How did you know it involved a blow job?"

He chuckled and glanced around, then backed her up against the nearest wall. "I don't think you can say the word *blow job* on the floor where all the sweet newborn babies are."

"You don't think those figure in to those sweet newborn babies being here in the first place?" she teased, looping her arms around his neck.

"Blow jobs don't result in babies," Conner told her, running his duck-free hand down her side to her waist and pulling her closer.

"They help."

"I think you need to study your reproductive anatomy more in depth."

"I might need some help."

"At your service."

They kissed, hot and hard.

Until Nate interrupted them.

"Stick with the blow jobs."

They pulled apart with a laugh and turned to face Nate, their arms around each other.

"Strange advice from a new dad," Gabby commented gently.

Nate looked like hell. His eyes were bloodshot, his hair tousled like he'd been running his hand through it, and his shirt rumpled.

"I think you have new gray hair already," Conner said, not as gently.

"I'm sure I do," Nate agreed. "I have a baby *girl.*"

Conner chuckled and nodded. "I know. In fact, I knew like five months ago she was going to be a she. As did you."

"But now she's here."

"And that's awesome," Gabby told him.

"She was up until three a.m. and she's demanding and loud and all about being the center of attention."

Conner laughed louder at that. "You've met her mom, right?"

"*That's* what I'm afraid of."

"Emma already decorated her nursery in a princess theme," Conner said. "What did you think this was going to be like?"

"I think this is going to be like *your* life raising girls," Nate told him.

Conner stared at his friend. He wanted to tease him, he wanted to say *better you than me,* he wanted to say *yeah, I'm a damned saint.*

But he couldn't.

He'd raised the four girls...but they'd also raised him. And he wouldn't trade any of it.

"You know what, Nate?" he asked. "I hope so. I hope you have every up and down that I did."

Nate groaned. But Conner grinned.

Gabby squeezed his hand. "I think I'm going to take Dr. Sullivan for some coffee."

Conner watched her put her arm around Nate's waist and steer him toward the elevators and his chest tightened.

She was taking care of the people that mattered to him and she was letting them take care of her.

"Hey, G!" he called as the elevator doors slid open. "We're going to have a *bunch* of daughters, okay?"

She grinned at him. "You got it, Dixon. We need some estrogen on my side of the family, for sure."

His heart full, a goofy grin on his face, he started in the direction of the nursery to see the newest female he got to dote on.

Thank you for reading Conner and Gabby's story! I hope you loved Why You Should Never Kiss Your Roommate!

Don't miss the series epilogue wedding (and baby!) novella, **Why You Should Definitely Kiss Your Groom!**

Go to **ShopErinNicholas.com**
and look for the title or
go to this link:
shoperinnicholas.com/b/1ypJH

Love protective guys who wear badges (and want to see where JD Evans (Gabby's brother Josh) ended up?) Check out the **Badges of the Bayou series!**

Love big groups of friends and family who are always there for each other... with plenty of teasing and trouble too? Check out my **Boys of the Bayou series!**

ღ

Just need more sexy rom com fun?
Find all of my books (including a printable book list) **at ErinNicholas.com**

ღ

And join in on all the FAN FUN!

Join my **email list!**

bit.ly/Keep-In-Touch-Erin
(be sure you get those dashes and capital letters in there!)

And be the first to hear about my news, sales, freebies, behind-the-scenes, and more!

Or for even more fun, join my **Super Fan page** on Facebook and chat with me and other super fans every day! Just search Facebook for Erin Nicholas Super Fans!

WHY YOU SHOULD NEVER... THE SERIES

Why You Should Never...

Kiss Your Boss (Ben & Jessica)

Kiss Your Blind Date (Sam & Dani)

Kiss A Grump (Mac & Sara)

Kiss Your Fake Boyfriend (Dooley & Morgan)

Kiss Your Ex-Husband (Kevin & Eve)

Kiss Your Brother's Best Friend (Ryan & Amanda)

Kiss Your Ex (Shane & Isabelle)

Kiss Your Enemy (Nate & Emma)

Kiss Your Best Friend (Cody & Olivia)

Kiss Your Roommate (Conner & Gabby)

MORE FROM ERIN

Want more hot protective guys who wear badges? Try my Badges of the Bayou series!

Badges of the Bayou
Gotta Be Bayou (Spencer & Max)
Bayou With Benefits (Michael & Ami)
Rocked Bayou (Colin & Hayden)

*

If you love steamy romance with big groups of family and friends, check out my Boys of the Bayou series!

Boys of the Bayou
My Best Friend's Mardi Gras Wedding (Josh & Tori)
Sweet Home Louisiana (Owen & Maddie)
Beauty and the Bayou (Sawyer & Juliet)
Crazy Rich Cajuns (Bennett & Kennedy)
Must Love Alligators (Chase & Bailey)
Four Weddings and a Swamp Boat Tour (Mitch & Paige)

*

ABOUT ERIN NICHOLAS

Erin Nicholas is the New York Times and USA Today bestselling author of over thirty sexy contemporary romances. Her stories have been described as toe-curling, enchanting, steamy and fun. She loves to write about reluctant heroes, imperfect heroines and happily ever afters. She lives in the Midwest with her husband who only wants to read the sex scenes in her books, her kids who will never read the sex scenes in her books, and family and friends who say they're shocked by the sex scenes in her books (yeah, right!).
Find her here:

facebook.com / ErinNicholasBooks
bookbub.com / authors / erin-nicholas
goodreads.com / author / show / 3155383.Erin_Nicholas
tiktok.com / @erinnicholasbooks

www.ingramcontent.com/pod-product-compliance
Lightning Source LLC
Chambersburg PA
CBHW061523210726

48287CB00006B/1796